"You're a barnacle, Jesse Rivers.

"You cling to the safe stone of home ground. You live a few miles from where you were born. You've always gone to the same church. You're limited in your outlook because you've never bothered to look beyond your horizons."

"You think you know everything, don't you? You sure think you know me."

"I grew up knowing guys like you. You think because you have a handle on your little corner of the world that you're some kind of god." Nan closed her eyes.

Jesse had no idea what to say so he leaned over and kissed her.

Nan smiled at him. "I guess I don't know everything about you, after all."

ABOUT THE AUTHOR

This is the eighth Superromance novel by
Sharon Brondos. Set in South Dakota,
neighbor to Sharon's home state of Wyoming,
the story is told with the flair and expertise
that will surely delight her readers. Prepare
for some heart-stopping thrills as the
hero takes to the air to perform his
daredevil stunts.

Books by Sharon Brondos

HARLEQUIN SUPERROMANCE

HARLEQUIN TEMPTATION

A Place To Land

SHARON BRONDOS

Harlequin Books

TORONTO • NEW YORK • LONDON
AMSTERDAM • PARIS • SYDNEY • HAMBURG
STOCKHOLM • ATHENS • TOKYO • MILAN

Published July 1991

ISBN 0-373-70459-3

A PLACE TO LAND

Dedicated to
Margaret Brondos
1910–1990

Special thanks to
Lee Hermann, M.D. of Cody, WY,
for information on planes and flying,
especially for the flight in the Cub
described in chapter 9.

And thanks to Judy Kneale of Casper, WY,
for inside info on running a
video rental store.

CHAPTER ONE

NAN BLACK WAS daydreaming when the small airplane touched down on the highway directly in front of her station wagon. For a millisecond, the danger seemed a part of her fantasy. Then it all registered.

She jerked back to reality, shrieked and put the car and the U-Haul trailer attached to it into a skid that avoided the aircraft, but left Nan and all her worldly possessions in the shallow ditch that bordered the South Dakota road. Dust swirled. The engine clanked and died. She clung to the steering wheel, grasping it so tightly her knuckles whitened. Breath caught in her throat and then couldn't come fast enough. *I'm hyperventilating*, she thought. She was going to faint.

But not before she skinned alive the idiot who had nearly killed her!

She released the wheel and managed to steady her shaking hands enough to unclasp her seat belt. Thank goodness using the thing had become a habit. She could easily have gone through the windshield if she hadn't been buckled in tightly. Nan's temper heated as her fear fled. By the time she got out of the station wagon, she was ready to spit nails. She climbed out of the ditch, her muscles still trembling in reaction. But she walked to the middle of the highway and took a determined stance, waiting.

The little plane was now a way down the road, moving slowly with the propeller barely turning. Even at this distance, however, she could see the machine was not in good shape. It looked battered and as if it were held together by baling wire and chewing gum. An accident on its way to happen, and it had very nearly happened to her! Her temper was at the boiling point. She quit waiting and started down the road toward the retreating plane, mentally daring the careless pilot to run away from facing her wrath. Boy, she was going to give it to him! Anger had overcome her usual reluctance to make a scene, and she was ready to fight.

The plane slowed even more, then did a maneuver that stopped her in her tracks. It turned, literally on a dime, and headed back toward her. Nan could make out the shape of the pilot through the distorting whirl of the propeller, but couldn't see enough to tell what kind of person she would be dealing with.

As the plane neared, she became absolutely certain she was facing some kind of homicidal maniac who had nothing better to do this sunny spring afternoon than to try terminating her life. The roar of the engine was deafening, the sight of the machine coming at her head-on was terrifying. Losing most of her nerve, she looked around wildly for safe shelter, but the featureless prairie afforded none. Not a tree in sight. Not even a good-size rock. Her only chance was to take refuge behind her car. Turning, she raced for the vehicle, wishing she had listened to the advice of friends who had warned her not to travel without her weapon handy. If she had her gun, she could at least defend herself. Her heart pounded as she crouched behind the car, wondering what she was going to do if the pilot rammed it. Wondering if she could actually shoot someone who was trying to kill her.

Wondering if this lunatic really was trying to kill her, and why?

He wasn't. She peered cautiously over the hood as the plane slowed and eventually stopped a distance from her. The engine wheezed and clanked. The propeller made one more painful turn before grinding to a halt. It sounded like a metal monster chewing scrap. Visions of the machine demon from the movie, *The Terminator,* flashed through her mind. She held her breath as silence settled and she heard nothing for a moment but the soft sigh of the wind in the dead grass by the side of the road. Only that and the rapid beat of her heart. Then the peace was shattered.

The cockpit door flew open with a clang, and a figure emerged, cursing. Nan listened, frightened but impressed at his variety of colorful phrases. He walked slowly around the plane, kicking the tires and discussing the machine's ancestry with no one in particular. She raised her head and watched.

He was not a tall man, but he had broad shoulders and a powerful build. The ratty old bomber jacket and well-worn jeans didn't disguise that. Paratrooper boots on his feet completed the costume of the barnstormer pilot. All he lacked was the white silk scarf! His features were difficult to make out because he wasn't looking in her direction; however, there was an air of tanned ruggedness about him. His hair was light brown and curly with blond highlights. Finally he stopped cussing at the plane and stepped away from it. He took a cigar from inside his jacket, jammed it in his mouth and lit the thing.

"Okay, lady," he called. "You can come out now. I'm not biting this afternoon."

"*I* am!" His sarcastic, impatient tone brought back all the anger. "You nearly killed me. I'm seriously thinking about pressing charges."

He took a step in her direction.

"And don't come any closer. I've got a gun, and I know how to use it!"

"What caliber?" He took the cigar from his mouth.

She thought with regret of the weapon packed deep in a box in the U-haul. "Uh, a . . . a forty-five. It could stop a freight train!"

"Maybe so." The cigar hit the ground and died under a boot heel. "But if you can hit anything with a forty-five without getting knocked into the next county, then my luck's really all run out and I might as well let you plug me. Now, come on out and let's get going."

"Get going?" She ducked, feeling a hard flutter in her throat. There was not another sign of life as far as she could see. Just blue sky and gold prairie, the man and his plane, her car and herself. "What do you mean?" She looked over the hood again and gasped. He had moved close enough to place his hands on the other side of the car. She hadn't heard a thing.

He smiled, and it was not a warm expression. "I mean, miss, that as far as I've been able to tell, we are the only folks in a hundred miles. We've only got each other, and I need you."

Nan stared, unable to move a muscle. Her imagination raced with the possibilities implied by his words, but her eyes and mind couldn't help studying his face. Up close, he wasn't too bad-looking. His eyes were green and his mouth wide and so firmly sculpted it looked deliberately carved. But his nose was an aggressive hook, and something about the set of his jawline gave him an almost brutal look. "Don't you forget my gun," she managed to say.

"Oh, for…" He took out another cigar. "You don't have any gun, miss. If you did, you'd certainly have waved it at me before this. I guess I'd even deserve it." He surprised her by sounding embarrassed. "I didn't think I'd scared you." He lit the smoke. "I thought you heard me pass over twice. My engine was going out, and I knew if I didn't land near you, I'd be stuck out here for who knows how long. The radio I carry got misplaced somewhere, so I can't call for help. As it is, I'm ready to pay for a hitch into town and for any damages your car got from going into the ditch."

"Pay?" She stood up slightly. "For a ride? For damages?" Now he was making some sense.

"Of course. I'll even drive, since that doesn't seem to be one of your strong points. What were you doing that you didn't hear me? Radio on? Stereo too loud?" A puff of blue-gray smoke blew past her. The smell reminded her of diesel exhaust. She'd ridden behind enough of that on this trip to last a lifetime.

Nan coughed and straightened. "No. I was thinking. I do a lot of that when I'm on an open road like this. I just didn't hear you or see you. Not until you fell out of the sky right in front of me, that is."

He laughed. "Must have been thinking about something pretty engrossing. What if I'd been a tornado? Would you have heard that?" The second cigar followed the fate of the first.

"Of course I would have. I always check the weather when I'm driving. There's not a cloud in the sky." She gestured at the wide, empty bowl of the Dakota heaven. "At least not a natural one," she added, glaring at him.

Jesse Rivers narrowed his eyes and really looked at the woman. He had been too preoccupied with his plane before to do more than note she was young and had shoulder-length blond hair. Now he saw she was extremely pretty. The hair was pale as the wheat growing on his father's farm, and her eyes far bluer than the sky she had pointed to. Finely drawn features and lips pink enough without lipstick. Her cheeks had a high color in contrast to her fair skin, but he figured that was from the anger he saw in her eyes. A moment ago they had seemed filled with fear, and that had bothered him. His gruff manners had never endeared him to women on a first meeting, although to cause panic was the farthest thing from his mind. "Look," he said, his hand automatically going to the inner pocket of his jacket and the cigars, "I didn't mean to scare you off the road. I just needed your help. Is that so terrible?"

Nan put her hands on her hips. "How about an apology, buster? You shaved ten years off my life with your little stunt." Relief, now that she knew he meant her no harm, made her voice shrill. She could see it grated on the man's nerves.

"Apologize?" Jesse frowned. "What for? I gave you plenty of notice. Anyone with half a brain on their driving would have heard me. It's not my fault you were off in never-never land, probably fantasizing about some guy or something." The cigar went between his lips, his teeth clamping on it out of long habit.

She blushed more deeply. "I was not fantasizing about some man. You have a very low and limited mind. I was dreaming about a place. It was a G-rated daydream, I'll have you know. And do you realize that's the third cigar you've lit in less than five minutes? What's the matter with you? Are you that nervous?"

He took the cigar out of his mouth and stared at it. "Damn. I didn't even realize..." A wry smile. "I'm trying to quit. Done pretty well for the past few weeks. Don't know why I... Nervous, no. Tension, I guess." The third cigar died under his boot. "It's a dirty habit and bothers other people. I promised myself I'd quit for good by Christmas. That gives me... what? Nine more months?"

"Well, that's the only decent thing I know about you so far." Nan came around the front of the station wagon and glared at him. Her courage had returned. He hardly seemed frightening anymore. "What are you going to do about that plane? You can't just leave it in the middle of the highway."

"I get the ride?"

She shrugged. "If you promise not to smoke. I don't suppose I can just leave you out here. The nights still get pretty cold, even though it's almost May." She pulled down the sleeves of her sweatshirt. The afternoon wind was already getting an edge to it, though the sun was shining brightly.

"Good." He nodded as if that was the answer he'd expected all along. "Help me with the plane, will you?"

"Me?"

"You see anyone else around here, miss?" The corners of that sculpted mouth turned down, the expression indicating impatience. "Yeah. You." He turned his back on her and strode toward the plane.

Nan stood her ground, hands back on her hips. "My name's not miss. It's Nan. Nan Black. And I'd appreciate a please when I'm being asked for a favor."

The set of his shoulders stiffened. "All right. Please, Nan. Help me with my plane. And if you do this for me, I'll thank you very much."

"That's better." She lifted her chin and walked past him. "Now, what am I supposed to do?"

"Push."

"Push?"

"We have to get it off the road. By dark, it'll be a hazard." He hit the side of the plane with a closed fist. "Not that it isn't already."

"I can't push a thing this size."

He gave her an appraising look. "Sure you can, Nan. You're young and obviously healthy. Put your shoulder right here and lean into it." He flashed the first genuine grin she had seen on his face, and it transformed him instantly. He was suddenly, startlingly handsome! "Go on, try," he added encouragingly.

With the image of this handsome, dashing new man in her mind, Nan obeyed. Thanking her stars she had chosen to wear just an old sweatshirt and jeans for traveling, she ignored the dirt and oil smeared on the side of the machine and pushed. To her surprise it moved several inches. "Oh!" she said.

"See, it's light. Easy to move." He stripped off his jacket, revealing a muscled torso covered by a black T-shirt. The jacket went to the ground and his hands to the plane. "I use it for aerobatics, so it has to be." Without apparent effort, he moved his side several feet. "Come on, help out."

She did, but stared through the windows of the cockpit at him. "Aerobatics? As in stunt flying?"

"Yeah. I love it." His shoulders bunched as he corrected the direction of the plane. "Closest thing to having wings yourself. Afraid of flying, Nan?"

They were nearing the edge of the road. "Not in big planes or in my dreams. But I'll pass when it comes to something like this. You might have been killed, you know.

I don't know much about engines, but this one sounded like it was dead before you hit the ground."

"Nah." He made another adjustment as the front wheel bumped onto the dirt and grass. "Even if the engine had given out, I could have glided down safely enough. The landing gear might have been damaged, though. That's why I hit the road before shutdown. So, you fly in your dreams?" He sounded mildly amused.

"Sure." She stumbled on a clump of dead grass. Further obstacles. "Doesn't everyone? Just how far are we pushing this thing anyhow?"

"Far enough so headlights won't pick it up unless someone's looking for it. I don't dream at all. I *live* flying instead of fantasizing about it." He shoved, and the plane skewed around a bit toward Nan.

"Everyone dreams," she said, pushing harder. "It's been proved scientifically."

"Not me. I haven't dreamed since I was a kid. Don't daydream, either." He stopped and looked back at the road.

Nan came around the front of the plane. "You're dead wrong, mister. Reliable scientific reports agree with me. Everyone dreams, and people's daydreams are either more structured or less structured. My own are very structured, but that's because I work at them."

"My name's not 'mister.' It's Jesse. Jesse Rivers. And I don't give a good—I don't care what the scientists say. I know my own mind." He seemed to think the subject was now closed. Then his expression lightened. Another grin, but this time a wicked one. "Although I have to admit I wouldn't mind knowing what your 'structured' daydreams are all about."

He watched as that blush reappeared. This encounter had started out as a royal pain, he thought, but now it was getting more interesting. He wondered where this blond blusher was heading with her station wagon, U-Haul and volatile temper. She was on the road to his hometown. If she had no place to stay the night, he could offer the spare bunk at his home and see what that might lead to....

No, no, Jesse. Not with Jimmy in the house. What in hell was the matter with him? He never had thoughts like this about a woman just a few minutes after meeting her. Preferred to have feelings for a lady grow on him gradually. Must be a reaction from the adrenaline that had shot through him when he knew he was going down. Not from fear, but rather because of the excitement. Kind of an affirmation of life. Yeah, he could understand that.

Then he saw he'd really stepped over the line. She looked shy and uncomfortable. "Hey," he said, frowning, annoyed with himself. Sometimes, he had worse manners than an old hog. "I didn't mean to embarrass you. Sorry. I was only kidding," he finished, feeling awkward and embarrassed himself. It was not a sensation he liked.

"It's okay." She shrugged, the gesture revealing that beneath the baggy sweatshirt she wasn't as delicately built as her face and slender hips suggested. Jesse felt his resolve to be coldly polite and distant fading before the sunny smile she beamed on him suddenly. Her shyness, or what he had thought was shyness, had disappeared.

"I asked for that," she said. "I tend to be kind of opinionated on the subject of dreams and fantasies, Jesse. It's true some people don't remember dreaming and perhaps don't recognize when their thinking habits fit into the category of fantasizing. But it is a distinctly human characteristic. Maybe you call it thinking creatively." She grinned at him, and he could have sworn her blue eyes twinkled. "End of lecture. Is this as far as we need to move this thing?"

"Uh...yeah." He opened the cockpit door and made some adjustments to the instruments, then took out the wheel chocks. "Go on back to your car. I'll be there in a minute." He needed that minute to do some creative thinking.

Nan nodded, a bit surprised at the sudden closed expression on his face. She had been about ready to make peace and try to be friends. After all, despite his bravado he had to have been under stress when he thought his plane would crash, leaving him out here all alone. His manners weren't the worst she'd encountered, either. Furthermore, the longer she was with him, the less brutal and the more handsome he looked. The kind of looks that grow on you, she realized. An interesting man.

She headed back to the car, wondering where he lived and if he would be a likely customer at her new business. She smiled to herself. Probably not, given his negative attitude toward fantasy. But you could never tell. People's private mental lives could be at extreme variance with their outward appearance. She thought about this while, back at the car, she busied herself making certain her possessions in the U-Haul were all right.

BY THE TIME he'd secured the airplane and taken out his stuff, Jesse was sure he had his errant erotic-romantic interests under control. He whistled a favorite tune to further calm his mind. The afternoon breeze had freshened and had all the promise of a cold night in it. All he felt was gratitude that he'd been able to catch an accommodating ride. He scooped up his jacket and shrugged into it as he approached the station wagon. Noting the angle at which it was wedged in the ditch, he decided it would be no problem getting the vehicle out, even with the U-Haul attached. "Nan?" he called. She was nowhere in sight.

"Around here."

He followed the voice to the back of the U-Haul. The sight that met him halted him in his tracks.

She was halfway into the U-Haul. Her rear was rounded and enticing, and her sweatshirt had ridden up to reveal a section of smooth-skinned back and narrow waist. As her upper torso worked on whatever she was doing inside, the muscles in the parts he could see bunched and moved in ways that made him break out in a sweat and long to touch her.

It wasn't fair, he thought, reaching for another smoke. Not damn fair at all. He was too experienced and smart to be caught by a face and body anymore. Then the humor of his thoughts hit him. He grinned at himself and removed his fingers from the cigar. According to his little brother, he was too old for such crazy, wild feelings. So be it. When Nan Black brought her front part out of the U-haul and smiled at him, he managed to just nod curtly.

THE DRIVE to the next town began in silence and mono-syllabic replies to Nan's questions. She had been alone for days and was ready to chat, even with a man who had little sense of social grace. Jesse Rivers, however, was having none of it. She wondered what had caused the moody sul-lenness and finally put it down to worry about his plane. Maybe even a belated sensible reaction to his close call, though she found that a bit difficult to believe. He was, she figured, the kind of man who was unwilling to face his own mortality. Certainly unwilling to admit he'd made a mis-take in judgment. That plane should never have been in the air, as far as she was concerned.

He had gotten her out of the ditch without mishap, demonstrating considerable skill when it came to maneuvering vehicles. When she had tried to be pleasant by complimenting him, however, he had only grunted a reply.

Once out of the ditch, she had taken the driver's seat, explaining that her insurance wouldn't cover another driver. He had taken the news without comment, settling in the passenger seat and turning up the collar of his jacket as if to shut out the sight and sound of her. He had thrown a battered briefcase in the back seat, and she'd wondered briefly what a stunt pilot was doing with such an item, although she doubted her curiosity would be satisfied on that score.

It wasn't satisfied on any score.

"I can drop you at the next town," she said as they sped along. "Or somewhere else, if you want. I'm going quite a ways more."

"Next town is where I want to go. Devil's Hole. I have a friend there who can help me get the plane back in the air."

"All right. I'm going all the way to Hennington. I'm staying there."

Silence. In his head Jesse heard the delighted cackling of some demon. Hennington was his hometown. He felt the need to hum, a technique that always helped him calm down under stress, but stopped himself just in time. She was still talking.

"I'm opening a new business there. The company I work for thinks it'll be a great market. Small, maybe. But steady and loyal." There. Maybe he would get curious.

Silence. Jesse was considering the unfairness of fate. Of all the people to be on the highway when he had to set down the plane, it had to be an alluring female who happened to be opening a small business in Hennington. Then he realized how stupid it was to overreact like this. She was cute, but her head was obviously full of feathers. He would feast his eyes all he wanted, because his mind sure wasn't going to let him get any more involved than that. His days of caring about the appearance of a woman more than her character were long past. He was ready to get involved again, all right, but with the kind of lady who'd make a good wife. He indulged himself, painting a mental picture of such a person. Then he listed his likes and dislikes. Highest on his list of dislikes was superficial attractiveness covering a shallow personality.

"After I get settled and open the place, I'm going to have a slam-bang grand opening. Would you like an invitation?"

"What kind of place?" he asked, not really wanting to know. Nan Black seemed tailor-made for his dislike list.

Nan glanced over at him. He was staring out the window. "It's a video store. You know. VHF, Beta. But it's not the kind of store where you can rent just anything. I'm going to be carrying old classics and family-type entertainment. A few quality art films. All suitable for a wholesome, small-town clientele. And the prices are unbelievably low. The company, Family Film Fantasies, believes in supplying a quality product at a reasonable cost to the consumer."

"Oh."

"You don't like movies?" This was getting annoying.

"No."

"Television?"

"News. Not much else. Sports now and then."

"I see. Just exactly what do you do with your time, Mr. Rivers? When you aren't crash-landing, that is."

Now he looked at her. "I live. Work and play. Just like most everybody else. Life itself is far too interesting to waste time in unreality. I prefer living my adventures in person."

"That can be fatal." Nan grew serious. "I've known guys like you—ones who live on the edge. They don't all get to see thirty, you know."

"Well, I will. Soon, too. I don't live on the edge, either. Everything I do is as safe as I can possibly make it."

Nan laughed.

"Okay, okay. I made a mistake and ended up having to put down on the road. I did it and I didn't get a scratch on me. Or you, for that matter. And don't tell me what you felt while you were driving into that ditch wasn't more excitement than any fantasy could provide."

"What I felt was stark terror. Who needs that? Besides, the daydream you so rudely interrupted was one of my better ones."

Jesse made a derisive sound. "If it was so great, tell me about it. If you have the nerve." They had another hour before they would reach the town of Devil's Hole. He was going to run out of items to list about his future wife, and he was trying his best to be bored with Nan so her California-girl hype couldn't get to him. Listening to some half-baked story was as good a way as any to achieve that, he figured.

He figured wrong. For the next forty minutes, he listened, unwillingly enthralled as she unfolded a tale of high adventure and romance. Not sex. *Romance.* For the first time since he was a small child, Jesse's full attention was on people and events that were imaginary and unreal.

Her tale involved a mythical land of summer plains and winter mountains, crystal lakes and fragrant forests. A lovely, spirited princess pledged to wed an evil wizard. A brave and loyal centaur who rescued her. A quest by the two of them to find a treasure that would release the girl from her pledge. And a happy ending that left Jesse amazed at Nan's cleverness.

"Hey, come on. The centaur died in the mountains after they found the treasure," he protested, questioning the logic of the ending. "How can he be the wizard?"

"He just is." She gestured with a small, well-shaped hand. "You see, he always loved her, but couldn't get past her fear and distrust while he had the wizard aspect on. When he changed into a centaur—"

"But he died!"

"You can't kill a wizard, Jesse. It's one of the rules. They are tricky creatures. Anyway, I've had a lot of fun finishing this. Thanks for listening."

"You mean you made it up as you went along?"

"Not entirely. I had the basic plot figured out before. It's just when I have an audience, even a captive one, I tend to elaborate more than when I'm only telling it to myself in my head."

"Ever write any of these things down?" In spite of himself, he was intrigued. She definitely had a talent, even if he was reluctant to admit appreciation of it.

She shook her head. "I'm a storyteller, not a writer. I really should have been born when folks gathered around the fire at night and listened to the bard spin the tales of the clan. If they let women do it, that is."

"They'd have let you. You're good." He spoke the words behind his hand as if he wasn't sure he wanted her to hear them, but she smiled at the compliment.

"Thanks."

Jesse settled back into silence again, relieved when she didn't try breaking it. Probably worn out from talking so much, he decided. Anyway, he had a few things to think about.

He had been charmed. Not by her beauty this time, but by her imagination. He had enjoyed hearing the silly story. *Liked* it. It beat the hell out of listening to the radio to pass time on the highway. Why, his own mind had conjured up pictures, scenes.... Fantasies...

Fantasies! He almost clapped a hand dramatically to his forehead. *She* was the one all those boxes were for. He'd received them down in Rapid City a week and a half before, merely noting they came from a company with a strange title and were for a person whose name he didn't recognize and who didn't have an address in Hennington. Contacting the company had only led to confirmation that the order was in the right place. He was to hold the crates until an N. Black called for them. Family Film Fantasies paid for the storage without a fuss. He considered telling her about the crates, then decided to wait. They were already on the outskirts of Devil's Hole. If he admitted he lived in Hennington, he'd almost certainly have to ride the rest of the way with her after he made arrangements with Charlie to rescue the plane.

Given the untrustworthy state of both his libido and his mind, that didn't seem like such a good idea.

Nan drove into the town, taking in the Western movie-set storefronts and the people moving casually along the sidewalk, stopping to chat with one another. This was just the kind of place she hoped her new home, Hennington, would be. A wholesome, sane haven of Middle America where she could rediscover the values she'd been taught as a child. Values far different from the ones she had lived with for the past few years.

"Where should I drop you?" she asked her passenger, feeling rather reluctant to part company with him. He intrigued her. Grumpy one minute, all smiles the next. His response to her little story had been gratifying, and she was sure she could make a convert to movies if she had time to be around him a bit longer. "Your house?"

"I don't live here." He pointed to a corrugated metal building at the edge of town. A sign over the door proclaimed the place to be a fix-it shop. A beat-up van and pickup were parked out front. "Just stop there and I'll get out. This friend of mine will help me with the plane."

"Okay." She eyed the structure dubiously. The area around it was full of dead weeds and trash, and she wondered how much help someone who owned a place like this could be. "If you're sure..."

"I'm sure." Reaching into the back, he grasped his briefcase and wondered how to get out most gracefully.

"Um," he said, turning back to her. "Well..."

She held out a hand. "Well, Mr. Rivers. It's been interesting. I certainly hope that if you get to Hennington sometime you'll drop by my store. Even if you don't want to see any movies, I'd enjoy renewing your acquaintance. I know it's not easy to make friends in a new place. Especially in a small town, and I'd like a chance to be friends with you."

Jesse took her hand. It felt so delicate, he was hesitant about squeezing it, but she gave him a firm clasp. "Yeah," he said. "I'll be by when I can." Then he was out of the car.

Nan studied his back as he pushed open the door of the metal building. He looked and acted like a man who couldn't get away from her fast enough. She shook her head and put the station wagon in reverse, steering carefully to allow for the U-Haul. First he had burst into her life in a manner befitting a romantic hero. He had acted both attracted and repelled, then unusually wrapped up in her verbal fantasy. Now he was gone, obviously as quickly as he could manage. Nan sighed. He was certainly flawed, and she wasn't sure if she would even like him if she got to know him better.

But she hoped that sometime soon she would see Jesse Rivers, stunt pilot, again.

CHAPTER TWO

"THIS IS AL'S DELIVERY, isn't it?" Nan said into the receiver of the telephone. She managed only with great difficulty to keep herself from snapping at the innocent, youthful voice at the other end of the line. "I have a letter here from my company saying you have all the merchandise."

"Well, this isn't Al's Delivery, ma'am. This is ALS Delivery. You sure you got the right town? I'd really like to help, but I'm just answering the phone for the boss before I have to get to school, you see."

"Al's...ALS Delivery, Hennington, South Dakota." Nan looked around at the bare shelves lining the walls of her store. She had to have those videos if she was to open tomorrow. "Is the manager there? I'd like to speak to someone who knows what's going on." She regretted her tone as soon as she spoke. The boy was trying to be nice. "Please," she added.

"He's out right now, ma'am, making some deliveries. Can I have your telephone number? I'll have him call you directly he gets in."

She sighed, gave her number and hung up. Staring with unseeing eyes at the empty shelves, she thought that she ought to have expected something like this. So far, everything else had gone much too smoothly to be true. Since that near-disastrous encounter with the crazy stunt pilot, she had experienced nothing but good fortune. On arriving in Hennington, where the storefronts and people were even more appealing than in Devil's Hole, she had gone immediately to the office of Alice Turner, the real estate agent with whom she had been in contact by letter and phone. The woman was warm and friendly and had shown her a rental house that so exactly suited Nan's needs and taste it seemed especially designed for her.

The store was even better. Located just off the main street, but highly visible from almost anywhere in town, it had originally been a grocery shop. Ample parking space in front, no partitions or walls to be knocked down. But it was all the storage area in the back that sold Nan. She phoned the home office immediately to get permission to sign a contract for the company. Alice had then demonstrated that Hennington was indeed a caring town by expressing delight for the man who owned the property.

"It's been sitting empty for so long," she said. "When Ed Mack retired, he couldn't get anyone else to keep the place open for business. Independent grocers just can't compete with the big chains anymore, you know. The money will sure come in handy for him. His wife's sick and needs nurses. You know what a drain that kind of thing can be."

The information had made Nan doubly glad to have rented the place. Not only was it perfect for her, but she was doing some good. That was important. She had been so selfish for so long.

She closed her eyes and let her imagination and memory take her back into the past. She saw herself leaving a loveless, dead-ended marriage. Leaving her family, too: Mom and Dad, and her siblings, Jenny and Sam—people who loved her but couldn't understand her ambition. Saw herself taking the money from a small inheritance left to her by her grandmother, buying a car and packing up her belongings. Saw herself in the car, heading for California. She was going to knock Hollywood on its ear with her brilliant ideas for exciting, unique movie scripts. Fame and fortune were within her reach.

Or so she had thought.

The picture shifted, and she remembered how it had really been. Discouraged and depressed by her inability to get any sort of attention from the film industry, she had gone the route of so many young hopefuls in Tinsel Town and taken a job waiting tables. Her funds had dwindled in spite of the generous tips she usually received—she did have a natural talent for serving customers—and she began to face the possibility she might soon have to return home in disgrace. A failure.

Then Scott had entered the picture. Entered her life and dragged her along a romantic raceway that made her breathless even now just thinking about it. Given her a job and responsibilities that opened a whole new world to her. She discovered then that her real talent lay in business. But in the final chapter, she'd been wise enough to run from Scott and his wild dreams, too. Found her own niche in the video rental business. She'd learned her lesson: depend on yourself, not anyone or anything else! Find your talent and—

"Don't tell me you aren't having a sexy daydream right now, lady. I won't believe you, and that's a fact."

Nan's eyes opened and focused. Jesse Rivers was standing right in front of her, his hands on the counter where her computer and printer rested. An unlit cigar was clamped between his teeth.

"Wh-what?" she stammered, her heart beating wildly. "I—I mean, how did *you* get in here?"

He jerked a thumb toward the front of the building. "Right through the old front door. I knocked. Saw you through the glass just standing there. But you were back off in never-never land. You expect to succeed in running a business when you apparently can't keep your mind on reality for five minutes at a time?''

"I *have* run a business successfully, Mr. Rivers. I know what I'm doing when it comes to retail merchandise. Do you think Family Film Fantasies would send a novice out here to open a store for them?'' She started to tell him about the video center she managed in San Jose, but decided he wouldn't be impressed. His next comment confirmed her suspicion.

"A company with a name like that? I wouldn't be surprised at anything they did.'' He grinned, taking the sting out of his gibe, and the skin at the corners of his eyes crinkled charmingly.

Nan looked him over. He was even scruffier than when she had first met him, if that was possible. In addition to the jeans, boots, T-shirt and jacket, his hair was tousled and his cheeks and jaw stubbled with a blondish beard. But he was still handsome in a go-to-hell kind of way, she had to admit. "Haven't been able to give up the cigars yet, I see,'' she said, reaching over the counter to pluck the offending smoke from his mouth. She dropped it into a trash can.

"Well, I'll be.'' He grinned even wider, though his eyes looked unexpectedly sheepish. "You know, I haven't stuck one of those in my face since the last time we met. You must make me nervous, Nan. Or at least real tense.''

She laughed. The soft sound echoed in the empty building.

Jesse kept the smile, but he was thinking about how true the teasing words were. Ever since he'd called the shop and gotten the message from Jimmy that Ms. Black wanted to talk to him, he'd been getting more and more uptight. Knowing he had no way of avoiding her, since he had mountains of her stuff in his warehouse, he had opted for an immediate confrontation. He hadn't wanted one, he told himself, but he'd have to have one. His emotions puzzled him, and added to his nervousness.

Only now, it seemed his uneasiness was equaled by his excitement. For the past ten days he had heard folks all over town talking about the new lady from California. How darned nice and pretty she was, and how lucky the community was she had decided to move here. How good it was going to be to have some decent videos to watch. The town received very little in the way of network television because of its isolated location, and satellite dishes were expensive. Then there was the odd way he felt when he listened to single guys wonder how she'd react to being asked out. If he didn't know better, Jesse would have sworn he was jealous.

Which was completely ridiculous, because he wanted nothing more to do with her than to receive the check she would write when he delivered her stuff tomorrow. "What did you want me for?" he asked.

"Not a thing." She looked surprised.

"Well, then why'd you call the office? Jimmy said you sounded real put out with him. He's just a kid, you know."

"You're Al?"

"No, I'm Jesse. Remember?"

"But the name of the delivery service..."

"ALS for air, land and sea. Don't be embarrassed. You aren't the first person to make that mistake. I guess I shouldn't have chosen such a confusing name. Kind of misleading, too, seeing as we don't exactly have an ocean in these parts. It seemed like a good idea at the time, though."

"So *you* have my stuff? All the movies and posters? The VCRs?"

"I do indeed. Got you scheduled for tomorrow. What time would you like it all delivered?"

"I need everything delivered this morning," Nan replied, trying to control her annoyance with him. "I'm planning on opening tomorrow, and it's going to take all day and half the night to set up. If you could leave now and bring it all to me right away, I just might make it."

"Oh." He shifted from one foot to the other. "Got a problem with that, Ms. Black. Sorry."

"Lose your problem, Rivers." She put both hands on the counter and leaned toward him. "I *have* to have my merchandise. I placed advertising in the weekly paper and on the radio station. I'm opening tomorrow. Bring me my delivery, please."

"The earliest I could get to it would be late this afternoon or this evening. I have a previous obligation. It's to the guy in Devil's Hole. Charlie. The one who helped me with my plane."

"Unobligate yourself. Get someone else to do it. You *owe* me!"

"Hey, I also owe Charlie. And he did a hell of a lot more than just drive me to town. I have to take some equipment to him and help him with one of his trucks. Now, I'm sorry about this, but I'll deliver your junk to you. I promise."

"Junk!"

"Sorry. I mean your merchandise. I didn't intend to let personal prejudice get into this."

"Sure, you didn't! You're putting doing a favor for a buddy over a professional duty. Now, listen to me, Mr. Rivers. If you won't provide me with the kind of service I need, I'll just take my business elsewhere. I'm sure there are—"

"There's no other delivery service in this section of the state." His smug expression said, *Gotcha!* "Too few businesses for the big carriers, and the post office is slow and expensive. I'm it, Ms. Black. Take me or leave me." Muscles at the sides of his mouth twitched. Clearly, he was enjoying himself.

Nan turned away for a second, forcing back the scalding retort that sprang to mind. He was right. She was going to have to deal with him. Before she started out for Hennington, she had been told by the district manager in Denver that ALS, a small private delivery service, was the best way to go for shipments and delivery. Translation: the only way. But she *had* to have the stuff today. Suddenly she felt so helpless that tears were a dangerous possibility. The last thing she wanted to do was break down and cry in front of this man!

But Jesse saw. Guilt, then anger went through him, leaving him feeling strangely weak and confused. "Hey," he said, reaching out to put his hand on her shoulder. "I didn't come here to upset you. I came because you called, and I thought it would be more neighborly to stop by."

"You knew you had my videos! Why bother to stop unless you were going to deliver?" She jerked her shoulder, dislodging his hand. It had felt too strong and warm. A tear fell from her eye and splashed on his skin. He wiped it off on his jeans as if it had burned like acid.

They stared at each other. The counter was between them, effectively blocking any further physical contact, but it was no barrier to the sexual electricity that zinged with power across the empty space. Nan felt her grasp on reality slipping. His eyes lost that steely look and became warm. His firm lips softened, parted slightly, ready for a kiss. She thought she saw miles into his heart and soul. While she didn't understand a thing, she *knew* this was a man who was far more than the rude jerk he seemed determined to portray. Her heart could open to him and her body...

Her body decided right there and then Jesse Rivers was the most desirable man she'd ever yelled at!

Jesse didn't analyze. He just knew if he didn't get out of the place at once, he'd be over that counter and making a complete fool of himself. Her eyes, skin and hair seemed to glow with an inner light that drew him like a moth to flame. His hands ached to feel the blond silk, to touch the creamy skin, to explore....

To get himself into a situation where he was either going to be thrown in jail, or worse—thinking he was crazy about her when it was clearly only the lust of the moment—was really stupid. Thinking about marriage as he had been lately was making him too vulnerable to women. That was all it was. Jesse looked away and cleared his throat. "I gotta go," he said. "Charlie's waiting on me. But I'll try and get your shipment to you today. I'll make a special effort for your delivery. That suit you?"

Nan shook herself. He sounded angry. All the softness and need had disappeared from his features, and he just looked tough. Tough and bad tempered. A man to be avoided unless absolutely necessary. "I suppose it'll have to," she replied. "But it's easy to see the only reason you have customers is because you're the only game in town. A taste of competition might change your tune and make you more eager to give service with a smile and some consideration." Any sense of desire was gone, and all she wanted was for him to get out of her store.

"You have a real smart mouth, lady. That's not going to get you anywhere. Not around here. It might have worked for you in California, got you the attention you want, maybe, but—"

"In California I didn't need a so-called smart mouth. I *never*, in all the time I was on the coast, *ever* met anyone as rude and temperamental as you! As for attention, I know you get more of that with kindness than nastiness. Think about it, if you decide to give your brain some exercise one

day." Nan forgot the desire she had felt, forgot her appre-
hension and knew only anger. She opened the gate in the
counter, letting it crash down after she came out. "Just put
my delivery out on your loading dock, if you have one. I'll
go downtown and hire some men to pick it up for me. I
don't need you! Maybe I'll start my own delivery service."

"I have a loading dock, but no one's allowed on my
property without my permission." He loomed over her,
glaring. "And good luck starting any other business here.
There's not a man in the county who'd work for a woman
who's off in a twilight zone half the time!"

"Twilight zone?" She stood on tiptoe, equaling his height
and matching his angry stare. "Well, that sure beats getting my thrills bopping around the sky in a plane that's
ready for the scrap heap. At least I can walk away from my
fantasies. Yours are likely to end up squashing you flatter
than a flyswatter!"

"F-flyswatter?" Unreasonably, Jesse found himself ready
to laugh. Found himself wanting to reach out and hug her.
Nothing sexy about the impulse. He just felt sudden affection for her. For her willingness to do verbal battle. For her
spunk.

So he did it.

Nan received the hug in astonishment. Jesse's strong arms
wrapped around her and pulled her to his chest. She was too
startled to resist. She breathed in leather, tobacco and man.
He felt…solid and wonderful. "Oh," she said. She shut her
eyes. And…

He was gone. Just like one of her dreams. "I'll be back,"
he called from the door. Nan opened her eyes and turned in
time to see him walking rapidly away from the store.

He was lighting a cigar.

"So, WHAT'S SHE LIKE? Huh, Jesse?" Jimmy loaded another box into the delivery van. "She sure looks pretty.
Turtle bagged her groceries yesterday, and he says she's real
nice. Friendly to everybody, you know. Prettier close up, he
says."

Jesse ached with weariness from the day's demands. If he
thought about it much, his head ached wondering why he'd
hugged Nan Black that morning. He regarded his brother.
"As far as you and Turtle are concerned, she's an older lady.
If she's not thirty, she's real close." Old lady? Not by a long
shot. But when he was sixteen like Jimmy, thirty had looked
like the first stage of senility. Was he an old man to his
brother? Well, he sure felt like one this evening. He was
tired, and his emotions were still jumbled. Why *had* he
hugged her? Fool thing to do! He started humming under
his breath. Mozart. It cleared his mind. Usually.

Jimmy grinned and shrugged. He could tell the subject
was getting to Jesse, and he enjoyed the power, however
temporary. The classical music was a sure sign Jesse was
bothered and doing his best not to show it. "So, she's old
like you. She's still pretty. I can dream, can't I?"

Clamping down on the impulse to lecture, Jesse made a
noncommittal noise. Jimmy was thirteen years his junior,
and at times he felt more like a father than an older brother.
But they both had a dad, and a good one. Jimmy didn't
need Jesse playing parent. The kid was only living here because it was easier for him to get to school. Jesse studied the
boy while Jimmy laughed and lifted cartons with ease.
Strength ran in the Rivers family, and Jimmy had gotten his
fair share.

His brother was growing up, Jesse realized. Lanky and
tall, with hands, feet and a nose still too big for the rest of
him, Jimmy already topped him by an inch or so. When he
filled in that bony frame with muscle, he was going to be a

man to be reckoned with. Jesse could only hope by then Jim had the good sense to control that man. And to do it better than *he* had.

"Go ahead and dream, if you want," he said, wiping his hands on his jeans. "That'n fifty cents will get you a good cup of coffee about anywhere in this part of the country."

"Aw, Jesse." Jimmy unconsciously imitated his brother's action, cleaning off his hands on his pants. "You really know how to hurt a guy." His grin was wide enough to show the silver retainer that was the only remnant of the braces he'd worn for years. Years during which Jimmy had rarely smiled, much less grinned.

Jesse grinned back. "Come on," he said, jerking his thumb toward the cab of the van. "You drive. I'll introduce you to Ms. Black. You can judge for yourself then, and tell Turtle and the rest of the guys to go looking in their own sections of the pasture."

"You got her roped off for yourself?" Jimmy's astonishment outweighed his delight at the permission to drive. His big brother was no Romeo, for sure, but something in his expression and tone of voice revealed that this Ms. Black was someone special to him. That made it all even more interesting!

"No, I haven't," Jesse snapped. "I just think she's too old for you kids to go talking about her, understand? It's not right."

"Yeah, Jesse." Jimmy hid his smile. Jesse was getting ticked again. This was great! "Yeah, I understand, all right. I sure do."

NAN WAS FURIOUS. She had called ALS three times in the past hour and had raised only an answering machine. He was doing this deliberately, she thought. Because he hated movies. Because she made him angry. Because... because he'd hugged her?

But that didn't make sense. He was a businessman with an obligation to her. He had said he'd be back, hadn't he? She looked outside. Although the sun was still shining bright as ever, it was almost six. She had forgotten how long daylight lasted in the north. A few more weeks and it would be light until nine or later.

Of course, that would be both a benefit and a challenge to her own business. It would have been better to start when the weather wasn't good and the nights long. On the other hand, people would wander in during the light hours of evening to find something to do after dark. Nan's mind shifted from her anger and her problems with Jesse Rivers and she began to think of ways to turn summer to her advantage. In a few minutes, she was seated at her desk, making notes on a yellow notepad. Ideas began coming to her in a rush. Good ideas! Absently, she reached over and turned on the local radio station. Country and western music blared. She concentrated so intently on her ideas that she scarcely heard it.

"DON'T SHE HEAR US?" Jimmy looked at Jesse. His brother's mouth was pulled into a tight line. They stood at the front of the old grocery store, banging on the door. The lady was clear across the room, though, behind a counter. She hadn't looked up at the noise. Her head was bent, and she fiddled with her hair, poking at it with a pencil. "What's the matter with her?" He did hear some music. Maybe it was too loud.

"Beats the hell out of me," Jesse muttered. Was she just sitting there, ignoring him because she was mad? He rubbed a hand over his face. He was feeling dog tired after helping Charlie with his truck as well as doing his regular runs and the office work. Jimmy was a big help with the physical stuff and answering the phone while he was busy, but the kid just wasn't ready for more office responsibility, and he still did have schoolwork to do in the afternoons. So Jesse had done everything. Now, he was delivering her damn movies a day early because she'd asked. If she thought sitting there and letting him holler at her was funny, she had another think coming. "I'm going around back," he told Jimmy. "Keep knocking. Maybe there's another way in." More trouble for him. This was the thanks he got for going out of his way for her. Special delivery, be hanged!

There was, however, another way in. Jesse opened the back door to the storeroom with no trouble at all. She hadn't even shut it all the way. Not only was she thoughtless, she was dangerously careless. True, Hennington was a virtually crime-free town, but you never knew. From time to time some hard cases passed through. She was probably going to have cash on hand, and she was a woman working alone. Music blared from the front. She'd never hear an intruder with that racket! He moved through the storeroom, noting how clean it was. She'd found something to do today, at least. He wondered how she'd react if he suggested she come clean up his place? Probably have a fit and declare she was no cleaning woman. He neared the door to the front of the store and imagined her indignant expression. It made him smile in spite of the situation.

"Who's in there?" The question came loud and bold. "Don't you move! I've got a gun, and I'm calling the sheriff!"

"It's just me, Nan." Jesse ambled wearily through the door. He froze when he saw this time she wasn't bluffing about the gun. The black muzzle of a businesslike pistol pointed at him for a moment before she raised it to the ceiling with a practiced gesture. "My God," he yelled. "Are you crazy!" Out of the corner of his eye, he saw Jimmy pounding the door, his young face twisted with fear for his brother.

Nan slid on the safety. "No, I am not crazy. You are, for sneaking up on me. I just now spotted the kid trying to break in the front, and then I heard...someone in the back. What was I supposed to think?" She put the pistol back in the desk drawer and turned off the radio.

Jesse almost sputtered, trying to find the words to fit his feelings. He settled for a simple recitation of facts. "The kid isn't trying to break in. He's trying to get your attention. He's my brother, and we're delivering your crates, Ms. Black. Tell me where you want them, and we'll be out of here as quickly as possible."

"Oh." Nan sat down. She glanced at the front door. The kid was standing there, no longer pounding on the glass. He had a very strange expression on his face. "I'm sorry. I guess I didn't think you were coming tonight."

Jesse didn't dare say anything. He was just too angry. He lifted the counter gate and went over to let Jimmy in. Before his brother could blurt out words, he said quietly, "Just start unloading, Jimmy."

Nan watched them, feeling like an idiot. Knowing she didn't need to be ashamed, she still couldn't help a paralyzing embarrassment. Jesse Rivers had a way about him that made her feel just plain old everyday Incompetent Female. It was an uncomfortably familiar sensation, and one she'd thought she'd left behind years ago. She glared at him, wondering how she could ever have thought he was attractive. How she could ever have let him touch her. *Hug* her.

But he and his brother were fulfilling his promise. As she sat unmoving behind her protective counter, the two brought in boxes and crates. They spoke to each other in low, masculine tones, shutting her out even further. She saw the resemblance between them. Jesse was stockier and more solid, but the boy was showing signs of growing into the same kind of rugged handsomeness. . . .

What was the matter with her! Nan forced herself to get up. Her legs still felt weak from the emotions that had run through her. Pointing the gun at another human being had been a terrible experience, even though she had prepared for it by training in California. Thank goodness it had only been Jesse and not someone she might actually have had to fear!

But how had he gotten in? She was sure she'd locked up the back securely. No matter how placid and friendly Hennington seemed, she wasn't dumb enough to leave her business and herself vulnerable. Turning her back on the two males, she went into the storage area.

The door was open. Nan shut it, and it popped open. "Well," she said. "No wonder." She leaned her weight against it and heard a click as the latch caught. The door was warped. She'd have to get a carpenter out to plane it. Good thing she'd found out about it now, before she started taking in cash and before her inventory was displayed.

"Anyone could have walked in on you." Jesse's voice was close enough to make her jump. "Where'd you get that cannon? You pull it on the wrong person, and you could end up in jail yourself, you know. Or worse, if you don't know how to use it."

"I know the law." Nan faced him, determined not to lose her temper or self-control. "I have a license. And training. I didn't have it on me in the car because I'd passed through some states where my documents wouldn't be legal, so I'd stashed it in a suitcase. I already apologized to you, but I thought I was securely locked in, and only a thief could possibly be in the storeroom."

"The door was ajar." He stood, legs planted wide, his arms crossed over his chest and a scowl on his face.

"I know." She slapped the door lightly with her palm. "It's warped. Know a reliable carpenter? I'd like to get this fixed as soon as possible."

"Jesse could tool it down for you tonight." The teenager had come through the storeroom door and stood behind his brother. "He's got all the equipment in his garage."

Jesse did not look pleased. "Jimmy, this is Ms. Black. My brother, Jimmy Rivers." He waved at the boy. Nan smiled and started to speak, but Jesse wasn't through. "I could do it," he added. "But what about the stuff out front? Someone could sashay right on in and help themselves."

"Oh, I'm liable to be here until morning. Setting up will take hours and hours. I'm willing to pay generously for the job if you'll do it. I'd feel much more secure knowing the door was fixed." She ran the tip of her finger down the uneven edge of the door. Maybe the brief rain yesterday had added just enough humidity to make it buckle.

Jesse watched her caress the wood. The gesture was unconsciously seductive, and it got to him, clearing away his anger and resentment and making him want to help her. Fixing the door would take him less than an hour. He cleared his throat. Jimmy poked at his shoulder and nodded encouragingly. "Um, I'll fix it under one condition," Jesse said. "A condition involving your safety."

"What's that?" Nan straightened and brushed stray strands of hair back from her face. She was tired and not in the mood to put up with any of Rivers's macho bull.

"Let Jimmy stay here. He's big enough to discourage any casual intruder, and he could be some help, too. He's strong for his age."

"Oh." The request surprised her. "Oh, okay. But wouldn't you rather be doing something with your friends?" she asked the boy. "I mean, it's liable to be boring just hanging around here."

Jimmy grinned. "Not much else going on, Missus Black," he said, pronouncing her name in a way that made it sound like "Mrs. Black." "It's a school night, and this town is pretty dead anyhow. I'd rather help you. I ain't like Jesse. I love movies, if that's what's worrying you."

"Well, I'm glad to hear one of you approves of my wares. Call me Nan, please, Jim. Mrs. Black makes me sound a hundred years old." She laughed, and Jimmy laughed, too.

Jesse couldn't laugh. *Mrs.* Black! His insides felt as if they were getting a coating of ice. She was married? Fortunately, Jimmy started firing questions and Mrs. Black came up with ready answers, and Jesse didn't have to reveal the distress he felt.

CHAPTER THREE

SEVERAL HOURS LATER, Jesse had a lot to think about. For one thing, he was sitting in her living room, doing that thinking.

Well, she was married. Jesse took a long swallow from his beer. *Was* married. And divorced, years ago. He squinted at the TV screen and waited, his curiosity at a high peak. His emotions were at a high something, too, but he had already decided to ignore them. To an extent, he was succeeding. Jimmy was a gold mine of information concerning *Ms.* Nan Black, and when he could manage to tear his attention away from the action on the screen, he was spilling it all to Jesse.

Which suited Jesse fine. He wasn't up to asking the questions directly. She stirred him up, and he wasn't sure just why.

"So after she dumped this turkey, Black, in Wyoming," Jimmy said, "she took off for California. Tried to make it writing scripts for a while, but that didn't pan out. So she started working as a business manager for this race car driver, Scott somebody." His voice trailed off as he became absorbed in the video again.

Jesse sat up from his slouched position on the sofa. They were both in Nan's living room, watching a video she had selected for them as part of her reward for their help. He had fixed her door, then pitched in along with Jimmy to set up her store for tomorrow. With the three of them working, it had taken only a few hours. Hours Jesse had enjoyed because of Nan's presence. Enjoyed? That was a weak word to describe the way his skin had felt electrified when she moved near him. By the time they were done, and she had made offers that ensured they'd be together longer, he was in no shape to resist. Not even when it meant having to sit and watch one of her silly videos. Besides, Jimmy's enthusiasm for the treat had been undeniable. To have refused would have made Jesse out to be a real wet blanket.

The movie was a war flick, and Jesse found the parts with the airplane sequences actually worth some of his attention. He couldn't tell you what the rest of the story was about. Jimmy seemed to like it, though. Jesse let his attention wander. His thoughts returned to their conversation. "Race car driver named Scott? Not Scott Fielding?" Jesse asked. "That his name?"

"Yeah, I think so." Jimmy didn't take his gaze off the screen as he brought a pizza round to his mouth. "Yeah, that's the guy's name. She kind of indicated he was a turkey, too." He made an appreciative noise and reached for another round.

The other part of their reward was dinner. Nan Black was out in the kitchen, fixing it. That part, Jesse had accepted enthusiastically, since he was hungry enough to eat anything. If the appetizers were any indication of her cooking talents, he thought, they were in for a treat. He looked around the small living room, noting how she had made it comfortable in just a short time. The furniture was old, though in good shape—a sofa, easy chair and coffee table, facing an entertainment center. The equipment in the center wasn't new, either, but it was quality stuff. One painting hung on the wall over the sofa. An amateur effort, but not bad. It showed a small farmhouse against a wide prairie sky. No family photographs or knickknacks. Books were piled by the easy chair, indicating she did more with her mind than sedate it watching endless fantasies. Except for the absence of personal trinkets, the room looked well lived in.

Jesse thought about what Jimmy had just said. Scott Fielding! She'd managed Scott Fielding? Anyone who followed sports knew of his skill and insane showmanship on the racecourse. What was she doing here, then, setting up a little business in an out-of-the-way spot like Hennington? If she'd had anything at all to do with the famous racer's career, she ought to be able to name her job and price anywhere in the country. "She say she knew any guys she didn't think were turkeys?" he asked, wanting to keep the flow of information coming.

"Jimmy's not." Nan answered his question. She must have heard all their talk. He turned and saw her standing in the doorway, wiping her hands on a towel. She still had on jeans, but had changed from a cotton sweater to an old flannel shirt. She looked slim, domestic and desirable. "I'm reserving judgment on you, Jesse Rivers." She smiled, making the comment into a joke. "Dinner's ready. Come on."

Both men jumped to their feet at the invitation. The hungers driving them, however, were not exactly the same.

Nan set the platter of spaghetti and meatballs on the kitchen table and sat down. It was a strange sensation to be serving dinner to men again. Particularly since the men kind of made a family, being brothers. She pulled her chair into place and was reaching for her fork when she saw they both had bowed their heads. She did the same and listened as Jesse uttered a simple prayer of thanks. Then she took up her fork and spoon and started eating. Jesse and Jimmy didn't start. They dived in.

"This's great!" Jimmy praised between huge mouthfuls. He was on a second helping before Nan could blink. "Jesse usually just opens a few cans and heats up whatever's in them for us after work at night.''

"It is good to have real food," Jesse agreed. "I can cook, but I rarely have the inclination by the time I get to the kitchen." He rubbed a piece of garlic toast around his empty plate and went for the platter again.

"You both act starved." She ladled out some salad for herself. No point in trying to compete for the meat. "Maybe I should be obligated to you on a regular basis. I really do appreciate what you did, and this meal is little enough thanks.''

"Well, you could—" Jimmy started to say.

"This is thanks enough," Jesse interrupted. "We get fed properly when we go home on the weekend. Mom's a terrific cook, too." He stared down at his plate. It had been far too long since he'd taken advantage of home cooking. Or home at all.

"Since when do you—" Jimmy tried again to have his say.

"Eat up, Jimmy," said Jesse. "We've got to get home. You have school in the morning, and it's after eleven already.''

"But I haven't seen the end of the movie."

"Some other time, okay? You need your rest."

"Aw, Jesse..." But Jimmy's brother shut down his protest with a look.

Nan felt a wedge of anger enter her good mood. She had no business interfering, but her impulse was to go to Jimmy's defense. She knew exactly how he felt, getting the law laid down by her older brother. It had certainly happened often enough to her when she was still at home. She bit off words that would undoubtedly start trouble and suggested they could watch the end of the show over dessert. She had strawberry ice cream, she said, and she was sure she had sneaked some chocolate cookies past her calorie conscience when she was at the store the other day.

"We'll pass on dessert," Jesse said, rising and picking up his empty plate. "Some other time, maybe. Thanks."

Jimmy's expression fell almost to the floor.

They helped clear and volunteered to wash and dry, but she wouldn't let them. If Jimmy's bedtime was so important, she said, they'd better get right on home. The sarcasm stung her tongue and cast a cloud over the evening to match the one Jesse had flung. Nan didn't care. Her anger at him for Jimmy's sake had grown to a feeling of intense dislike.

But at the front door, after sending Jimmy on to start the van, Jesse Rivers redeemed himself somewhat. He paused under the porch light and looked at her. The yellow light caught the gold in his hair and haloed him. "He's my only brother," he said. "I love him like he was my own kid. I may not always do what's right by him, but it isn't because I'm not trying. Understand?"

"I guess I don't." She frowned, regarding him as directly as he was staring at her. "I'm the baby in my family, and I tell you, I got real sick of everyone thinking they knew what was best for me. You're probably right about tonight. It is late. But you didn't have to cut him off like that."

"Like what?"

"You really don't know, do you?" She studied his eyes. He looked confused. "You interrupted him at least three times. Didn't even let him finish the sentence. You might as well have stomped on his feelings with your work boots, to judge from his expression."

"God, did I do that?" He rubbed a hand over his face. "I'm sorry."

"Don't apologize to me. Talk to Jimmy." She crossed her arms over her chest. The night was chilly, getting cold. So why did her face feel so warm?

Jesse smiled. "Yes, ma'am. I'll do that. I got careless with his feelings. Thanks for pointing it out to me." The smile erased the brooding lines on his face. "And thanks for one of the best meals I've had in a long while. I don't actually get home most weekends, though Jimmy usually does." He leaned forward and brushed her temple with his lips. "Thanks, Nan. For everything."

"Anytime." She stood still, tingling, while he walked away. He climbed into the passenger side of the van, and she saw Jimmy turn to him as he spoke. They talked. They smiled. When the van drove off, they both waved cheerfully to her. Nan watched until the red rear lights disappeared.

Then she went back into her house, wondering what in the world was going on with her and Jesse Rivers.

BY THE NEXT MORNING, she had relegated that question to a very low place on her priority scale. She had much more important matters to deal with. Thanks to her helpers, she was set and ready for customers at ten, when she unlocked the front door. She had deliberately chosen a Friday to open, hoping she would draw the TGIF crowd in the evening. While she hadn't expected the morning to bring a horde of potential clients, waving money, she had hoped for more than the trickle of interested folk that actually came by. At ten-forty, a little old lady, who walked with the help of a stout cane, wandered in, browsed around, glaring at the video box covers and the television, ignored Nan's offers of assistance and wandered out. Nan shrugged, changed the video in the display from *Star Wars* to *Bambi* and rearranged a few posters. Know your audience, she reminded herself. Adjust to it.

At noon several women came in, greeted Nan cheerfully, checked out her wares, declared they were just looking and left, talking soap operas. Nan put *Somewhere in Time* in the display. If they wanted romance, she'd give it to them! No one else, romantic or otherwise, showed up for the next few interminable hours.

Relief came at three-thirty. *Time* had come to its tear-jerking conclusion, and she had put in *The Black Stallion*. Just as the movie opened, a crowd of noisy children poured in the door. They were followed by two women, who were talking and laughing as loudly and freely as the kids. Nan's smile when she said hello to them all was genuine.

"Hi," said the taller of the two women. She had ginger-colored hair and a wide smile. Energy fairly crackled off her freckled skin. "You're Nan Black." She put out her hand. "I'm Sue Petersen." They shook. "My husband, Walker, and Jesse are good buddies. Jesse said we just had to come here and check out your place!"

"Oh?" Nan kept the smile in place. Jesse had actually recommended her wares? "What kind of videos would you like to see?"

Sue Petersen introduced her friend, Bertie Reynolds. Bertie was in town for the day to shop. She lived with her two children on a ranch about fifty miles out, she explained. "We want a 'kiddie' movie," Bertie said. She was short and dark, with carved, gorgeous features that made Nan wonder if she was a Native American. Her next words confirmed it. "But no cowboy and Indian stuff, please."

"Bertie's kids root for the Indians," Sue explained. "Makes it awkward, given the usual ending."

"I may have just the thing." Nan lifted the counter gate and led the way over to the science fiction section. She took down a box with a lurid front. "Don't judge this by the cover," she said. "It's really a delightful adventure story. And the hero is an American Indian in charge of a human colony on another planet in the future. I think all the kids will like it.''

Bertie grabbed the box and read the blurb on the back. "This is fantastic! I didn't even know they'd made this movie.''

Nan shrugged. "It never was released. That's the beauty of videos. You get to see material that wasn't thought to be commercial enough for the theaters, but is still good stuff. A lot of it isn't good, of course. I try screening everything on my shelves, so I know what I can recommend.'' She tapped the box. "This one, I loved!''

"Jesse said you were enthusiastic.'' Sue smiled as if at a private joke. "He and Walker got together at my kitchen table this morning to plan a fishing trip, and he had trouble talking about anything but you.''

Nan raised an eyebrow. Sue Petersen did not elaborate.

The two women chose a few more children's movies, and Nan suggested a romantic one for Sue and her husband to watch after the kids went to bed. It was easy to tell she and Walker had a good relationship. The sparkle in Sue's eyes when she spoke of him was a reliable indicator. Her voice even took on a different timbre when he was mentioned. Nan felt a slight itch of envy for her happy marriage. If she had found someone who made her feel like that, she'd still be married herself.

"I know you're real busy with your new business,'' Sue said before she and Bertie took their charges and left. "But I'd like us to get to know each other. How about lunch?''

Nan laughed, delighted to have an invitation, but disappointed she couldn't accept. "I'd really like that, but without an assistant, I'm stuck here. Sunday's the only day off I give myself.''

It had been a toss-up between Sunday and Monday, but she had decided business on Saturday would be better if people didn't have to return movies until Monday. Sunday had been a marketing choice, but she was comfortable with it. She thought she might even try attending church, a practice she had abandoned after leaving Wyoming.

"Sunday, then." Sue wrote down an address on a scrap of paper. "My house about one o'clock. It'll be family and some other people, but we can still talk."

"I'd love it!" Nan took the address. "What can I bring?"

"Just yourself and a good appetite. There's always too much food, and I hate dealing with leftovers."

They chatted a bit longer, then Sue and Bertie left, kids in tow and entertainment for the afternoon under their arms. Nan put the address in her desk drawer. An invitation to lunch on Sunday at a private home was a precious gift, she thought. It made her feel more welcome in the community than anything else that had happened so far.

The rest of the afternoon was slow, but not dead. She rented out several VCR players as well as movies and made a note to herself to investigate stocking machines to sell. Once people got into the habit of watching the videos, they would want their own machines, rather than going to the trouble of renting one every time. She was beginning to see the wisdom of her company's decision to set up small operations in out-of-the-way places. Properly handled, such a place could be a very profitable market. And she was just the person to handle it! Indeed, she was loving it.

Though she refused to admit it to herself in so many words, as the evening progressed, she hoped Jesse Rivers would walk through the front door. After seven, the number of customers increased. Some just came to look, among them several men who seemed more interested in her than in her movies. Nan gave them scarcely a glance. She was too busy with the people who wanted her help, who wanted her videos.

Lots of people wanted movies she didn't and wouldn't carry. "I'm sorry," she said to a teenager who looked about Jimmy Rivers's age. "I don't carry any X-rated videos. Just family stuff. Can I recommend...?" The boy left before she could finish. A woman standing in line behind him sniffed disapproval. Nan smiled at her as she picked up the comedy the woman had chosen and put the video in the box.

"I know that boy's mother," the woman said, her voice tight. "She'd be so ashamed."

"He's young," Nan commented soothingly. The boy's mother was undoubtedly going to hear of the incident. Too bad, considering the rather sour source. "Kids are entitled to do some silly things, don't you think?"

From her expression, the woman thought no such thing. Nan didn't continue the discussion, she felt a prickle of uneasiness over the encounter. It was likely she could have been in deep trouble if she had chosen a company that insisted she stock the racier material. She would have to use discretion in choosing selections from the monthly order sheets. Keep it clean, she thought. Clean material and good quality!

Jesse didn't show up. Neither did Jimmy, which surprised her a bit. She had kept the video he hadn't finished watching in hopes he'd get a chance to view the rest over the weekend. Maybe he'd gone back home, she reasoned. But he could have taken a machine and more movies with him. She certainly owed him more than dinner and part of a video for the help he'd given her.

Of course, in fairness, Jesse had been a big help, too. The back door now shut as tight as a drum and had a big deadbolt lock. Once she shut herself in, she was as safe as can be. He'd done a first-rate job. And he had refused any payment for his work. She felt uncomfortable with that. Sure, she'd fed him dinner, but that wasn't anything. She still owed him.

"Got any James Bond stuff?" The big, blond woman sounded impatient, as if she had asked the question more than once.

Nan came out of her thoughts and concentrated on her customers.

By the time she closed up, did her accounts and left the store locked front *and* back, she was so tired that if Jesse had come by and begged to watch a movie with her, she would have refused. She drove home, yawning, and fell into bed after forcing herself to eat half a peanut butter sandwich. She was going to have to look for part-time help soon, she thought just before she went to sleep. She was too tired even to remember her dreams.

Saturday passed in much the same pattern. Slow in the morning and afternoon, but picking up by evening. Nan was well rested after her deep sleep and didn't feel so exhausted by the time she turned the Closed sign around on the front door.

In fact, she felt restless. She wanted to be with people. Be with someone. Talk...

She thought of Jesse Rivers... Be with someone...

Make love... With someone...

Well, that wasn't possible, she told herself angrily. She had chosen this road, and she was determined to follow it. Even if she were the type to go out looking for companionship on a Saturday night, she would be extremely unwise to do it here. She was the "new kid on the block" in Hennington, and if she wanted her business to be successful, she would do well to behave in a manner in keeping with the values of this place. That meant closing up at ten and going directly home to her bed alone. Too bad! Eventually, she would surely find a social life. But for now, discretion was the better part! She picked out an old favorite from the shelves and tossed the video on the passenger seat. That would be her companion for the rest of the evening!

Nan unlocked her front door just as her phone started shrilling. She raced over and grabbed the receiver, hoping irrationally. "Oh, hi, Mom," she said, when the familiar voice on the line asked if she was catching her at a bad time. "No, I just got in from the store. I'm glad you called. Really!" She pulled a kitchen chair away from the table and sat down. Taking a deep breath, she began to fill her parent in on the events since she had arrived in Hennington. Most of the events, anyway. She did not talk about the handsome stunt pilot-deliveryman.

As she talked, however, she got rid of some of her feelings of guilt. She had actually been disappointed to hear her mother's voice instead of Jesse's! And she ought to have called home instead of waiting and letting her mom make the move. She ought to have called the day she got to Hennington. Her dad came on with a gruff hello and wished her good luck. Nan sensed their love and concern, but couldn't react to it. Their worry made her feel like a little kid. Like the baby, who had to be taken care of by everyone. Well, she was far from a baby anymore, and the only one of her parents' children who had left home by more than a few miles. They had trouble with that. That, and the fact she'd divorced and wasn't about to remarry. By the time she hung up, she thought she had soothed them adequately, although she felt far from soothed herself.

She poured a glass of milk and went into the living room. Popping the video, she sat in the easy chair, which had belonged to her grandmother, and stretched out her legs. The movie began playing. Nan saw none of it. Her mind was on other matters.

JESSE SCOWLED at his beer. He'd nursed the drink for most of the evening. Two inches remained, and they were flat. He glanced at his watch. Eleven-ten. She ought to be out of there and home by now. A lovelorn country and western ballad grated on his ears. The noise in the bar acted like sandpaper on his nerves. The Canteen was a place where locals gathered on Saturday night for relatively low-key partying. The roadhouse just outside town was for the rowdier types. Jesse liked the crowd here, and he usually relaxed and had a good time. He'd been here for hours. Been here since he had found himself driving toward the video store and changed direction before he made a fool of himself again.

A moth to the flame.

The funny thing was, he couldn't figure out why he felt this way. Why he was attracted on the one hand and scared spitless on the other. Jesse laughed automatically at a joke made by one of the other men sitting at his table. He hadn't heard a word of it. A woman, wife of one of the guys at the next table, came over and said hello. She sounded as if she'd had too much to drink. Jesse lifted his hand an inch in greeting, then retreated into his thoughts. The wife wandered on to more attentive company.

What was wrong with him? So she was pretty, clever, a good cook. She wasn't any more or any less than other women. So why couldn't he get Nan Black off his mind? He looked around the bar. Two single women were giving him the eye. He dated them both from time to time. Some of the married ones were watching him, too, but that was not his style. Not his style at all.

Neither was sitting around on a Saturday night, mooning over a woman who was nothing special. Jesse drained his beer and stood up. This was stupid. He was going home to bed.

NAN JAMMED her hands deep into her jacket pockets. The night was cool, but not cold. The air tingled, and the stars were bright. Walking was helping her relax—something the movie had failed to do. She knew what was going on. A lot of *stuff* was churning up inside, and she wasn't dealing with it. She couldn't. Old stuff from her break with her parents after her divorce. Stuff from her years in California, where her social life had been full, if not fulfilling. New stuff from the ambitions burning in her... That was the stuff that mattered. What she needed to do was clear her mind and emotions and get on with the job!

What was so hard about that?

The sidewalk ran out as she left her neighborhood, and she walked on the edge of the street pavement. The houses became smaller, the front yards less cared for. Nobody was really rich in Hennington, she reflected, but some folks had coped with the life better than others. She stopped and looked around. The lot on her right had two decaying automobile bodies as decor on the front lawn. In the next block, the pavement ceased and the road was merely graveled. Another block, and town ran out altogether, giving way to flat prairie. What would keep people here all their lives, she wondered?

What would keep a man like Jesse Rivers here?

Thinking of him increased her inner turmoil. Face it, she had really hoped he'd come by this evening. Nothing Jimmy had told her indicated his big brother had a steady woman, but she couldn't imagine a man like that living a monastic existence. Not by a long shot!

She tried picturing him with one of the local lovelies. It was easy to see, and it really bothered her! She hunched her shoulders and stalked on out toward the prairie. Her sneakers scrunched softly on the gravel. She stepped off the road and walked on the dirt and grass. *If it bothers you so much,* she thought, *then do something about it.* She kicked at a dirt clod. *Ask him out yourself! See Jesse Rivers socially and get him out of your system.* She stopped and looked up at the wide sky. Taking a deep breath of clean, fresh air, she realized she felt much, much better.

JESSE CRUISED the street, feeling ridiculous. He had a tape blaring classical music from the player, filling the truck cab with wild string sounds. It might as well have been heavy metal. He was certainly behaving like a teenager! he thought. Sweaty palms, jittery stomach, horny body... Her lights were still on. He could stop and knock.... He could...

He could make a complete fool of himself! It was after midnight. What would she think he wanted at this hour? To gaze soulfully into her eyes? To take her to bed?

Jesse slowed his pickup and grinned wryly. Both ideas had a lot to be said for them. Who was he kidding? He wanted to see her socially. Liked the idea of taking her to bed. *Grow up,* he told himself. He turned down the music. *You want to see her? Do it. Call her and ask her out. You're acting like Jimmy, not like an adult male with a temporary case of the hots.* He made a U-turn in the middle of the street and headed home. He felt better. Much better.

CHAPTER FOUR

IN SPITE OF not getting to sleep until after one in the morning, Nan woke bright and early Sunday. Sunlight blazed through the window, giving the tiny bedroom an airiness that lifted her spirits. She literally bounced out of bed, full of energy and a sense of anticipation.

The shower picked her up even more. By the time she sat down to a breakfast of hot oatmeal and toast, she was in such a good mood she could scarcely sit still. She had come to some wise, simple decisions regarding her yen for one Jesse Rivers, she had a luncheon invitation this afternoon from a woman she felt would become a friend, her business was up and running.... It just couldn't get much better than this right now.

She had a great deal to be thankful for.

She decided to go to church.

In Hennington that didn't involve much choice, she found when she checked the phone directory. There was one church in town. Hennington Community Church, an uninspired but practical title. Other denominations were listed, but folks had to go the distance to get to them. There was also a small advertisement for a home church, but she dismissed that as being probably closed to a newcomer with no spiritual credentials. In any event, she wanted just a plain old, regular church. She wanted to become part of this community, she reminded herself, so she ought to check out the local congregation. Noting the hour of the service and seeing she had plenty of time, she went into the front room and sat down in her grandmother's chair.

She spent an hour writing personal letters to friends back in California and penned a conciliatory note to her parents, promising a visit one of these days. A twinge of guilt turned inside her as she sealed that envelope. Such a visit would only bring back all the old hurts. She was never going to make that trip, and they knew it. However, the letter was a way to show she still felt love.

Forty minutes before eleven, she went into the bedroom to dress. Girl clothes today, she told herself. Jeans were fine for work in this country, but she would bet a nickel and more the women in Hennington dolled up on Sunday. Choosing a light purple dress in a blend of wool and silk, she tossed it on the bed and rummaged in a drawer for panty hose.

Pulling on the hose, she reflected once again how much she hated the things. Someday, some saint would design stockings for women that were not only pretty, but comfortable. Now *that* would be the way to make a mark on the world! Nan grimaced and reached for the dress.

Its soft folds fell over her arm, and memories streamed into her mind. She had bought it and worn it when she was with Scott. Dear, crazy Scott. She patted the material. He had seemed so perfect at first. So handsome, very romantic, adventurous, exciting. The ideal fantasy man.

But he was just that: a fantasy. She lifted the dress and dropped it over her head. He was a child, really, not a man. A man in disguise, pretending. He had all the flash and dash and none of the solidity that marked an adult male. None of the dependability. She fastened the buttons and snaps and set the belt at the right notch.

Well, she would always care for him a little and be grateful to him for making her realize she was unlikely ever to find the ideal man—one who combined all those wild, exciting qualities with the kind of nature a woman could depend on all through life. She went into the bathroom and put on a touch of makeup. Such a man probably didn't exist except in her mind. She pulled her hair back on both sides with barrettes, decided the style made her look too young and redesigned it into an upswept twist.

Then she grabbed a long silk scarf, a light wool coat and went to church.

JESSE SAT in his place up front, wishing like mad he hadn't agreed to do the music today. Ordinarily, when Walker asked him to do some special stuff, he jumped at the opportunity. Today he'd have given his right arm to be just about anywhere else.

Nan Black sat out in the congregation, staring up at him as if he were from outer space and had green skin! She, on the other hand, looked as if she had just stepped down from heaven.

Well, so what? She sure had every right to be here, just like anyone else. It was his problem that he hadn't expected her to be a churchgoer. Jesse shifted in his seat and tried to concentrate on the organ music. He'd been doing this far too long to let some woman make him self-conscious about it.

Music soothed him. Not all music, but a lot of it. He listened to it while he worked when he was alone. He walked to the rhythm of it in his head when he strode around the acres of wheat at his old family home. And, most important, he soared to the wild strains of it when he flew. He closed his eyes. Bach took him aloft. Swung him in his imagination through an intricate aerobatic sky dance. Jesse relaxed. Then Walker's strong voice welcoming the people to worship brought him solidly back to earth. Jesse felt good. He was home.

Nan stood with the rest of the congregation and sang the familiar words of the opening hymn. Her hands shook with nervousness and embarrassment, and she prayed the older woman standing beside her didn't notice. She had gone to church often enough when she was little to be comfortable with the service. That was not the problem. There were several others.

First, when the two grown men had followed the teenage acolyte bearing the cross up to the front of the church, she had thought for a heart-stopping moment Jesse Rivers was the minister. But the other man wore the black suit, shirt and collar. Jesse's suit was gray. He looked magnificent in it! It was clear she had misjudged him badly, figuring as she had that he was just a jeans and T-shirt type who'd probably not even own a tie, much less a dress suit. She wasn't ready to deal with this new dimension to him. After her carefully thought-out decisions last night, she didn't feel ready to be shaken up so soon.

Then, there was the other man. The minister's name was Walker Petersen. She shut her eyes and suppressed a groan of embarrassment. She ought to have noticed on the bulletin or the board outside. Walker Petersen. The Reverend. Sue's husband.

Sue Petersen, who had waved cheerily to her from a front pew when she first came in. They didn't speak because Nan was a little late and the organ was already sounding. Sue, to whom she had rented a fairly racy romantic movie the day before. Hardly fare for a preacher and his wife! Nan felt a hot blush covering her face.

So much for cementing her reputation with community leaders. She looked up at Walker's stern visage as he surveyed the congregation. He had dark hair, tinged with silver, receding at the temples, and piercing black eyes. He did not look like a man who would be amused by her little film and the romantic rompings therein. She suppressed a small shiver.

Actually he didn't look like a man she'd expect a woman like Sue to be fond of. Too uptight, too little warmth. A puzzle. She studied the back of Sue's head. The ginger-haired woman was in the second row, the length of the pew next to her filled with small children. Four of them! Like little stair steps. She remembered the crowd of kids that had come into the store on Friday. Well, maybe he had some time for warmth, after all. She shouldn't judge him on first appearance, especially when he was "in role."

But that hardly let her off the hook. She sank back in her seat after the hymn was finished, then sprang back up when she saw no one else sitting. Her blush deepened. Was she doomed to go through the morning in a state of total embarrassment? She had committed one faux pas with the movie and another with her choice of outfit. She was way, way overdressed. While Jesse wore a suit, he was one of the few men so garbed. Many wore jeans. So did a number of women, and nearly all the kids. Everyone looked scrubbed and fresh and nice, but not fancy. Rather as if they were at an informal family gathering instead of a solemn worship service. Apparently the rules she had learned as a child didn't apply here. She watched Petersen's back as he intoned the words of contrition and forgiveness. He sounded grim and solemn. The congregation was silent.

And then the man astonished her. He turned around and raised his hands. His face was changed completely by a joyful smile. "We are forgiven!" he said. "Greet your brothers and sisters!" Nan stood frozen as the sound of happy laughter rose around her and people started shaking hands and hugging. Jesse and the minister embraced and slapped each other on the shoulders, their grins as big as could be! Their friendship and love was open for all to see.

"Mrs. Black?"

Nan turned at the soft voice. The tiny, white-haired woman smiled up at her and held out a small hand. "My name's Inge Frank," the lady said. "Welcome."

"Hi. Thanks." Nan shook the hand carefully, wary of its frailness. But the grip was strong enough. "How...how did you know my name?"

"Oh." Inge Frank smiled. "Word does get around, you know, in a place this small." She surveyed Nan. "It is so nice to see a young woman dressing up for church." Nan hadn't noticed her clothing before. Now she did and regretted her inattention to her neighbor. Inge wore a suit of rose-colored wool and a little black hat with a scrap of veil. "We all used to, but few bother anymore." Her smile took any censure out of the words. Obviously Inge accepted things the way they were, not the way she thought they ought to be. Nan found herself smiling back, relieved of embarrassment about her clothes, at least.

"Ms. Black!"

She turned around and smiled at the Reverend Walker Petersen. The tall man grasped her hand and shook it warmly. Nothing in his expression censured her, and she now felt an instant liking for him similar to what she had felt for Sue the other day.

"I understand you're joining us for lunch today," he said, grinning. "Looking forward to it, I must say." He glanced over to the other side of the room where Jesse mingled with another family. "Though not as much, I bet, as my best singer is."

"Singer? You mean J-Jesse Rivers?"

The minister's smile widened. "Just wait, Ms. Black. Wait and listen!" He moved past her and hugged Inge Frank.

Jesse never did come by her section of the room, though she saw him cover the rest of the place like a politician seeking votes. He was obviously at home and well-liked. She shook hands with a few other people, then she sat down next to Inge.

"Young Mr. Rivers seems a little nervous this morning," the older woman whispered. "I expect it's because you're here."

"Why would you say that?" Nan looked closely at her companion.

But Inge just shrugged. "You're new. You came from California. You must get to listen to some fine singers in a big place like that. He's just a local boy. No training, you understand."

"Oh."

They were silent for a while, listening to the lessons. Walker Petersen had real style, Nan thought. Odd that he should be in such a small place—with his presence and voice, he'd be able to fill a huge cathedral. Then it came time for the Psalm. Jesse stood up, no book in his hands. Inge nudged her gently.

Nan sat transfixed. His voice and style were untrained, a bit unsure on some of the notes, but the effect was raw and powerful. He sang the ancient words without accompaniment, pulling her back from the present into the time when the words were at the heart of a society. His voice painted pictures of beauty and devotion. She felt tears stinging her eyes by the time he finished and sat down.

Walker got up to read the Gospel, and the congregation stood. Nan glanced around to see if anyone else was as moved as she. All seemed unaffected.

Of course, they had heard Jesse Rivers sing for years. Some of them, the younger ones, all their lives.

She listened in a slight daze to Walker's sermon. It was short, to the point and uplifting. The message from the Scripture, he said, was about new beginnings. He drew some simple analogies with springtime, laid down an admonition about missed opportunities and reminded his people they were able to start anew today. She glanced around again, carefully, and noted that most folks were paying attention. Only one ancient man was sleeping. What kind of church was this? When she was growing up, she remembered long, boring sermons, kids misbehaving and most of the men snoring. These people acted as if they were accustomed to listening, to being enlightened by words from the pulpit.

It was over before she was ready. Jesse sang once more, a moving melody in a language she didn't recognize. Inge helped her out.

"That's Norwegian," she whispered. "His grandmother taught it to him. A very old hymn," she added, nodding her head. "Very old."

"I see," Nan replied softly, thinking perhaps she was beginning to. Rivers wasn't exactly an ethnic-sounding name, but it could have been changed from some difficult and complex Scandinavian surname. Apparently his roots went far back, certainly deeper than hers. From her grandmother, she had inherited a chair. Jesse had music. Fine, old music. A heritage to perpetuate.

After dismissal, she was surrounded by people welcoming her to the church. Inge seemed to feel she had adopted her, and took her around to meet neighbors and friends. Nan recognized some as customers. Everyone was pleasant, though she sensed a reserve from time to time. That was okay, she thought. After all, she was a stranger.

"Hi, stranger," a man's voice said from behind her back.

Nan almost jumped straight out of her skin. She whirled and Jesse stood there, grinning at her like a little kid. "Hi," she said, smiling herself and feeling stupid. For no reason she could think of, she had the same sensations of awkwardness she had suffered as a teen when a boy she liked spoke to her.

"How did you like...?" Jesse seemed to struggle for words.

Nan recovered quickly and first. "Your singing was wonderful and quite a surprise," she said. "If I had no other reason, I'd be glad I came for that."

"You sure look nice." His green eyes were bright, brighter that she'd ever seen them. "Like you stepped out of a fashion magazine."

"Thanks." She was starting to blush again, darn it! He had avoided responding to her compliment and had returned with one of his own. That threw her back off balance. "I'm afraid I overdid it a little. But I didn't know what most people wore to church around here."

"It's nice." His tone was low, caressing. "Very nice. Don't you ever worry about anyone else. You'll do just fine. Very...pretty..."

"Jesse Rivers, you let her come on and meet some more folks," Inge interrupted, taking Nan's arm. "She's got better things to do than stand here listening to you tell her she's pretty. She already knows it, or ought to." Her tone was scolding, but Jesse just smiled.

"Mrs. Frank was my Sunday school teacher for years," he explained to Nan. "I still ask 'how high' when she says 'jump.'"

"Sometimes you toed the mark," Inge said, looking up at him. "Sometimes you didn't. But you were always thinking. That made you a good student."

Jesse shrugged, but Nan digested this bit of information as the three of them continued to move around and meet people. So he had been a thinker, a good student, when he was a kid. Did he still "think"? Or did he live his life at the no-nonsense level he claimed to prefer without bothering to ponder meaning and possibility? And if he did meditate, did he keep it all inside, John Wayne-style? Or would he share it with someone he loved and trusted . . . ?

Did she really care to find out?

Jesse followed the women around, content to let Inge maintain her role as Nan's chief escort. He wasn't exactly ready to take over. His tongue felt glued to the top of his mouth, and he knew if he tried to converse, he'd trip all over himself. Hadn't he done it first thing with her? Hi, *stranger!* Good Lord! Then she misunderstood his asking how she liked Walker's sermon. She thought he was fishing for praise for himself. She ought to have laughed in his face!

But she hadn't. Instead, she'd gifted him with a million-watt smile and a sincere compliment. Then he'd gone on, sounding like an idiot actor from one of her grade-D movies. *You look nice.*

She didn't look *nice.* She looked . . . wonderful, stunning, elegant, sophisticated. She was pretty enough without any trimmings. Decked out as she was now, well, she almost took his breath away. She was . . . beautiful. No other word for her.

And how smoothly she moved among his friends, talking to each one as if she had known them for years, but without seeming overly familiar. She was, still, a newcomer and she played that very well. People liked her. It was easy to see.

She was making good business contacts by the minute!

That realization hit him like a fist in the face. Sure, she was making an impression. She hardly needed to exert herself to do it. But how much did she really care about the people she was doing it to? Jesse studied her face from the side. He couldn't tell by looking. She seemed sincere enough, the light dancing in her blue eyes, the laughter that seemed genuine. The firm handshakes. The blush of pleasure at a kind word. Was she true or false?

And did he really care?

Sue Petersen came up and gave Nan a hug, speaking to her in a low voice. Jesse couldn't hear, but he saw Nan laugh and look as if she felt relief about something. His curiosity grew when both women started blushing. He knew Nan blushed, but he'd never seen the ginger-haired wife of his best friend do so, no matter what the provocation. Interesting.

"I'm heading off to the kitchen," Sue said, waving her arms to round up her children. The youngest of them hung at the hem of her denim skirt, clinging. "See the three of you in a little while."

"Could I help?" Nan held out her hand.

Sue looked at her for a moment, then gave her the toddler, a chubby boy with bright red hair and a tired, sulky expression. "Sure," she said. "Bring Tommy along for me. I'll put you right to work." She turned her back and shooed the three other children toward the door.

Jesse watched. Nan looked at Tommy. Tommy looked at Nan. There was no way she could win this one, Jesse thought. No way.

She didn't. And she did. Tommy waited maybe ten seconds before setting up a banshee yowl for his mother, who was already outside and almost out of earshot. Nan looked mildly distressed for a second, then she gripped the child firmly, settling him into position on her hip with her left arm wrapped around him. Well, she did know that much about kids, he thought. She pointed to the coatrack. "Jesse, mind getting my coat?'' she asked, modulating her voice to take advantage of the breaths between howls. ''It's the gray one with the white scarf.'' The little boy, sensing he had been relegated to minor nuisance, cried louder.

Jesse complied, barely resisting the urge to laugh. Tommy could bring down the roof with his complaints, he knew from experience. Bitter experience. She was in for it now!

But when he brought back her coat, she turned the situation. Unable to control his mirth, he started to sputter laughter. Nan ignored it. Extending her right arm, she slipped into the garment and maneuvered the screaming child right next to Jesse's chest. Tommy, recognizing a familiar adult, reached. Before he knew how it happened, Jesse was holding him. Tommy still yowled, but he buried his sobs against Jesse's shoulder, soaking the material with tears and slobber. His little arms gripped Jesse's neck like a vise. Nan smiled sweetly as she shifted into the other side of her coat.

''Nicely done,'' Inge said. She had gotten her own coat and was fastening the buttons. ''You have a good touch with men and children, my dear.''

''Not because of practice,'' Nan said, leading the way out the front door. ''That was pure inspiration.'' She glanced back at Jesse and his yelling armful. ''I only gave him what he deserved. If the man hadn't snickered at my plight, he wouldn't be lugging the child.''

Somehow, Jesse found himself doubting that.

SUNDAY LUNCH at the Petersen household, Nan reflected as she carried an armload of dishes into the dining room, was clearly an institution of long standing. The family lived in the large, rambling brick parsonage right next door to the church, and anyone who didn't have family, felt lonely or just didn't want to bother fixing dinner themselves that day showed up. Some brought food, most did not.

The reason for that became apparent as Walker and Jesse hauled out great platters and tureens from the kitchen and set them on the sideboard. "Cooking's a special hobby of mine," the minister informed her. He had shed his clerical garb and wore a Western-cut shirt with the sleeves rolled up. "I like doing it on Saturday night. Kind of clears my mind for Sunday and the sermon."

"I liked the one I heard today." She glanced over Walker's shoulder. Jesse was standing in the kitchen doorway, talking to another man. "But what really surprised me was..."

"Ol' Jesse's pipes?" Walker grinned. "Shocked the life out of me first time I heard him myself."

"When was that?" Taking another look past Walker, she saw that Jesse's companion, a short, florid-faced person, was clearly pouring a tale of woe into his ears.

"Oh, let me see." Walker made a playful grab at his oldest daughter as she slid by teasingly. The little dark-haired girl giggled and came back for a hug. After she was gone, he continued. "About seven years ago. We'd just moved here. Jessica wasn't born yet. He'd just moved back—"

"Jessica? She isn't by any chance...?"

"Named after Jesse? She sure is! She was due right around the middle of February. Sue went into labor early. All kinds of problems, ones Doc Muller couldn't handle alone. Jesse flew her over to Rapid. Tricky flying in bad weather. But it saved her and Jessica." Walker turned and looked at his friend. "I owe him more than I can ever repay."

Nan itched to quiz the tall man some more, but diners began crowding into the room. She saw Jesse pat the little man on the shoulder and saw tears in the other man's eyes.

Was he helping out another friend? Just what sort of man was he, really? It was one thing for him to fly crazy for fun or to take risks for his business. Quite another to put his life on the line for someone else.

She regarded him with increased interest as he came toward her. He had taken off his coat and tie and rolled up his shirtsleeves. His muscular forearms looked extremely sexy. The reddish-blond hairs glinted in the afternoon sunlight. She felt the breath catch in her throat. *Don't fail me, brain,* she wailed wordlessly.

Jesse saw something in her eyes that hadn't been there before. Walker must have blabbed something that bothered her, he decided. He ought to talk to his friend and make sure...

Heck, why shouldn't Walker talk to her? She was likely to become a parishioner, if she was sincere about church and hadn't just attended today out of boredom or curiosity. What difference did it make to him what she talked about with anyone?

God, she was lovely!

"You seemed quite involved with that man's problems," she said softly, indicating Charlie, who was busily filling his plate. She raised one hand and pushed back a stray, blond curl.

Jesse swallowed hard. Her hairdo was coming loose, and he was itching to help it along. "That's Charlie," he said. "Remember? The friend from Devil's Hole?"

"Oh." She looked again and nodded as if she understood volumes. "He comes here to church?"

"He comes here for free food. And when he's in trouble and needs to talk to me." Jesse stuck his hands in his pockets. "We go back years, Charlie and me. But they haven't been as kind to him. I help out when I can. He still is the best damn mechanic in the state. Taught me more than any man alive about machinery and fixing it.''

"I see." She did, she thought. Charlie ate heartily, but his hands shook, and his complexion indicated a fondness for stronger libation than the coffee and tea Sue was serving this afternoon. Nan's ex-husband wasn't like that yet, probably. Give him time.

"You disapprove?" Jesse watched her closely. She had suddenly gotten a hard glint in her eyes. He didn't like it much.

She shrugged. "It isn't any of my business."

"That's right. It isn't.'' His mouth was set in a flat, hard line.

"Where's Jimmy?" She felt a strong need to change the subject, to clear up the strained atmosphere between them. "I would have thought he'd be at church with you."

He seemed to relax a little. "He's at home. The family all go to a ranch church not too far from my dad's place. Sometimes Walker goes out there and preaches.'' He grinned. "Boy, you ought to see him then! He really pulls out the stops for the rural folks. He can preach the hay right out of the rafters."

"You are really good friends, aren't you?"

"We are." He was smiling sincerely now. "I don't think I could find a better one.''

"I think he feels the same.'' She slid her arm through his bent elbow. "Come on. Let's eat. I'm starved!"

Jesse accepted the invitation. Nan relaxed, sensing a truce had been called. For a time, they related harmoniously, enjoying each other's company.

Two other things happened that afternoon, however, that kept her from relaxing completely. One was good and one wasn't.

The first was the reaffirmation she had not made a social error in renting the Petersens the sexy video. While Sue had whispered her thanks earlier, letting Nan know how much she enjoyed it, Walker had remained silent until most of the guests had wandered off back to their own homes.

"Are you selling memberships in that store of yours?" he asked Nan while the four of them sat around the kitchen table. Kids played under the table and in and out of the room. The noise bothered Nan, but the others seemed oblivious. "For folks who'd like to be regular customers and could use a deal on the prices?"

"Why, yes." Nan set down her coffee cup. "I plan to start offering specials in a week or so, when I see how the flow of business goes."

"Put us down first on the list." Walker grinned again, a decidedly unholy expression. Sue laughed. A sexy sound. "We surely enjoyed last night's entertainment," he added, looking at his wife.

"Don't tell me I'm going to be a godfather again?" Jesse mugged disgust. "I can't take the responsibility, I tell you!"

"Don't worry." Sue patted his hand. "We just thought the film was fun. You ought to watch it, Jesse. You need a little romance in your steely soul, you know."

"I don't . . ."

"Mom." The plaintive voice of the Petersens' oldest girl interrupted Jesse's reply. Jessica had raced in from outside, slamming the back door behind her. Nan watched and listened as the girl was gently reprimanded for impoliteness. She was both impressed with the sincerity of the apology, which Jesse solemnly accepted, and upset over the words that followed.

"Mom, I was outside playing with Billy and he said we weren't really God's people." Her blue eyes filled with tears.

Walker rubbed his face and looked skyward. Jesse grunted and stared down at his coffee cup. He was scowling deeply.

"Why'd he say that this time, honey?" Sue put her hand on her daughter's shoulder, encouraging.

"'Cause of the movies." The child swallowed and tried to smile. "He's wrong, isn't he?"

"Well, we think so, dear." Sue hugged her. "Why don't you take off your coat and stay inside now? It's getting chilly." Jessica grinned, rubbed away her tears and took off. Nan heard her running up the stairs, yelling for her sisters to follow.

Walker said something under his breath. His expression was angry. Jesse's was worse.

"Movies?" Nan felt a little sick. "*My* movies?"

"Don't think anything about it," Sue said, patting her hand. "It's just there are some people around here with some rather old-fashioned ideas of morality."

"Strange, intolerant ideas," her husband said.

Jesse said nothing at all.

"Let's change the subject," Sue stated.

"I need a ride home, Jesse." Inge, who had been out in the front room with some friends, came in, effectively limiting the topic. Jesse started to rise at her command, but Nan offered to act the chauffeur, saying she really needed to get home herself. Inge accepted the change of drivers cheerfully, but Nan thought she detected a look of regret in Jesse's eyes. Was it because he liked driving Inge home?

Or was it because she was leaving?

CHAPTER FIVE

THE NEXT DAY, however, Nan figured Jesse had no regrets whatsoever concerning her. He hadn't called, hadn't made any attempt to see her. With only moderate success, she tried putting him out of her mind and concentrating on the important things in her life—her business and her future.

She drove to work Monday with a high sense of anticipation, still hoping he'd show up, even though she wasn't expecting a delivery from him. The sky was gray with clouds. The wind was howling across the landscape, but she welcomed the buffeting, knowing it was a good sign of warmer weather in the plains.

She was wrong. Neither Jesse nor the better weather materialized. The wind was only a harbinger of snow. Wet, messy spring snow that blanketed the town and surrounding countryside. It didn't last for long, but what did fall turned the soil into a dark, chocolaty mess. The ranchers hurried to rescue newborn livestock, glad the temperature and depth were moderate, and the farmers rejoiced over the moisture. Others were neither glad nor grateful.

Nan found her business booming. Mothers who were willing as a rule to let kids play outside in cold temperatures balked at the results of boots in wet snow and mud. Children were kept indoors. Restlessness, fostered by the nearness of summer, hung heavy in the air. Nan picked up on all this by listening to conversations as the weekend videos were returned that morning. At her gentle proddings and suggestions, kiddie rentals soared.

"I can't believe this town got along before you opened," Sue said to her on Monday afternoon when she returned her movies. In addition to Sue, there were at least six other women browsing the shelves, apparently desperate to garner fresh entertainment before school let out and their darlings returned home. "My goodness, all I heard at the grocery store this morning was how everybody hoped their favorite video would be in by this evening. You're going to make out like a bandit with this weather!"

"I feel sorry for the ranchers." Nan stacked Sue's films and started checking them off on the computer. "I remember when I was at home...in Wyoming. A bad spring snow could cause a lot of damage."

Sue sobered. "True. We're lucky this time. It's messy, but not too deep."

"I'd forgotten how much the weather affects life." Nan glanced over to the little table she had set out for children. Sue's two younger girls and several other preschoolers were seated around it, playing with the crayons and coloring books. "Around this part of the country, that is," she amended. "In California, it took an earthquake, fire or bad mud slide to get attention. Weather just isn't a big factor in people's plans or lives out there."

"It's a daily factor here." Sue shifted Tommy, who rode on her hip. The boy was eyeing Nan with a wary expression, two fingers in his mouth. He sucked on them neatly, not drooling. "But you know that, don't you?"

Nan smiled, including the child. "At times, I feel like I've gone back rather than moving forward. It's so much like the place where I grew up. I swore I'd never go back there."

"Why did you come here?"

"Opportunity, pure and simple. This is a place to start. A first step, so to speak. I intend branching out and up as soon as I can." She was ready to elaborate, to tell Sue about her ambitions, but the other woman's eyes clouded slightly, and she turned her attention to her children. Nan wondered if she had hurt Sue's feelings, or if she had inadvertently touched a deeper wound. From what she had seen, Walker's abilities were far greater than she would have expected from a small-town preacher. Sue's life was clearly tied up with her husband and kids. But was it enough? Could she be chafing at the limited life she had here?

Well, she was not a close enough friend yet for Nan to pry. "I want to say thanks again for lunch yesterday," she said, when Sue turned back. "That was fun. And I felt so welcome at church. *That* was wonderful."

Sue's eyes warmed. "That's family," she said. "We had a lot of choices about the kind of career Walker could have. He is now a happy man."

Nan wanted to ask just what that meant, but two customers came over, interrupting the private conversation. As she checked out their movies, the four of them chatted pleasantly. The front door opened and shut, letting in a chilly draft. Nan noted a male customer out of the corner of her eye. It wasn't Jesse, naturally. She promptly forgot his presence.

Forgot it, until the scream of a frightened child tore through the air and the man appeared around the corner of one of the stacks, hauling Sue's little girl, Callie, by the arm. The child was crying, and the man was red-faced with fury. He wasn't a large man, but he had a considerable paunch and a high hairline with salt-and-pepper wreathing the bald part.

"Mrs. Petersen!" He thrust Callie at her mother and Sue gathered her in, almost dropping Tommy in the process.

"Your child was inspecting the lurid covers of this woman's movies." He pointed a finger at Nan. "A child of a man of God! Looking at the Devil's own pictures! With her mother standing by, ignoring it. You should be ashamed!"

Nan and Sue found voice at the same time.

"Get out of my place!" Nan yelled, pointing back.

"Don't you ever touch one of my children again!" Sue screamed, holding her daughter tighter. Both her children were crying now. The other women and children stood mute, dumbfounded by the suddenness of the conflict.

Nan pushed over the counter gate and slammed it down. "Out," she said, advancing on the man. He gave ground before her, looking as if he were astonished she would take the offensive. She had him out the door and scurrying through the snow to a beat-up pickup truck in just a few seconds. Only when he drove away, splashing up dirt and slush, did she realize how angry she was. Hearing the ragged sound of applause, she turned and saw the rest of her customers were on her side.

"Did he hurt her?" she asked, hurrying back to Sue. "I'm calling the cops."

Sue, who was still kneeling, shook her head. "She's not really hurt, just scared a little. Don't bother with the police," she said. "He's not worth the trouble." She brushed her hand over Callie's dark hair. The child wasn't crying aloud now, but her little body shook with stifled sobs. "Are you okay, honey?" Sue asked.

"Billy's daddy scared me," Callie said. She looked up at Nan. She stopped shaking. "But you scared him." Her big blue eyes glowed and a smile formed on her delicate little mouth.

"Boo!" said Tommy, who sat on the floor, no longer crying and clearly fascinated by all the action. He waved his chubby arms.

Nan bent and picked him up. He grabbed a handful of her hair. "Billy's daddy, huh?" she said, remembering the incident yesterday with Jessica Petersen. "And no cops? You're sure."

"He's nuts," one of the other women said. Several nodded. "Harmless, though." She laughed. "You probably scared him halfway to Devil's Hole, going at him like you did."

Sue straightened, lifting Callie. "Every town has one, it seems. Thinks he has a direct pipeline to the Almighty. He runs a little maverick church of his own out of his house. I feel sorry for his family." She looked at Nan. "Thank you for standing up to him for me. I was just too shocked to think."

"Billy's daddy's mean," Callie said, still watching Nan closely.

"Honey, now." Sue cradled Callie's head against her shoulder. "He didn't do it on purpose. He's confused. You just forgive him and forget about it, okay?" Callie nodded. Her little body relaxed.

Nan felt this was carrying forgiveness a bit too far, but she kept quiet. If that had been her kid...

But it wasn't. It was her store, however, and she made a mental note to check out the boxes behind the stack to see what might have set off "Billy's daddy." As far as she remembered, all the covers were pretty benign.

There was, of course, an exception or two. Film artwork sometimes got ahead of reality when it came to design. She needed to be more discerning, she supposed.

Before leaving, Sue asked a strange favor. "Don't say anything to Jesse about this, will you?" she said to Nan when they had a moment of privacy. "He really dislikes Douglas Neilson. That's the man's name. They are not friends, to put it mildly. It goes back a long way, I understand."

"Sure, I won't say anything," Nan agreed. "But..."

"Thanks." Sue took Tommy back. The little boy hung on to Nan's hair, and when she gave a mock yelp, he giggled. He waved bye-bye to Nan all the way out the door. Through the plate glass, she could see him continue to wave, even after he was strapped securely in his car seat by his mother.

Nan went back, then, and checked the covers. Try as she might, she couldn't understand why any of them would have put someone into such a rage. It was a mystery, as was Sue's reaction to it.

Now, why would she specifically ask that Jesse not know about the encounter? Nan wondered. She could understand if it had been Walker who was to be kept in the dark. He was the injured party's father, after all. Not Jesse. And why did she think Nan would get the chance to tell the tale? Was he still talking about her to his friends? Was she going to find out what he said from himself or from gossip?

She had no chance, since she didn't see him, and nobody talked to her about him. By Wednesday, she had just about put the incident out of her mind. There had been no repercussions from the self-styled censor, Douglas Neilson, and no one else mentioned the event, not even those few who had witnessed it. Bad water under the bridge, Nan figured. There was plenty of good water to be thankful for.

The first part of the week had gone amazingly well, volume-wise. She sent in a preliminary report to the home office, requesting more movies, cautioning them about covers, just to be safe, and outlining some ideas for promotional deals for better customers. Walker's question on Sunday had spurred her to think in terms of accommodating the existing market, rather than imposing programs developed from outside. She had one or two rather innovative ideas and was eager to hear how they were received by the higher-ups in the business.

She also knew that soon she would have to hire help. The frantic pace of the first days had not yet let up. Undoubtedly, it would, but she couldn't expect herself to maintain this alone for long. She was only human and needed time off as much as the next person.

Well, almost as much, anyway. She did thrive on her work, and her ambition was a driving force she lived with day and night. But life demanded more mundane attentions from time to time.

She went grocery shopping Wednesday evening.

The snow was almost all gone, leaving the ground soft and gooey. The air was warm, in the forties even after sunset, and she could smell spring—a heady, musty, earthy, sensual odor that rose from the damp land. Something stirred within her in response. She pulled into the parking lot at the Safeway store and sat thinking in her station wagon for a few minutes.

All her time in California, she hadn't been particularly sensitive to nature, taking it for granted as it went about its business around her. Odd, that now she would find the very breath she drew full of promise because the dirt smelled wet. Nan shook her head, amused at herself, and consulting her shopping list, went inside.

She was bent over the produce, trying to pick out some decent fresh vegetables, when he spoke. "Not much to choose from this time of year. Wait a bit, though. I start flying in the fresh strawberries next week."

"Jesse Rivers!" She straightened and turned. He was standing right behind her. "You startled me," she said, trying to stop her heart from racing in her chest.

"Sorry." He reached past her and picked up a small tomato. "I should have announced myself, I guess." He didn't smile and didn't look directly at her. Stony, closed expression, just like the one he had given her when they first met.

He was also back in his scruffy costume of jeans, boots and bomber jacket. The black T-shirt was replaced with a sweatshirt so old and worn she couldn't make out the logo on the front. He didn't have the cigar in his mouth, but he hadn't shaved since Sunday, to judge by the stubble of beard. It glinted in the harsh light of the store, giving him a strange kind of burnished look. Very sexy, Nan thought.

"You've been busy?" she asked, trying to be pleasant.

"Yeah." He tossed the tomato back and selected another.

"Jimmy, too?"

"He's got schoolwork." That tomato passed. He placed it in a paper sack and went over to the potatoes.

She followed. "Well, tell him to drop by, please. And you don't have to be a stranger yourself, you know. We didn't really get to talk privately much Sunday, and I'm curious." He looked at her sharply. "After hearing you sing," she explained. "I'd like to know why—"

"Why're you curious about me or anyone else around here?" He sounded and looked angry.

"Excuse me?"

"Yeah." He threw down a potato. It rolled off and fell to the floor. "Why do you give a damn, since you only plan to use this place? Use us all, until you don't need us anymore."

"I know I've missed something here." She had no idea what was going on, but his pugnacious attitude was making her blood start to heat up. She had only tried to start a pleasant conversation. Be friendly. Now, it seemed, they were at war over something she didn't understand at all. "Just what are you getting at, Jesse?"

Jesse took a deep breath. He hadn't intended on losing his cool. Hadn't intended on saying much at all to her. His skin started to tingle when he saw her, though, and by the time he got close enough to speak, his mind was out of gear. Out of gear, out of the damn universe! He tried to cover up his inner turmoil by shrugging. "I mean," he said, looking at the onions now, "why go to the trouble making friends when you're out of here first chance you get?"

At first Nan had no idea what he was talking about. Then she remembered. "I know what's bugging you! I told Sue the other day that Hennington was a starting point for my business. That I want to move into the region eventually. Cover more and more territory. What's wrong with that?"

"Nothing." He seemed fascinated by the parchment skin of a particularly large onion. He flipped his finger across a loose section of it. The rattling sound of the skin punctuated his word.

"Isn't that what you do? Cover the local needs and the region? You couldn't possibly survive just on the business you'd get in Hennington."

"Sure, but...forget it." Jesse kicked himself mentally. He was out of line. He'd overreacted to what Sue had told him about her. Made a fool of himself. "I'm just in a bad mood, that's all. You happened to get in the way. Forget it."

"Jesse, what's wrong? Is it Jimmy?" She placed a hand on his arm.

He thought he could feel the warmth of her palm all the way through the leather of his jacket. Her face showed her concern for him, for his little brother, for...him. His resentment at her attitude toward his town faded, slid away to a hidden place where it could grouse in peace, without the distraction she so naturally provided. "You want to go out for a beer after you finish shopping?" he asked.

"Sure," she said, smiling at him. "That is, if you aren't ashamed to be seen with an old carpetbagger."

"Carpetbagger?"

"You know, someone who comes to town to exploit the citizens, then move on. Like in *Gone with the Wind?* Well, I might have to move on, but I have no intention of exploiting anyone. I like it here. I like the people I've met...so far."

"But you have doubts?" He probably fit in the doubtful group, Jesse decided.

"I wouldn't be realistic or reasonable if I didn't. Now, do you want to get a beer or not?" She had her hands on her hips and her chin lifted. A challenge.

He *almost* played her game. Almost. Jesse had seen the movie as a kid and he was sorely tempted to call her "Miss Scarlett, ma'am." But he didn't. "I asked you, didn't I?" he replied, without expression.

THE BAR WAS REALLY a modern version of the cowboy saloon, Nan thought. Instead of a piano player, country and western music yowled from the jukebox. No spittoons at the rail, and hardly anyone was smoking a stogie, but smoke hung in the air. No clean-air ordinances here. No dance hall girls luring drunken cowhands upstairs, either, but sexual action was being contemplated by some patrons, she was sure. The beer was cold and foamy and definitely not light. The place was dark, but not so dark you couldn't see the face of the person next to you. It was great!

"This is a terrific place," she told Jesse, raising her voice a bit so he could hear her over the music. "You come here often?"

"From time to time." He took a drink of beer. They had arrived separately, using their own vehicles, and since entering the Canteen, he hadn't said much. It was noisier than usual tonight. Someone had apparently loaded the jukebox with quarters. He'd have preferred more quiet, so he could actually attempt communicating with her, but she seemed happy. He tried to relax. "It's kind of a neighborhood place," he said.

"I saw the one outside of town," she said, tapping her finger in time to the music's beat. "Looks sort of rough to me."

"Stay out of there, if you know what's good for you. Not the kind of place for a lady."

Nan almost sputtered in her beer. So, now she was a lady? News to her. What a John Wayne kind of line!

But she liked it. Nan pondered that for a moment. She liked the idea, at least, that he was concerned about her. That he would bother warning her not to get into a situation that would be unpleasant, if not actually dangerous. Just as she would advise him not to show up at an assertiveness-training class for women. Very much the same thing. "I'll remember," she said. "Thanks."

Jesse was about to murmur a noncommittal reply when the music cut out abruptly. End of the quarters. The sound of conversation from the other patrons continued unabated, but where they sat in a private booth, silence seemed suddenly a tangible thing. Now, he felt, everything he said had to be significant. Meaningful.

So he said nothing.

"You've lived here all your life?" Nan asked.

"It's my home."

"Family?"

"There's Jimmy. You met him. Everybody else lives out on the farm." He took a drink of beer and set down his glass. He watched her.

"But you don't."

"I'm not a farmer."

Nan smiled. This was like pulling teeth. She had almost forgotten the game of coaxing information out of the strong, silent types. Most of the men she had encountered socially in the past few years were so eager to talk about themselves that you knew about their relationships with their fathers and mothers, their birth signs and lifetime dreams before you were sure you gave a darn. Little boys, they were, really. So eager to be at the center of attention. So enthralled with the intimate details of their own lives. She still wasn't sure if she cared all that much about Jesse Rivers, but this was a refreshing change.

"Did your dad want you to be a farmer?" she asked.

He shrugged. "He's got my sister and her husband. They've got their own place out there. Jane and Steve love the land, love working it." He grinned. "I love it, too. From the air, especially. Lays out there like a quilt. Just don't see spending my life depending on seeds to sprout and the weather to hold."

"But your flying. It depends on the weather. However, I can't see what your business has to do with love of this land."

"Everything!" He sat up straight. "See, the people are what makes the land. It's them I love. And they need me for—"

"Many things, don't they?" She remembered Walker's story. "Not just business and delivery. Safety, health? Contact with the rest of the country."

His expression became warm, and he looked a little surprised. "You understand. I do a good business, and I help folks. That makes me a happy man. I can't think of a better life."

Not a bad life, Nan thought. But she could think of better, if she put her mind to it, she would bet. There was his musical gift, for one thing. He'd settled for singing in church every so often. Life could offer him much more than the view he'd taken. His had serious limitations. But if that was all he wanted, fine. No surprises from this man. What you saw was what you got. Limited.

Though what she saw looked pretty appealing tonight. That had to be why she wanted to move closer to him, wanted to feel the warmth of his body on her skin, even through the clothing they wore. She could smell him, too. That special scent that was his, and the leather of his jacket. No stink of cigar tonight. Only clean, sexy things. It was a sensual yearning he roused in her, she realized. He was a man, and she found him desirable. Found herself wondering how he would be in bed.

It was a long time since that had happened.

"What about you?" he asked.

"Huh?" Coming on top of her sexy fantasizing, the question threw her off balance.

"What about you? What kind of life do you want? You said you might have to move on. That by choice?"

"Oh. By necessity." She recovered and settled in to recite what she believed her dream to be. "See, I start small in this company. I take a market they have few prospects for and turn it into a real money-maker. Then I get promoted. Take over a region, do the same. Eventually, I'll rise to the top. Control the business at a national level."

"Wow." He hadn't stopped watching her. Now his attention seemed to intensify. But his exclamation fell flat as a pancake. In fact, he looked amused.

"What's wrong with that? I'm good. With the proper drive, there's no reason I can't make it."

"No, there certainly isn't."

Nan felt her blood pressure rise. He was laughing at her, just because she had big dreams. Making light of her ambition. The story of her life! She was about to launch an attack, when she felt a damp hand settle on her shoulder. A man's voice rumbled a question.

"Say, ain't you the lady rents them dirty movies?"

Nan looked up. The man didn't look like a redneck goon. Jesse actually fit that image more closely tonight with his unshaved face and old clothes. The newcomer wore a pullover sweater over a white shirt, and his hair was neatly combed. A little too neatly. Like it had been slicked down in an effort to prevent any freedom. He looked like a mild-mannered office-worker type. But there was something in his eyes....

"I have a video rental shop," she said, keeping her tone calm and polite. "However, I do not—"

"Yeah, I heard what kind of filth you got there." The man's gaze moved from her to her companion. His eyes flickered a bit. "Hi, Jesse. Keeping bad company, I see."

"I'm having a beer with my friend, Les," Jesse said, his eyes narrowed. "I'd kind of like to know what you're doing, though." His voice settled into a low drawl. "I know you ain't a drinking man, so I'm wondering what business you got in a bar at all." He sat quite still, but Nan sensed tension in the lines of his body. His hands rested lightly on the table.

Les licked his lips quickly, the tip of his tongue dipping out like a snake's. "I want to let this *lady* know how some of us felt about her opening a porn store in our town. Corrupting the minds of our children and all."

"A *porn*...!" Nan came out of her seat. Jesse's hand on her shoulder pressed her back.

"Les," he said gently, "get the hell out of here. Mind your own business for a change."

"I got a right—"

"Sure you do." Jesse nodded. "Just keep on exercising it. But not in my face or where it bothers my friends. Understand?"

The other man seemed to consider his options. Jesse's hand slid down Nan's arm and held her hand. Tightly. After a moment, Les seemed to deflate slightly. "All right," he said. "I'm going 'cause I don't believe in violence. But—"

"Butt out, Lester," another man yelled. Other voices chorused agreement.

Nan looked around. She had been so angry and so absorbed, she'd failed to notice their confrontation had drawn the attention of the entire bar. Lester, seeing he was seriously outnumbered, rushed for the entrance and disappeared to the sound of applause. The whole event reminded her uncomfortably of the encounter with Douglas Neilson two days before.

"You okay?" Jesse asked. He still held her hand. His palm was warm and dry and comforting.

"Of course I am. Who was that man?"

"Just a local guy with a narrow attitude." He smiled at her. "Didn't they warn you about this kind of thing in the big city?"

Nan laughed. "Everybody's a critic. And you can't please the world. Like you said, he has a right to his opinion."

"Don't let him worry you. Big mouth, small brains. No action. That's the style of people like that." He frowned, showing anger for a moment. "We have a few around here, just like anyplace else. Nothing to worry about, though. Usually, they stay under their private rocks, feeling righteous. It's their problem, not yours."

"I suppose." She gently removed her hand from his grasp. Jesse sat straight, startled, as if he just realized he was holding her. "Thanks," she said. "I could have lost my temper and made a needless scene."

"You?" He drained his beer. "Lose your temper? Make a scene? No way."

"Sarcasm does not become you, Rivers."

Jesse was trying to think of a reply when two couples came over to their table. "Nice going, Jesse," Ben Starks said, slapping him on the back. "Old Lester's getting a bit big for his britches these days."

"He's such a throwback," commented Lisa Starks. "Nan, don't you mind what he said. We love your store!"

Nan smiled and welcomed their words. Both couples were people she had met Sunday at church. While Jesse invited them to sit down and join the party, she was thinking. Although he didn't know it, and was treating the matter as a joke, this was the second confrontation over her films. She needed to work on a strategy to avoid more trouble. Just because no real problem had arisen yet, didn't mean she could sit back and relax.

She had to prepare for battle. If it never came, so much the better. But she had to be ready. That was her responsibility.

That was her job. She flinched back slightly as her knee touched Jesse's under the table. She tried to ignore the tingles that ran over her skin. That was her life!

After a while, she left, making her exit quickly so Jesse didn't have time to offer to leave with her. She had things to think about that did not include him. Once again, she thought she detected regret in his expression, but since he did nothing, she figured it was all in her overheated—at least where Jesse Rivers was concerned—imagination. He was not one of her worries.

At least, not now.

CHAPTER SIX

THE NEXT DAY Nan's worries were confirmed. Hennington's weekly newspaper, the *South Dakota Weekly,* ran an article about her store. That was fine. The writer, a young woman who was fascinated by Nan's business ambitions, did a flattering but accurate job. Even the photograph was all right—surprisingly, since she usually looked about fifteen in such pictures. But the editor also ran a series of letters to one side of the article. Most of them were from people vehemently opposed to her merchandise.

Nan drank her morning coffee through clenched teeth. "Pornography...lewdness...moral destruction..." Just *where* had those people been looking? Surely not at her videos! She knew the letter writers represented only a small percentage of the population, but this was not good. Negative publicity never was. Not one to stay meekly on the defensive, she prepared herself mentally for battle as she showered and dressed.

Right after she opened for business, she went to work on the problem. Jesse Rivers scarcely crossed her mind, and when he did, she pushed his image aside. She needed all her energy for the important matters!

By noon she had a date to tape a talk show for the local radio station. She had called the paper and asked for another interview. She wrote a guest editorial on the issue of pornography and constitutional rights, emphasizing the point that she was not defending ugliness and immorality, but rather her right to operate a business renting films to a free people. Then she called the local school superintendent and offered to give a talk at the school assembly.

"I wouldn't be promoting my business," she explained, "although I would hardly be lecturing in a vacuum. The kids know about the store."

"This could be an interesting exercise in Civics," Dick Tanner, the super, said. "Let me call Genny Weaver. She's the high school principal. I'll get back to you."

He did, almost immediately. Nan's talk was scheduled for the next day.

Sue came by right after the phone call. "I read this stuff," she said, plopping the paper down on the counter. "I figured you might be upset. Want to talk about it?" No one else was in the store.

Nan explained the steps she had already taken. Sue agreed she was taking the right tack—bringing the battle to the enemy by responding publicly. Then Nan switched the subject. "Where are the kids this morning?" she asked. "I hardly recognize you without them."

Sue laughed. "This is my working day. I belong to a babysitting co-op kind of thing. We switch off three days a week. Gives us each a chance to get out and breathe. Or in my case, get in a few hours of work without someone hanging on my skirts and demanding attention."

"You work?" Nan poured them both a cup of coffee and opened the counter gate. Sue came in and took the extra chair at the desk. "Where?"

"At home." Sue took a sip of coffee and reached for the sugar. "I write articles for religious publications. Nonfiction, family stuff. Sometimes I knock off a short story or a poem, but I'm mostly into how-to and personal experience material. There's a wealth of it right in our congregation, believe me."

"I'm impressed!" Nan sat down. "I figured you were giving it all to..." She let the words trail off, feeling awkward. She had misjudged her new friend.

"Walker and the kids?" Sue leaned back. "No, indeed. He and I worked that out years ago. See, when we first married, Walker couldn't decide which was more important to him, me or his church. We didn't have kids, didn't think we could, and I saw him slipping away from me week after lonely week. He was beyond workaholism. He thought he was God's only foot soldier! It was insane. I tried to tell him and got nowhere. He loved me, but he wouldn't or couldn't listen to me. So I decided to do something about it. Something that got his attention finally."

"You started writing?" Nan was fascinated.

"No, I left him."

"You what!"

"Shocking, isn't it?" Sue grinned and sipped coffee. "A minister's wife and all, packing up and leaving. It happens more often than you might think. But I wasn't divorcing him. I went down to Casper to take some summer school classes. We were located in a little place called Advance in Wyoming, then."

"I know it. It's not too different from the town where my family lives. Where I grew up."

"Then you know what it was like for me. Day in day out. Even if we'd had a family right away, eventually I'd be alone and without anything for myself. Walker is everything to me, but he is not enough, if you know what I mean."

"I think I do. So you left him, took some classes. How did he handle it?"

"Not well."

Nan listened as Sue explained the road to understanding she and Walker had taken. Through an English professor, Sue discovered she did indeed have a talent for communicating through writing. She found a market for her material. Walker learned to give up his dependence on his congregation and his ministry for his sense of identity. To be a husband and friend first, a minister second. And before it was all settled, they were more in love than ever. "The conflict and the pain was really the making of our love," Sue said.

"Not for me." Nan set down her cup. "My ex-husband wanted me to stay home and literally chew his food for him. When I said I wouldn't, he got mad and sulked, just like a little child. We didn't last. We couldn't have lasted. I don't think I'm cut out for marriage."

"Maybe someday some man will change your mind."

"I don't know. I thought I had one when I was in California. He was everything my ex hadn't been. Wild and free, and he liked me wild and free. But he had no...sense. If Paul Black was a worm, Scott was a big, beautiful butterfly. Neither one was much good for me."

"I think you need to find a man who isn't some lower form of life."

Nan slapped the newspaper. "I do begin to wonder about them all from time to time. All this stuff is written by guys. Where're their women? How do they feel? Do they agree, or what?"

"You may never know." Sue frowned. "I don't pretend to understand it, but some women are still content walking three paces to the left and rear of their men."

"Good position to aim a kick from."

They laughed at that and chatted for a while longer. Then Sue left, declaring Nan needed no more cheering up and that she had a deadline to meet. It wasn't until after she was gone that Nan figured out her new friend had put her before her work.

Would she ever be willing to be that unselfish? She doubted it.

Not many people came in during the afternoon, and no one rented anything. Nan put it down to the day. Thursday was usually slow for video rentals. The rush would come on Friday afternoon. She spent the quiet time writing a letter to her company's PR director, advising her of the problem and how she was meeting it head-on. The PR specialist might have some suggestions, and Nan was certainly open to any ideas she might have.

While she wrote, she ran a favorite adventure film in the store VCR and watched the familiar tale unwind as she worked. About halfway through, she realized she was seeing Jesse Rivers's face instead of the actor's when the hero was on the screen. She fought it for a while, telling herself she was being silly, then she let her imagination take over. Jesse became the hero, and the subject of her fantasies. She finished her letter and pushed back from the desk, closing her eyes and relaxing.

It was easy to see him as a romantic star. He was ruggedly handsome enough to fit the mold. In reality, of course, he was just too stodgy and ordinary to be a hero of the silver screen. But she could invent her own reality any time in her mind.

That was the beauty of a fantasy.

By the time the movie ended with a crescendo of music, her imagination was off and running with a story of its own. Her Jesse-hero was a warrior king on another planet in a future time, and her heroine—herself, of course, only much prettier and smarter and possessed of a great deal more dignity—was the queen of a peaceful people who defied him and eventually defeated him with her love. Of course, together, they defeated an evil enemy as well. She didn't care for stories that had romance only as the conflict. There had to be a bad guy. She put Douglas Neilson's face on him and gave him a truly gruesome, spectacular end to pay him back for scaring Callie and upsetting Sue.

The fantasy entertained her until closing time that night.

And well into the wee hours of the next morning in her dreams.

Because her appointment at the high school was for nine o'clock, she didn't bother going to the store first. Instead, she put on a business suit, packed brochures and leaflets on constitutional rights in her old briefcase, loaded some visual aids in a box and drove directly to the school. On her way in the front door she was met by Jimmy Rivers.

"Hi, Nan," he said, grinning and blushing. "I mean, hi, Ms. Black. I'm your escort."

"Well, I am honored." She smiled and handed him the box. "Where do I go?"

"Down here." He waved a hand. "This ain't...isn't much of a school, I guess. We don't have a real auditorium. The lunchroom acts as one, though."

"The lunchroom sounds fine to me. I hate being up on a stage, myself." They continued to talk as they walked down the hall. Nan noted that the building smelled relatively new. It was, in any event, clean and modern, cheerful and brightly lit. She felt positive about the place.

When Jimmy opened the lunchroom door for her, she had sudden qualms, however. The room was packed with teenagers, all talking at once, it seemed. Several boys let out wolf whistles when they saw her, but Jimmy's scowl put an end to that behavior.

Jimmy's scowl, that is, and the ringmaster voice that boomed over the sound system. "Come to order!" the voice demanded. As the echoes died, Nan could have heard a pin drop.

"Our fearless leader," Jimmy whispered, pointing to the front of the room. "Mrs. Weaver, the principal."

A woman stood on her tiptoes to reach the microphone. She had a wildly curly head of red hair so bright Nan wondered if it was artificial. Her half glasses rested on an imperious nose that hooked like an eagle's beak. She glared at the students. Not one of them moved a muscle.

"We have a special treat this morning," Mrs. Weaver said, her deep voice at odds with her delicate appearance and bizarre hair. "A local businessperson is going to speak to us on the subject of constitutional rights." There were some low moans. They ended abruptly as the principal scanned her audience over the top of her glasses. When all was quiet, she spoke again. "Jimmy," Mrs. Weaver said, waving her hand, "will you please come on up and introduce our guest."

Nan kept from smiling with difficulty. Under his bronze-gold hair, Jimmy's skin was deep red with embarrassment. But he led her forward and strode manfully up to the microphone. He cleared his throat several times, and kids started to giggle. Then, Jimmy Rivers got control of himself.

"Ms. Black is from Wyoming, originally," he informed his peers. "But she lived in California for a long time. So she knows what it's like in both kinds of places. That's important for us, 'cause we just know what it's like here. What's more important, though, is that it's all part of America. And we got...we have the constitution, no matter where we live. That's what she's going to talk about." He stepped back. There was scattered applause.

Nan stepped forward. "How many of you like movies?" she asked. Hands went up. Soft snickers sounded.

"How would you like it if the police wouldn't let you go to them?" Hands lowered. Silence fell.

For the next twenty minutes, she talked, filling them in on the basic rights of the First Amendment as applied to the arts. It was sketchy and superficial, but she didn't have the time to cram a whole course down their throats. When she called for questions, however, she knew she had made her points.

"Can I go to any movie I want?" one boy asked. His dark hair flopped in his eyes, and he pushed it back with his left hand while his right remained in the air.

"No, dummy," a neighboring kid informed him. "You ain't old enough yet."

"That's right," Nan said, dominating due to the microphone. "The movie company can make any film they want. That's a right. But until you're an adult, you need permission to attend or can be barred. That's a privilege, too."

"How come?" A slender, pretty blond girl asked that question. The set of her full mouth indicated a sullen attitude. "What's so 'privileged' about being kept out?"

"You have a right to be protected from material until you're emotionally mature enough to deal with it." Nan held up a poster. She had chosen the promo for a particularly gruesome horror film. A chorus of gags and groans greeted the sight. "Would you want to let a really little kid, say your younger brother or sister, see this? Do you think it would be good for them, or not?"

She made her point, judging from the response.

Questions went on for a few more minutes, then a bell rang, and Mrs. Weaver took over. "We all want to thank Ms. Black for taking her valuable time to speak to us." Applause. "Dismissed!"

The resulting commotion left Nan a little dazed. By the time she recovered, the lunchroom had emptied except for herself, Mrs. Weaver and Jimmy.

"Sorry I didn't get to meet you earlier, Ms. Black," the principal said, shaking Nan's hand. "I'm Genny Weaver and am delighted to meet you, finally. I wanted the privilege of escorting you in myself, but someone had to be here to keep the troops in line." She grinned.

"I understand. Please call me Nan." Nan returned the handshake and the smile. "You are good at your job, Mrs. Weaver."

"Genny, please. So are you." She looked over at Jimmy, who was shifting his weight awkwardly from foot to foot. "And you did a fine job of introducing our guest, Jim. You may return to class now."

"I, uh, thought I'd help Ms. Black take her stuff out."

"Oh, that's all right," Nan began. Then she saw something in his expression. "Well, I suppose I could use a hand, after all." She turned to the principal. "If that's okay with you, of course."

"It is." Genny Weaver's drill sergeant stance softened marginally. "Just don't dawdle, Jim."

"No, ma'am. I won't."

"Ms. Black, thank you again." More softening. "I'll be in touch with you later."

"I'll look forward to it," Nan replied, meaning it. This small woman with the strength of personality capable of controlling close to a hundred kids using only her voice intrigued her. They said goodbye and Weaver left.

"She's really something, ain't . . . isn't she?" Jimmy said as he picked up the box. "I was really scared of her when I came here from junior high."

"And now?"

"I'm still scared." He grinned. "But in a different way."

"You're growing up and getting smarter." Nan thought about that for a moment. It must be wonderful for Jesse to watch this process in his brother, she reflected. If he was aware of it, that is. They started walking down the hall toward the front door.

"Uh, speaking of that kind of thing . . ." Jimmy began.

"Yes?"

"Uh, I really liked what you said in there. About our rights and responsibilities and stuff."

"Thanks."

"I mean, I'm really interested." He held the door open for her, reminding her strongly of his older brother's offhand chivalry. "A lot of us knew what you were talking about. About those jerks who don't want you renting any movies in town."

"Now, Jim. I thought I made it clear. They are entitled to their opinion. Just as long as it doesn't infringe on my freedom or yours."

"Yeah. Well, I was thinking. . . ."

"What?" She stopped and faced him directly. "Out with it. If you have something to say to me, say it."

"Do you need help, Ms. Black? I mean, I'm working for Jesse, sure. But he just needs someone to haul and load and answer the phone. Anybody can do that. I ain't . . . I'm not learning anything. I think I could, working for you."

Nan thought quickly. "I do need help. I can't continue to run things all by myself much longer. Won't this cause a problem for you, though? I need someone who can work weekends, and you go home."

Jim shrugged. "I can stay in town. I'm old enough to make a decision like this. Mom and Dad will understand. Jesse don't actually pay me, see. I'm sort of working for him for room and board."

"Ah. Family business, eh?"

"Yeah. For you, well, it'd be a real job. The sort of thing that would look good on a college application. And I'd be learning stuff, wouldn't I? I mean, Jesse don't talk about my constitutional rights ever. We just work, if you know what I mean."

"I think I do. Can you start tomorrow?" She smiled at the grin that lit up his face. "No, come in this afternoon after school. Unless you have things to do for your brother, that is."

"Jesse's out of town this weekend. He's got some deliveries up in North Dakota for a bunch of veterinarians. He didn't ask me to do anything while he was gone, since he expected I'd be heading home right after school. I can call Steve and tell him not to drive in for me."

"We aren't open Sunday, if you'd like to go home. I could even drive you out."

"Oh, that's okay. I don't want you bothering. I just want to learn." His enthusiasm was plain.

"Well, Jim Rivers, then you're hired. I'll pay only minimum at first, but you work hard and you'll get rewarded. I'm a fair employer." She held out her hand, and they shook on it. "And call me Nan, for goodness' sake!" His grin widened.

After Jimmy went back into the school building, Nan sat for a few minutes in her car. She had taken steps this morning that would surely have positive results for her future, and she was happy.

Glancing at her watch, she saw it wasn't ten yet. She would run home and change before opening the store, she decided. Delaying the opening time for a few minutes wouldn't hurt anything. No reason to spend the rest of the day in her good clothes, especially if she was going to be busy.

Hopefully, she would be busy.

JESSE BANGED ON THE GLASS, wondering if she had wandered into the storeroom and was back there daydreaming instead of opening at ten as her sign declared. Her station wagon wasn't parked in back, though. He had already checked. Maybe she was plain lazy and sleeping in. What a way to run a business, he thought in disgust. He looked at the time. He had to be on his way. Didn't have time to hang around, waiting for her to show. Didn't have time to run by her house. Damn.

He wanted to ask if she'd go to dinner with him Sunday evening. He'd be back from his delivery trip by then. She'd made him a little angry the other night when she just up and left him at the Canteen. No reason for him to feel that way, of course. She had her own car. But it rankled, nonetheless. He'd had some intentions of getting a bit closer to her that night, and nothing had happened. It was an unsatisfactory date, if it could even be called that. He had made that promise to himself to ask her out, hadn't he? What was so complicated about it? It ought not to be at all complicated. She sure wasn't. She was just another woman. Just a hard-charging, hardheaded woman who had plans she thought were good ones. Plans that were only so much pie in the sky, as far as he could see. So the whole mess ought not to be bothering him at all.

But for some reason, it was more complicated. In spite of what had nearly happened with other relationships, he had never been in this kind of a tangle over a woman before, never had this sense of...awkwardness before. Not only did that make him feel uneasy, it made him oddly anxious to be with her. He did want to talk to her, get to know her better.

He wanted to figure out why he couldn't get her off his mind.

Jesse stuck his hands in his pockets and went back to his truck. As he drove away, the feeling of emptiness that had been plaguing him for several days grew sharper. It did not improve his mood. He was fairly sure nothing was going to, either.

SUNDAY MORNING, Nan slipped the folded check into the collection plate with a feeling of thankfulness suffusing her heart. She had never tithed before, never wanted to, but she felt like doing it today. She had a great deal to be grateful for, she thought.

First, no more hassles from the porno criers. She had feared some nasty phone calls or, at worst, picketing of her place. Nothing had happened, and no one who came into the store had said anything in favor of the conservatives. Those who had had something to say on the subject were strongly in favor of her and her business. She definitely had the support of the majority in the community, it seemed.

Second, Jimmy was working out remarkably well. He had shown up minutes after school on Friday, dropped off by a friend with a car, he told her, so he wouldn't waste time walking over. She had already made a list of things for him to learn and was impressed with his quickness. He was a highly intelligent boy. His enthusiasm and cheerfulness infected everyone who came in, and she was sure her rental rate was up because of him. He was going to get a raise sooner than she had promised, she decided. She did lose him late Saturday afternoon when his brother-in-law Steve came into town to fetch him home. She didn't meet Steve, since she was swamped with customers, but as he went out the door, Jimmy shouted out that he'd be in on Monday afternoon.

She was looking forward to it.

The third thing she figured she had to be thankful for was just being here in the same pew, beside her new friend, Inge Frank, for the second Sunday in a row. Inge had greeted her warmly and had complimented her again on her clothes. She wore the business suit she had used on Friday morning, but had dressed it up with a frilly blouse and jewelry. Inge's approval pleased her, and she realized, absurdly, that she had anticipated it as she dressed earlier. Though she had spent only a few hours with the woman, Inge was already important to her. Her emotions were stirred as she listened to the junior choir sing. The childish voices seemed to tug right at her heartstrings.

Later, as she mingled with the rest of the congregation, she was almost overcome by her feelings. Tears gathered in her eyes for a moment. For the first time in years, she actually had a group of people who welcomed her into their midst without question and without ulterior motive.

And to her relief, no one mentioned the controversy about her business.

Over at the Petersens' she pitched right in, helping with lunch. She was heaping her plate with food and laughing at a joke when a warm hand touched her arm and a voice spoke to her from behind. A thrill ran through her at the sound.

"Don't stuff yourself here this afternoon. If you're not busy, I'd like to take you out for dinner tonight."

She turned, almost spilling mashed potatoes on Sue's dining room carpet. "Hello, Jesse," she said, feeling her heart bounce around in her chest. The cardiac action left her a little breathless. He looked sexy as all get-out in a white dress shirt and gray slacks with a blue crew-neck sweater. No tie, but he was shaved and his hair was combed down. Bronze-brown curls were starting to spring free from the grooming, and she itched to touch one that threatened to fall across his forehead. "Back in town?" she asked, hoping her tone was casual enough.

"Yeah. And glad of it. The weather wasn't any too kind to me, but the vets were sure happy to get the parvo vaccine."

"P-porno vaccine?"

He laughed. His eyes showed both amusement and sympathy, however. "Parvo. It's a killer disease of dogs. Nothing to do with your troubles." He sobered. "I hear you took a beating in the paper the other day. I didn't see the letters, but I heard about it. Sorry."

"Hardly anything for you to be sorry for." She moved aside for several people who were going through the food line. "In fact... Never mind," she added, remembering she wasn't supposed to tell him about Neilson. "Did you say dinner? Sure, I'd like that. But—"

"Let's get out of here, Nan." He guided her into the kitchen. "Go some place we can talk, okay?"

"Jesse, you have no claim on Nan's time," Sue sang out from her position by the sink. "She promised to help me clean up today."

Jesse made a face and pushed up his sleeves. "I guess that means I gotta get to work myself if I want her company." He winked at Nan. "Darn."

Not too much later, they were alone. Nan drove her vehicle home. Jesse followed.

"I want to change," she told him when they had both parked. "Come on in and make yourself at home for a few minutes."

He eyed her. "You look just fine." He stayed in his truck. "Let's go. It's a long drive."

Nan smiled wryly. "Where're we going for dinner? Unless you're planning on flying us someplace, I expect I'm not really properly dressed for the occasion."

"Do you care?" The green depths of his eyes had an impish light. The edges of his mouth twitched, though he kept a straight face.

"You rat!" She grinned and turned toward her house. "You're taking me to some place where I will stand out like a sore thumb in this dress-for-success suit! Stay put, if you want. I'll be right back."

Jesse watched her until she disappeared. She did look just fine to him, actually. He tapped his finger on the door frame. Looked like a high-powered lady executive, all right. Just what she planned on being. He almost sighed, then caught himself.

Well, so what? If that was what she wanted, that was fine. All he was doing was taking an attractive woman out to dinner. He wasn't asking her to marry him, for goodness' sake! She was so far from his ideal of a wife, it was laughable. All he was doing was scratching a small emotional itch he had concerning her.

All he was doing . . .

All he'd done all weekend was think about her. The flights had been routine and boring in spite of the chancy spring weather, so he'd had plenty of time to think. She'd probably call it fantasizing, he thought, tapping again. But he had only been thinking to pass the time. Just . . . thinking.

Thinking wasn't going to hurt him.

Was it?

CHAPTER SEVEN

GOOD AS HER WORD, Nan was back out in a few minutes. She had changed into a calf-length denim skirt and a white shirt. She carried a black shawl and wore a pair of dressy black cowgirl boots. Leather belt at her waist. Classy. Very simple, very Western.

Very un-high-powered executive.

"So where are we headed?" she asked as she climbed into the passenger seat. She had moved too quickly for him to get out and open the door for her. He wasn't sure she'd appreciate the gesture anyway. "You say it's far?"

"A ways." Jesse slid the truck into gear. "Mind a drive?"

"Of course not." She ran her hand behind her neck, lifting her blond hair free of her collar. "It's a beautiful afternoon."

Jesse stared at her profile. "Yes, it is."

Nan relaxed as they drove out of town. The snow from earlier in the week had melted and disappeared, leaving the ground clean and bare. Patches of green were turning greener, a sure sign the world was accepting spring and readying for summer. The sky overhead was clear blue without the slightest trace of a cloud. "You must love flying in this kind of weather," she said. "It's so clear you could go on up forever, it seems."

"Don't let appearances fool you." He leaned over and turned on the tape player. Soft classical music wafted into the cab interior. "Those 'clear' skies are full of updrafts and downdrafts this time of year. You can be flying along and drop a thousand feet all of a sudden. No warning." He grinned. "And no stomach, either. Not recommended after a heavy meal."

"Yikes." She shivered. "I think I'll stick to the good old wide-bodied jets, thanks."

"I'd rather depend on myself and my own plane, thanks. I hate airplane food, anyway."

"I can understand that, I guess. You're a professional. You know what you're doing. Safe, dependable flying must be your trademark." She laughed and put her hand on the seat near his thigh. "Except when you're landing on the road out in the middle of nowhere, and nearly scaring the life out of an innocent passerby."

"That was an exception. I admit I made a mistake in judgment, taking that old junker out that day. She's up on the blocks right now. Won't fly her until I'm sure she's airworthy. I only keep her for sentimental reasons anyway."

"Hey, don't get tense. I'm teasing." She patted the seat.

Jesse looked down at her hand. A few more inches, and she'd be touching him. He wanted that. *Really* wanted it. Could imagine just how her small, warm fingers would feel on his thigh. "I know," he said, feeling the words stick in his throat slightly. "It's just I'm kind of sensitive when it comes to my safety record. It's something any pilot takes seriously."

"And if not?"

"He ends up grounded. One way or another."

"Oh." She pulled her hand back and curled it in her lap. The tape switched. Softer music followed the clicks. Nan looked out the windows at the smooth fields flashing by. Some had been plowed, their dark brown surfaces lined with neat furrows. In others, last year's yellow stubble still covered the soil. A picture was forming in her mind, but she tried not to see it. A small plane...smashed against the ground...

"Let's talk about something more cheerful," he suggested. "Your business going all right in spite of those jerks who did the letter-writing campaign?"

"Yes, in fact, I—"

"Oh, that reminds me. I found a VCR player and some tapes at home. I know Jimmy hasn't got any money, so I figured you gave them to him because of the work he did last week. You paid us back with dinner. I don't want you feeling any more obligation."

"Jesse, I don't feel any obligation. Those films and the VCR are part of Jimmy's work for me. He started on Friday afternoon, and I had some videos I hadn't had time to review myself. I asked him to take them home and give me an opinion on—"

"Work? For you? What're you talking about?"

"I hired Jimmy. Part-time, of course. I—"

Jesse almost drove off the road. "You what? Hired him? Behind my back! While I was gone!" He overcorrected and ended up in the left lane.

Nan yelped in terror. "Watch out! Oh, my God!" They barely missed a truck coming the other way. The driver honked angrily as Jesse swerved back into his own lane. He slowed and stopped, pulling off onto the shoulder. Both of them sat there for a moment, not looking at each other, breathing heavily.

"Sorry," he said finally. He leaned on the steering wheel, resting his forehead on his hands.

"I hope so!" She unfastened her belt and faced him squarely. "Are you nuts? And if you aren't, what's your excuse? I just told you I gave your little brother a job. I am *paying* the boy. He is learning! Does that deserve this kind of reaction?" She waved her hands in the air.

Jesse raised his head and looked at her. "No, it does not. When did all this happen?"

"Just now... Oh, Friday. I went to the high school and gave a little talk on constitutional rights. Part of my offense against the offensive stuff in the paper, and that... man who spoke so nastily to me in the bar. The kids seemed to like it and understand what I was trying to get across. Most of them, anyway. Jimmy was particularly enthusiastic. He asked me for the job. I did not deliberately go out of my way to offer it to him, but I did need help. And Jesse, he is a bright kid and a wonderful worker."

"I know." He still looked at her, no warmth in his face. "You really are a carpetbagger, aren't you?"

"Pardon?"

"Come into town. Stir up folks. Lure away the young. I mean, it'd make a great movie, wouldn't it?"

"Are you teasing? Or is this serious?"

"I don't know, Nan." He faced forward again, and shifted gears. "Buckle up, will you?" He pulled out onto the road as she complied. "What I do know for sure is Jimmy can't go on working for you."

"Why not! You don't pay him. Surely you could afford it."

"I can. I don't. That's not the point."

"Well, I would really like to know what is! What's the matter? Afraid of losing a little hero-worship time?"

He glanced at her. It was a glare. "That's not fair. You don't know anything about us. I'm his damn brother, not his hero."

"I can sure understand that! Jimmy, at least, has some discernment about people."

"Just what do you mean?"

"I mean *you*. What kind of a role model for him are you, anyway? You fly planes. Granted that has some kind of glamour, but not really. Not the way you do it. Probably safer these days than driving a truck. Certainly safer than you were a few minutes ago. You're a barnacle, Jesse Rivers, clinging to the safe stone of home ground. You live a few miles from where you were born. You go to the same church you attended as a kid. You're limited in your outlook because you've never bothered to look beyond your own horizons.''

"Now, just wait a damn minute! I—"

"No, you wait! Do you want to know why he asked me for work? It wasn't because of the store or the money. It was because of what I talked about. He wants to learn, Jesse. Wants to grow. He wants to reach outside his present experiences."

"I know that."

"Then why...?"

"Nan, excuse me if I sound trite, but you sure think you know everything, don't you?"

"I do not!"

"You sure sound like you think you know me."

His voice was low, barely audible over the music. She leaned forward and cut off the player. "I do, Jesse Rivers. I grew up knowing guys like you. I married one once."

"Oh, really?"

"Yes, really." She clutched her hands in her lap to keep them from trembling. She felt an anger so deep it hurt. "You think that because you have a handle on your little corner of the world you're some kind of god. I was raised in a place just like Hennington. All I knew was local stuff— who had money, who didn't, who was sleeping with whom, who was drinking—"

"Sleeping with *whom?*"

"Don't you dare make fun of me! My parents, my brother and sister, they all love the place, don't care if they ever leave. Don't want a taste of the world outside. My teachers in high school were just as bad. Civics was local politics, gossip, really. World history? Forget it. What was taught was dull as dishwater. English? The teachers wouldn't have known a good story if it had bitten them. All any of us wanted to do was get out of school and get married. Anything to escape the boredom."

"So, by those standards, you were a success." He slowed the truck again. She scarcely noticed.

"So successful, I nearly died of suffocation." She closed her eyes, her mind writhing with memories. "I did love Paul at first. I don't question that. I really thought we could have a wonderful life together. I had so many plans. Such high hopes."

"What did happen, Nan?"

She opened her eyes. They had parked again. The sun was much lower in the sky, burnishing the landscape with late-afternoon rays. Over to the left the flat land fell into a series of intricate trenches and rose into stark, low hills. Badlands. Jesse was watching her closely.

"He couldn't dream," she said, gazing at him. Tears burned, then spilled. "He tried to take *my* dreams, too."

Jesse sat, spellbound. He'd expected to hear common gripes—more complaints about boredom, poor sex life, drinking, laziness, maybe abuse, even. But not this. Not this almost spiritual cry. This yearning that *had* to be fulfilled. He had no idea what to say.

So he leaned over and kissed her.

Nan felt his lips on hers before she realized what was happening. And before she could realize anything else, she had put her arms around his neck and opened her mouth for him. Their seat belts prevented any closer contact.

It wasn't necessary. She felt as close to him for a moment as she ever had to anyone. His kiss was gentle, tender and sensual. Giving as well as taking. He tasted her with the tip of his tongue, but he didn't press. She could smell his clean skin, his after-shave—a plain, simple scent—feel his warm breath on her cheek. Her fingers touched the soft hair at the back of his neck, the prickly stubble where his barber had shaved it, felt the firm cords of muscles move. Felt herself ease into a boneless state...

Jesse was poised on the brink of an endless drop into a dark, warm abyss. And abyss that would enfold him with delicious pleasure while it took him inexorably downward. Her lips were so soft, her mouth so wet and willing. Her taste so sweet and real... The point of his tongue captured the clean flavor of her toothpaste, the moist, natural taste of her mouth. Her hand was touching his neck, fingertips stroking the sensitive skin behind his ear.... His muscles bunched. He was ready to rip loose from his seat belt and swarm all over her!

He let her go and pushed away. "Sorry," he said, gripping the wheel and looking out the front window. "Shouldn't have done that."

"Speak for yourself." She was breathless, but in control now. "I liked it. I guess I don't know everything about you, after all. I would never have thought you were such a good kisser."

She was smiling at him. Her lips were parted and still wet looking. Alluring. Her cheeks had high, bright spots of color. Touchable. With some effort, Jesse pulled himself together and smiled back. "Want to keep on arguing?" he asked.

"No." She reached over and gave his arm a squeeze. "I let my past intrude on the present. That wasn't right. We're friends. We can discuss our differences without heat." She looked around. "Where are we? This is beautiful. Look at the way the sun is hitting those hills. I can see purple and green and gold. Red, too.''

"Some people might call it desolate." He pointed to the broken terrain, trying not to consider what she meant by saying they were friends. He was not feeling much like just her friend at the moment. "That's a small outcrop of the Badlands. The colors come from the composition of the rock and soil. The best way to see it is from the sky, though. You'd think you were flying over another planet.''

"Really?" She looked at him again, and there seemed to be stars in her eyes. "I'd like—"

"Would you like to? I'll take you, one of these days. When it's . . .''

"Safer?" She smiled, taking the sting from the words.

"Yeah. Anything wrong with that?''

"Don't get defensive. I thought we weren't going to argue." She tilted her head slightly to one side, studying him. "Jesse, have you ever been married?''

"No.''

"Close call, though?''

"Yeah, once." He started the engine. "Let's go. I don't know about you, but I didn't get lunch, and I'm hungry.''

They drove on, without speaking. Nan ached to ask about his "close call," but kept her curiosity on a tight rein. It was none of her business and none of her concern what he had done or would do with his romantic life. She put his kiss and her reaction to it out of her mind. That was the result of the heat of the moment, surely. The only issue she needed to get straight with Jesse Rivers concerned his brother. She was prepared to fight for Jimmy's rights and independence.

Because she had been unable to fight for her own when she was his age.

The restaurant was on the outskirts of a town so small it made Hennington feel like a metropolitan center. This place looked like an accident that happened to the prairie land, jutting right up out of the ground with no warning, no rhyme or reason to it. The appearance of the restaurant itself did not fill Nan with confidence. Constructed out of cinder blocks and clapboard, it had a neon sign announcing EAT in pink letters. But the graveled parking lot was filled with cars and trucks of every description. She looked at Jesse.

He smiled. "Trust me," he said. She rolled her eyes and looked heavenward.

He was, however, right. When she walked in the front door, the aroma of good food made her hungry. The decor was dreadful—false wood paneling, black velvet paintings of big-eyed children, brass eagle clocks and peeling plastic on the chairs. That didn't seem to matter to the enthusiastic patrons, who were, one and all, chowing down with relish. A number of them greeted Jesse and regarded Nan with open curiosity. She was glad she had changed clothes. The hostess was a large woman with white hair and a friendly smile that widened when she spotted Jesse.

"Hello, stranger," she said, including Nan in her greeting. "Been a long time, Jesse."

"Hi, Sarah." He put his hand on Nan's elbow, proprietorially, she thought. He introduced Sarah to her as the owner and manager. "Got a No Smoking table for us?" he asked.

Sarah laughed heartily. "This little gal gonna get you to give up those cigars permanent, Mr. Rivers? We'll sure miss the perfume!" She made a face, then led them to a booth in the far corner of the place. No Smoking, Nan realized as they sat down and Sarah removed the ashtrays, just meant that you didn't. There was no separate, privileged section.

But the food was wonderful. At Jesse's suggestion, she had the roast beef. It was so tender she could cut it with her fork. The rolls were fresh, hot and yeasty. The only negative was the drinking water. When she reached for her glass, he stopped her with his hand on hers.

"Don't even try it," he warned, keeping his voice low. "You'll be picking minerals out of your teeth for a week. Hard as I've tried to talk Sarah into ordering bottled water, she still insists on using the stuff out of the tap here. Says it's more 'natural.'"

Nan picked up the glass and sniffed the contents. "I'll say," she commented. "I think I'll have a beer, instead."

He ordered one, taking a soft drink, himself.

"No beer?" she asked. "Designated driver? Do you expect me to get soused or something?"

"No." He rested his chin on his hands and regarded her. "I'm flying this week. Tomorrow, actually. I make it a practice not to drink before I go up."

"Not even a beer?" He shook his head. She was impressed. "You're a very disciplined man, Jesse Rivers," she said.

"Just cautious. I like a drink as much as the next person, but I've seen the havoc it can cause. My friend, Charlie..." He broke off when the waitress appeared with their food.

"I figured he had a problem," Nan said after they were alone again. "Last Sunday, he looked—"

"Don't judge him." Jesse spoke softly but firmly, his eyes gazing hard at hers. "Charlie's come a long, long way in his fight."

"I'm sorry." She reached out and touched his hand. "I admit I have trouble not being harsh. You see, that was one of my ex-husband's endearing traits."

"He drank?"

"Still does, I hear." She blinked and looked down at her plate, suddenly losing her appetite. "Whether I want to know or not, my family keeps me informed."

"You are carrying a lot of baggage from your past, aren't you?" He paused for a forkful of food. Chewing, he regarded her speculatively. "Suppose that's why you have such firm ideas," he added after swallowing.

Nan smiled. "That another way of telling me I'm stubborn and opinionated?"

He grinned back. "Yeah." His tone was kind and understanding in spite of the affirmative word.

She found her appetite returning with a vengeance.

Over dessert, however, Jesse returned to the discussion. "You're wrong about a lot of things, you know," he said.

"Such as?" She was in no mood to fight. The meal had filled her to the point of being stuffed, and she was feeling extremely relaxed. He couldn't get a rise out of her if he tried standing on his head to do it, she decided. She was just going to laugh at him if he made an attempt.

"About me, for one thing. Jimmy for another. He really can't go on working for you."

"Why not?" Anger started to stir, and she put it down with some effort, surprised at how easily he could rile her. "Give me one good reason *I* can understand."

"I know you're paying him, and I appreciate that. I guess I should have offered a while ago myself. He's worth it, that's for sure. But he needs to learn about business, about the world. Not about... well, about dreams and fantasies."

She felt her muscles tensing. "And you think that's all he'll get from me?"

"You talk about dreams a lot. You sell fantasies."

"We all need them! I do a proper business."

"Maybe. You've been open a week or so. You're a novelty. A controversial one, at that. Face it, Nan, by your own admission, you are fly-by-night. Here as long as it does you some good. What's Jimmy going to get out of an experience in a place that has no...permanence?"

"I don't believe I'm sitting here, listening to this!"

"He can't let his mind wander off his schoolwork, either. He has to keep up his studies, his grades."

"Of course he does! Even if he ends up like you!"

Jesse sat back. "Like me? No chance. I plan to see to that. I'm all right now, but I wasn't for a long time. I made lousy grades in school. Very nearly didn't graduate. I was too busy yearning for the future. Dreaming, if you want to call it that."

"You? Don't make me laugh."

"Me. See?" He leaned forward again, pointing a finger at her. "That's another thing you're wrong about. You called me a barnacle. Well, I had legs on my shell for a while."

"You did?"

"Nan, I went to work for someone when I was a little younger than Jimmy. Before that, I worked at home on the farm for my dad. He tried teaching me farming, but I wanted to fly."

"And you did."

"Sure did. The guy taught me to look up at the sky and the clouds, not down at the ground. First time I went up in his plane, I knew I was home. By the way, it was the same plane I landed nearly on top of you that day we met. He can't fly anymore, and I—"

"Charlie?"

Jesse nodded. "After I graduated, I took off. By then, Charlie was starting to drink pretty heavy, and I wasn't old enough to deal with that. I did a hitch in the army, then went on my own, free-lancing for small airlines, private planes, anything I could find. I wasn't a barnacle, I was a rolling stone, and no moss clung to this rock!''

"I believe you. What brought you back?" Nan was fascinated. She certainly had been wrong, but it did explain that undercurrent of excitement she sensed in him. Maybe he wasn't such a dull stick, after all.

Or, at least, he hadn't been. Now...?

"I came back because I wanted to, needed to. This is my home. I was free out there, sure. But I wasn't happy. I was also getting a little dangerous. To myself and anyone near me."

"That's when you almost married?"

He grinned. "Boss's daughter. Can you believe that? I can't believe I was ever really that stupid. I was flying private for a big corporate CEO down in Georgia. Daddy's little girl came along from time to time. She was beautiful and rich, and I guess I was just plain dazzled."

"I bet she was, too." Nan set her elbow on the table and rested her chin in her hand. She was seeing something else in him now, but wasn't quite sure what it was.

"That was the problem." He held up his hand, indicating to the waitress he was ready for the check. "I thought we were in love. I was willing to put up with all the snobs who thought I wasn't up to her social class. And then one day— it was like waking up from a good dream and finding out reality is the nightmare—I knew she wasn't really in love with me. Not Jesse Rivers. She loved her daddy's pilot, the guy who presented this romantic image to her."

"Oh, I see." But Nan didn't. How could anyone mistake Jesse Rivers for anyone but Jesse Rivers? Romantic image? Sure, he was sexy and could kiss, but he certainly had no aura, no special image. "That's a sad story."

"Not really. Soon afterward I decided to come home. Someday..."

She didn't get to find out what his "someday" held for him. The check arrived, and Jesse handled it. She felt no need to fuss about that. After all, he had invited her out. She relaxed once more, feeling friendly vibes toward him.

On the way home, however, he started in again. "So, do you understand now why I don't want Jimmy working for you?" he asked as they drove through the now moonlit landscape.

"I do not. I don't see any correlation between your experience and his. Maybe you say you don't like fantasy, but it strikes me you've lived out one or two of your own. What I can do for Jimmy is teach him some solid business principles. It wouldn't matter if I was renting out kumquats. Those principles would be the same."

"Maybe." He sounded a little less sure of himself.

"Besides, Jesse, it was his idea. Are you willing to take the risk of barging into the situation and becoming the 'bad guy'?"

"I don't get your point."

"Did your father raise objections to your working for Charlie?"

"We had a discussion or two about it."

"I just bet you did. And he came off as a stodgy drag on your dreams, didn't he? You knew he didn't understand you, didn't you?"

Jesse didn't say anything.

"Look, no offense. But regardless of how romantic you must have seemed to your little Southern peach, to Jimmy you've got to be much like your dad was to you at that age. Older, unexciting, predictable. Let him alone for a while. I promise to make sure he doesn't neglect his studies."

"You're saying I'm boring? Dull? That Jimmy must see me already halfway in a rocking chair?" There was an edge to his voice.

"Hey, I asked you not to take it personally. I'm just trying to see it from a teenager's point of view. I think you're . . . nice, myself."

"Good Lord."

"Well, Jesse, let's face it. You are a nice guy. You have a business, a thriving one, I think. You own your home. You have good personal habits—go to church, don't drink much and you've given up smoking. To most women, you're an ideal they long for."

"You don't see me that way, though?"

"I like you! Don't be so sensitive. You're just . . ."

"Dull?"

"Jesse . . ."

"No, really. I want to know."

"You aren't exactly Errol Flynn." She paused, looking at his profile carefully. He didn't appear upset by her criticism. In fact, if she could judge accurately by the turn of his lips, he thought it was all pretty funny. Okay, pile it on, she thought. "Much less Indiana Jones," she added.

"Who?"

"Never mind. Jimmy knows who he is. And how good he is for business. He's *the* hero of the decade, I believe. You're almost culturally illiterate if you don't know—"

"Oh, yea, he's that guy with the hat and the whip. That's your idea of a hero?"

"Well, one of them."

"A man of action, willing to take risks?"

"Well, yes."

"What're you doing next Sunday?"

"Huh? Oh, I don't know. That's too far in the future for me to be sure."

"Save the afternoon. Tell Sue you won't be going to lunch."

"It this another date invitation? Because if it is, I think we need to get a few other things out of the way before I decide whether or not to accept."

"Like Jimmy?"

"I did have him in mind."

"Okay." Jesse slowed the truck, and Nan saw they were inside the Hennington town limits already. He had taken a shorter route home, she realized with a stab of disappointment. In a hurry to get rid of her and her unflattering comments, possibly.

"You may be partly right," he said. "I told you before, I tend to get a little narrow in my view when it comes to the boy. I'll let you both give it a chance for a week or so. But if he starts mooning around and daydreaming—"

"I'll fire him, myself. Fair enough?"

"I guess so. You made a good point about my interfering. It'd be a mistake, and he'd resent the hell out of it. Just swear to me—"

"I won't swear anything to you except to promise I'll be fair."

He didn't respond right away. Instead he drove on to her house and parked. Nan put her hand on the door handle.

"Don't get out just yet," he said softly, staring out the front window. "We still have one or two things to clear up."

CHAPTER EIGHT

NAN FELT a sensual shiver pass down her spine. "Like what?" she asked.

He reached down and released the buckle on his seat belt without looking over at her or answering. Moonlight spilled through the windows, filling the interior of the truck with that special silvery-gray light of northern prairie spring nights. Jesse's strong features were highlighted and shadowed, giving him an ominous, but exciting appearance. She knew she couldn't move, even if she wanted to.

"When we kissed back there by the Badlands," he said, "I didn't want to stop."

"Neither did I." She was having trouble getting enough breath, but she didn't want to sigh. It would sound fake. Deliberate. Corny. Ruin the mood of the moment. The magic of it!

"You have an effect on me I didn't go looking for from you," he said, still looking out the front window. "We haven't much in common at all. I just can't figure it, myself."

"Do you really need to?" She itched to touch him, if just to give him some comfort. He seemed very ill at ease. "Why can't we just enjoy what's happening?"

Now he looked at her. "That what you want? Just to take the moment? Enjoy it? Play out a fantasy in real life?"

"What's so bad about that? Jesse, it strikes me that you have too much reality on the brain." Now she did touch, putting her hand on his shoulder. "You could use a little fantasy, I think." She moved closer, slipping her hand across his back, feeling the hard muscles tensing under her palm. "Maybe even a dream or two," she added softly. "You're entitled, just like anyone else."

"You aren't playing fair," he said, his tone almost a low growl. He frowned, but she could see his lips trying not to smile. "Not fair at all!"

"I know," she said, letting her fingers play over his hair with just a feather's touch. "You said we have things to clear up? Well, I think it's pretty clear we like each other. In some ways, if not others. Would you agree with me there?"

"I'd be a liar if I didn't."

"True." She inched closer, so close she could feel the heat of his body. She felt extremely sexy, but in a playful way. Not serious sexy. The windows of the truck were closed, and she could see a fine mist beginning to fog the glass. With any other man, she would never have tried this, she realized. But she trusted Jesse. She *knew* she was safe with him. Resisting the need to giggle at the situation, she trailed her fingertips across his neck and jaw to his mouth. There, she traced the finely carved lines of his lips.

He groaned, leaned back and shut his eyes. "You're playing with dynamite, you know," he said, his voice hoarse. "If I should come unglued, there's no one to rescue you. No knight on a white horse. Just me."

"You'll do," she whispered, kissing his neck. His skin was hot, and she could feel the jump of his artery right beneath her lips. His pulse was racing. "Just fine," she added, tasting him with the tip of her tongue.

He was enjoying himself, Jesse thought, as he rode down hard on the need to escalate the situation into a full-scale clinch and kiss. In a perverse sort of way, though. Like an exquisite pain that was so close to pleasure it was impossible to tell the difference. Her breasts were millimeters from his arm, her thigh even closer to his leg. Her scent was filling his nostrils and clouding his mind, sending his senses soaring and screaming for more. But it was sweeter not to take it all. Not now.

Later? Maybe...

Nan understood what was happening. Or so she thought. He was letting her do this, letting her tease him. Actually, he was fully in control. That was why she felt so safe. She wanted to change that, to drive him far enough so he lost it. Make him lose that iron control. Make him crazy! She started to run her hand down his chest, then hesitated.

This was not her style, so why was she persisting? She sat back and looked at him. He was watching her out of half-closed eyes. She could read no expression on his face. Not that she needed to. His body was showing his desire clearly enough. "You like this," she said. "You're having fun and egging me on, aren't you?"

"Well, I'm not exactly ready to scream for help, if that's what you mean." The edges of his lips twitched.

"Jesse Rivers, you are a . . ."

"Helpless love slave?"

"Rat!"

Now he grinned broadly. "Kiss rats on the neck often, do you? Kind of weird, don't you think?"

"Maybe." The joking tones they took killed the highly charged mood, but not the romance. She smiled and leaned against him. "But it was nice. You thought so, too."

He shifted in his seat. "I suppose I did. Even rats tend to get excited by the proper stimuli. And you are properly stimulating, believe me!" He put his arm around her shoulders.

Nan rested her head on his chest. "When can we get together again? This week is going to be a little crazy for me, but with Jimmy to help out . . ."

He shook his head. She could feel the movement. His hand caressed her arm gently. "I've got a busy time, too. And when I see you again like this, I don't want to be worried about time. Sunday?"

"All right. How about—"

"No, don't make plans. I have a few things in mind. A surprise or two. I believe you're the kind of person who enjoys surprises."

"As long as they're good ones." She looked up at him.

When they broke off the kiss, the windows were completely fogged. Leaving him then and saying good-night was one of the most difficult things Nan had done in a long, long time.

THE DAYS PASSED SLOWLY, when she thought of Jesse, and rapidly when she managed to turn her mind to business. Having Jimmy working for a few hours in the afternoon or early evening made a big difference in her efficiency, and she enjoyed his company. She had worried a little that he might be harboring a teenage crush on her, but that didn't prove to be the case. She found it easy to treat him as if he were her own brother, in fact. A younger brother she could guide and advise gently.

There was only one thing about him that bothered her. He didn't mention his real brother. Not once.

Tuesday evening, Genny Weaver came in. She wandered around the store, greeted Jimmy and nodded to Nan, who was busy with a customer. When he left, Genny came over.

"I'd like to talk to you," she said. Her manner was friendly, relaxed, but Nan sensed an edge in her tone.

"Sure, what's on your mind?" Nan leaned her elbows on the counter.

"Well." Genny glanced at Jimmy, who was busy dusting shelves. He seemed absorbed with his task. "You were terrific with the kids the other day. I wanted to thank you again. Your talk generated some real discussion in some of the classes, the teachers tell me."

"Great! I like to make people think and talk about ideas."

"I'm afraid not everyone in this town agrees that's such a good thing. I did feel I should tell you that your actions to defend yourself may be causing you more trouble."

"I don't understand."

"That small group of people who are offended by your merchandise are even more horrified by the fact you have taken the initiative against their accusations and threats."

Nan blinked, unable to absorb what she was hearing. "Threats?" Her stomach turned over. "I haven't been threatened."

"Not directly, I know. And it doesn't mean anything, really. I don't think. But my sister had the bad judgment about fifteen years ago to marry a man named Douglas Neilson. I hear from her that you've caused quite a stir in the ultraconservative circles. Douglas is beside himself at being kicked out of your store."

"He asked for it!"

"Undoubtedly, but the group sees it as an attack against all of them. I'm afraid you've acquired some enemies you don't even know, Nan."

"I didn't mean to. I only wanted to defend myself. They're entitled to their opinions, as I said Friday. Just so long as they leave me to mine."

"It's not that simple," Genny said, lowering her voice. "And unless you're really naive, which I doubt, you know it isn't a simple issue. You've challenged them. You're a woman, to boot. That makes it even worse."

"Oh, give me a break! What decade is this?"

"Something wrong, Nan?" Jimmy came over, dirty dust rag in his hand. "Mrs. Weaver?"

"Jimmy." The principal regarded the young man. "I didn't mean to include you in this matter, but as long as you're working here, I suppose you ought to know. Ms. Black has angered some people in town."

"Yes, ma'am," Jimmy said. "I know. Some of my buddies are watching out for the place when we aren't here."

"Good grief!" Nan slapped her palm down on the counter. Several customers in the store looked at her. "What is going on? Do I need to get police protection just because I'm renting out movies a few people don't like?"

"No, it's not that serious," Genny Weaver said. "I expect you'll be accepted as a necessary evil soon. But Jimmy's right. You may experience some minor harassment or vandalism before they move on to another target or feel they've made their point with you."

Nan sighed. "I don't like what you're saying, but I appreciate your taking the time to come in and talk. I never anticipated this sort of problem. Not with the kind of videos I carry."

"It wouldn't matter now. You humiliated Douglas in front of people, and he can't handle that. It happened once before and..." Genny looked at Jimmy.

"What?" Nan demanded. "What happened?"

"It was Jimmy's brother, Jesse."

"It was about Charlie," Jimmy said. His manner indicated reluctance to talk about the matter. Nan suspected it was because the topic involved Jesse. "He wanted to open a service shop in town, after...after he lost his pilot's license, and old man Neilson . . . I mean, Mr. Neilson got the town council to deny him a license on account of . . ."

"His drinking?" Nan asked. "Jesse told me."

"Yeah." Jimmy looked at Mrs. Weaver. "And Jesse didn't take it good at all. He, uh, challenged Mr. Neilson's reasons. In public. He said Neilson was just scared 'cause Charlie's so much better at things. Even dead drunk, Jesse said, Charlie could pick apart and put back an engine while Neilson was still looking for his hind end with both hands." Jimmy turned red. "'Scuse me, Mrs. Weaver."

"That's all right. I was there. Those were his exact words, James. *Almost* his exact words. I believe he was a little more . . . colorful."

"So there was an economic factor involved." Nan tapped the counter with a fingernail. "I don't suppose another video company has considered opening here? One that Neilson has interests in?"

"Oh, no." Genny shook her head. The red curls flew and bobbed. "This time it's truly a matter of conscience for him and the others. They really believe you're going to be renting porn, even if you aren't right now."

"I won't! I never would. But I would defend the right of anyone to rent it, if I did. That's a matter of *my* conscience."

"Right!" Jimmy held up a fist in a salute. Genny laughed in approval, but Nan saw more than a trace of worry in the other woman's eyes. After she had rented a movie for herself and left, Nan pulled Jimmy aside, speaking low so no other customer would overhear.

"Neilson was in here last week," she said. "He scared Sue's little girl, and I chased him out. Told him never to set foot in here again. I'd do it again, but I need to know. Have I set myself up for some real trouble?"

Jimmy paled. "Does Jesse know about this?"

"Not unless someone else told him. Sue asked me to keep it quiet, which puzzled me. She specifically told me not to tell Jesse."

Jimmy nodded. "Jesse'd be likely to kick his ass. Neilson's a snake, but he ain't dumb. Last time he crossed with Jesse, he ended up with a bloody nose. Coulda been worse, but Jesse got himself under control. Neilson was real scared, though. He got a lawyer to convince a judge he was in real danger. Jesse's got a restraining order against him where Neilson's concerned. If he lays a hand on him, Jesse'll end up in jail. See, Jesse didn't lead a peaceable kind of life when he was my age. Got into some trouble and all. He had a quick temper. Bad one, sometimes. Folks remember that kind of thing."

"I see." Nan covered her eyes with a hand. She imagined Jesse caged, and knew why Sue had cautioned silence. He'd be like a wild thing, an eagle, in prison. "Well, let's just hope it all blows over quickly," she said. "The last thing I want is trouble."

"Yes, ma'am." Jimmy grinned. "But I got an idea like Jesse, you wouldn't run from it if it came to you."

"Maybe." She thought of the gun hidden deep in her desk. She had never dreamed she might be in a position to even think about the need for that kind of protection. The idea made her feel sick. "Maybe not."

JESSE EASED UP on the throttle and turned his plane in a gentle curving arc, taking the approach to the runway advised by the man in the control tower. He chewed the end of the unlit cigar in his mouth, letting the bitter taste of the tobacco serve to aid his concentration. He landed without a bump.

"Smooth as silk on ice." He grinned, remembering how he had felt when Charlie first used that phrase to describe his young pupil's landing all those years ago. Good old Charlie. He was doing better now. Much better. Bad habits sure were the very devil to break. Sometimes they would break the man before he managed to conquer them.

He waited until he was well within the safety zone before tossing out the unused smoke and taking a fresh one from his jacket pocket. This one he lit. He puffed, letting the gray smoke cloud around his head.

"Hey, Rivers!"

Jesse turned and smiled. Patrick Wall was an old friend. One he'd made while helping Charlie through his troubles. "How are you, Pat?" he said, grasping the other man's hand when he came up to him. "Been a while."

"I'm great, you old dog." Pat gave him a slap on the back. "What's with you and the stogies, though?" He waved a hand through the cloud and coughed. "Thought you'd sworn off. Something going on in your life make you need the crutch again?"

"No!" Jesse saw immediately that his defensiveness had alerted Pat. He took the cigar and stuck it in a bucket of sand set against the wall. Pat watched every move. "I'm just fine," Jesse added.

"Want to talk?" he asked. "Got a pot of coffee brewing in the office."

"It's nothing, Pat. Just hard to break the habit. That's all. I'm fine. Charlie's fine. Don't worry about us."

"Well, okay." Pat gave him another friendly slap on the arm. "But don't forget. If you need to jaw out something..."

"I won't forget. And thanks." Jesse chatted for a few minutes then moved on, looking for the clerk who had the papers on his cargo. His hand moved back to the pocket with the cigars, but he stopped himself. This was getting out of hand.

It had started getting that way Sunday night as he drove away from Nan Black. The urge for a smoke had been so overwhelming, he had actually stopped his truck and rummaged through the glove compartment until he'd found a cigar so old it had begun to crumble in his hand. But he had struck a match and lit the thing. Smoked it down to a nubbin. The next day he'd bought a new box. Hidden it so Jimmy wouldn't find it. . . .

Jesse stopped and looked at himself. Deep inside. Pat was a veteran of A.A., and a man used to helping his fellows kick the demon of alcohol addiction. If he saw a problem brewing, Jesse likely had one. Was he becoming addicted to nicotine?

Or was he just reacting to his unfulfilled desire for Ms. Nan Black? If so, what was he willing to do about it?

NAN WAS BRAVELY belting out the last verse of the first hymn Sunday morning when Jesse eased into the pew beside her and took one half of the service book in his hands. Since Inge held the other half, on Nan's left, Nan just stood between them, enjoying the music as Jesse sang.

As they sat down, he whispered, "I'm running late." He touched Nan's arm, his fingers putting gentle pressure on her skin. "Sorry."

"God doesn't mind," Inge whispered back. Nan managed to keep from smiling when Jesse blushed and let go of her arm as if it had suddenly turned red-hot.

For the rest of the service, he sat close, but not too close. Only when church was over did he touch her again.

"Let's go," he said, taking her by her elbow. "Before we get corralled by anybody." He hustled her outside and over to her station wagon. "Go home and change. Meet me out at the airfield."

"Change into what? And just where's the airfield? I haven't had much time to explore, you know." She felt a wave of affection for him. In the bright morning sunlight he looked so young. Almost like the wild boy he must have been when he was young. The boy she was learning about, the one who had become the man standing before her today. She reached out and touched his cheek.

"Ah, don't do that here, Nan," he said softly. "I won't be responsible for what I might do." His smile was tender. He put his hand over hers, taking it away from his face, but continuing to hold it. "I missed you this week."

"That's nice to hear." She wanted to tell him the same, but the words stuck in her throat. She had seen him once through the window of her store when he had picked up Jimmy. He waved then, but hadn't bothered to come in. She had felt hurt and a little angry. Angry, she had told herself, *because* she felt hurt when there was really no reason. The next afternoon, Jimmy had explained his brother was running behind schedule. Okay, she thought. He had a business to operate, too.

"It was one hell of a week," he said, still holding her hand. "The good weather always makes for good business. But it means I get to fly my tail off."

She leaned to one side, observing. "Doesn't look to me like you..."

"Get in the car, will you! The airfield's two miles south of town. You can't miss it. See you there in a little while." He released her hand and stepped back. His eyes showed a gleam that she found extremely intriguing.

"Jesse, what—"

"See you there." He saluted, grinned and was gone.

Nan drove home slowly. She had no idea what was going on in his mind, though it was a good bet she was in for a plane ride. No big deal. She'd ridden in small planes before, even if she didn't particularly like them. No big deal. He was probably planning to show her the Badlands from the air. The weather had provided a spring dream of a day, perfectly safe for flying. Okay. That would be fun.

But there was something more. She knew it as sure as she breathed. He had something else planned for her. Something she couldn't guess at. Excitement tingled and grew in her as she changed into jeans and a sweater and pulled her hair back in a loose ponytail. Then she threw a windbreaker into the station wagon, just in case, and headed south.

The airfield was a paved strip of runway in the middle of a field. A dirt road led from the highway to a pair of buildings by the runway. She pulled in beside a concrete block structure that proclaimed itself ALS Delivery Service. Jesse's office. The other building was a classic curved-roof hangar. All the doors of the first building were shut. The hangar doors were wide open, and Jesse's truck was parked beside it.

Nan got out. She called Jesse's name. No answer. She closed the door of her station wagon and started toward the hangar. The runway, she noted, was clean as a whistle. Not a single blade of prairie grass, no leaf of any weed poked through the dull gray surface. Where cracks had formed, they were repaired with snake-streaks of black tar. Jesse Rivers took good care of his property.

The building was bigger than it seemed from outside. There were three planes inside. Nan stuck her hands in her pockets and wandered around. The biggest plane had two engines. Jesse's official logo was painted on the side. His main delivery vehicle, she reasoned. The little bomb in which he had dropped out of the sky a few weeks ago was stationed at the back, its engine parts strewn around on a canvas drop cloth. She suspected the order was haphazard only to her. Jesse would know where each nut and bolt lay.

She called his name again. Her voice echoed in the high space. But he didn't answer back. Nan felt a rise of annoyance. If this was his idea of a joke, she didn't find it funny. She went over to the third plane.

It looked to be in almost as poor shape as the wreck at the rear. She had no notion how old it was—probably older than she was. The instrument panel was simple. The material on the two seats was real leather. She reached in and touched it. Patched and worn, but leather, nonetheless. Jesse had a penchant for old machines, it seemed. She sniffed and smelled the fresh odor of oil and gas. Feeling the front of the old plane, she sensed warmth. He had been here and recently. Where the heck was he now?

She jammed her hands back in her pockets and ambled outside. She was hungry. Her stomach was growling in protest at missing the feast at the Petersens'. If he didn't show in five minutes, she was gone, she decided. She raised her head and stared up at the wide, blue sky.

At first, she didn't see it—just heard the low, wasp buzz of the engine. Responding to a primitive instinct, she stiffened and looked around for the source of the sound. The little plane dropped right out of the heavens before she could grasp what was happening. Nan screamed.

The machine looked like a toy as it skimmed inches from the ground. She saw Jesse in the pilot's seat. He waved, grinned and, she was absolutely certain even though she couldn't hear it, gave a "yee-ha!" yell of exhilaration as he aimed his vehicle back up to the sky.

Nan stood there and watched the show. He put the tiny plane, and her heart, through a series of maneuvers that seemed destined to splatter him all over the neat runway. She was rooted to the ground, unable to move as she followed his flight. He turned and twisted, performing unimaginable feats in the air. Once, he took a path straight up to the sun, and she heard the engine stop completely before he turned tail to death and revved it up again on the way down. Her leg muscles turned to jelly then, and she sat down hard on the pavement.

Jesse saw her fall and figured he had pushed it a bit. After all, she'd had no warning.

But she had deserved it! She had all but called him a coward, certainly accused him openly of being dull and boring. Predictable and safe. Well, he was that, for sure. But he was this as well! He felt the blood rushing through his heart and veins as he put the little Cessna Aerobat into the pattern of another Hammerhead, adding a quarter roll. Music soared in his mind as he climbed skyward. He was a little mushy in the maneuver and needed more practice. He adjusted the melody in his head to match the beat of the straining engine. Show season was coming up! They'd be hearing his music on the ground if this were a real performance. He worked the ailerons carefully, rejoicing when he felt the plane move exactly as he wanted. The judges would have loved it! The crowd would have gone crazy for him!

He turned into the start of a Cuban Eight, then backed off. He was showing off shamelessly like a schoolboy. His point had obviously been made. Jesse glanced over his shoulder at the small figure down on the ground. Her blond hair framed a face that looked white as snow. A bolt of guilt hit him, and he turned, preparing to land.

Nan breathed again when the wheels hit the ground. Her heart, which had taken up residence in her throat, settled back to its proper territory. She stood, feeling her legs tremble. Terror flowed away from her nerves.

And Nan got mad.

She stalked over to the toy plane, ready to ream him out verbally, just as she had the first time they met. But the sight of his face when he jumped to the ground made the harsh words stop before she uttered them.

"Hey, I didn't mean to scare you," he said, his smile like that of a kid caught in the cookie jar. "I was showing off, that's all."

"Jesse, I was *terrified!*" She felt the tears now and willed them away. It didn't do much good. She was crying for him! For what could have happened, did happen several times in her imagination. "Why did you do that? The engine stopped! I heard it!"

"It's supposed to." He reached over and caressed the wing of the plane. "It sure gets the crowd's attention every time."

"Well, it got mine!" The tears dried up. She put her hands on her hips and glared. Then she realized what he had said. "Crowd's attention? You do this for people to watch?"

"Sure do." He came closer and put his hands on her shoulders. "You said I was dull, boring, didn't take risks like your fantasy heroes. Well, maybe I'm guilty as charged, because what I'm doing isn't really dangerous. It just looks like it. I fly professionally at air shows all over the region during the summer, Nan. Daredevil stuff. Aerobatics."

"Oh, my Lord!"

She was still as white as a sheet. Jesse drew her closer with one arm across her shoulders. He led her over to the plane. "Look at this baby," he said. "She's designed for the stunts. Special structure, special features. I wouldn't take just any plane through a Hammerhead Stall."

Nan touched the metal skin. "H-hammerhead? Like in shark?"

"It's a stunt classic. Drives the crowd wild, like I said. I have the director stop my music when I go into the climb, so the engine stall is clearly audible."

"You're serious! You actually do put on shows. I can't believe this!"

"And why not?" He stepped away from her. "Prefer me dull and predictable? Safe? Boring?"

"I . . . I didn't mean . . . That is, I hardly expected . . ."

"Exactly." His expression was cold now. "You never expected me to be anything other than what you had decided I was. Ms. Black, forgive me, but I don't think you'd recognize a real-life hero if he came up and bit you. You've been dreaming too long."

"You're right." She stood straight, shoulders squared, accepting his accusation. "I did misjudge you. I apologize." She held in reservation his comment about her fantasies. Those were hers, and not his to touch!

"Well." Jesse felt the wind of righteousness go right out of his sails. "All right. Not that I'm claiming to be any kind of hero, mind. It's just that I thought you were being unfair."

"I was." She looked right at him, her gaze never wavering. "You were right to correct me."

Jesse felt worse than he had before his little exhibition. She was taking it like a trooper, leaving him looking silly. Now, she was going to think he was just a show-off. And she'd be right. He'd been grandstanding, pure and simple. Hadn't even taken the precaution of having a safety man out at the runway in case something did go wrong. Careless. He'd better watch it! Carelessness could get him killed!

"This wasn't the only surprise I had for you today," he said, digging the toe of his boot in the dirt by the runway. "And I think you'll like the other one better."

"It wouldn't take much. What is it?"

"That other plane. The little one with two seats. I'm going to take you for a ride, Nan. Take you over some Badlands formations, and if you're willing, later on, I'd like to take you to meet my folks. We're both expected for Sunday dinner. Will you go with me?" He almost held his breath, waiting for her response.

CHAPTER NINE

TO MEET MY FOLKS. Nan ran the words around in her mind as she gripped the metal rod running from the top to the side of the small plane. They had been aloft for some time now. Her hand was beginning to cramp from the tension she put on it. Why would he take her to meet his parents? Unless she was misreading him badly once again, she doubted he hauled his women friends home as a general rule. He seemed to love his family, yet keep himself separate and private from them.

Maybe it was because she was also Jimmy's employer, and if they had heard negative rumors about her business, Jesse might want to dispel their fears. Although she knew there was some tension and conflict between the brothers, their devotion to each other was just as clear as the problems were. Yes, he was probably thinking of Jimmy.

The plane dipped to the left and she gasped, grasping the side of the seat as well as the strut.

"Will you relax, please." Jesse's voice came in faintly through the protective earmuff things he had required she wear. "You're perfectly safe."

Nan didn't even try to reply. The ancient plane had no windows. The noise from the engine and the wind made conversation impossible. She had tightened her seat belt to the point of strangulation, but still felt as if she would fall out any second. They were flying hundreds of feet up from the ground, and there was nothing between her and the earth but air.

She had to admit, however, that the takeoff, specifically because there was nothing between her and the air they rode, had been exhilarating to the point of joy. She had never experienced anything quite like it.

To further the point, she had never experienced anyone quite like Jesse Rivers! She had been wrong, wrong, wrong about him and didn't mind admitting it.

Never in a million years would she have expected the daredevil aspect in him. Not now, at least. Perhaps when he was a younger man, just out of his teens, it might have been consistent for him to risk his life for the thrill of it. But he seemed so... settled. It didn't make sense.

It did, however, make him much more interesting. She eased her death grip on the strut slightly, trying to make her muscles relax. Jesse had explained about the old Piper J3 Cub, telling her of its origins and how reliable the machine was under almost any circumstances. "Planes don't live this long unless they have what it takes to survive," he said. "You're much safer with me in this plane than you are on the highway in your station wagon." Then he had grinned, raised his eyebrows and added, "Trust me." She had been laughing so hard, she hadn't resisted when he boosted her into the cockpit and strapped her in.

The plane dipped again, and she turned to express her complaint to the pilot. He smiled at her, however, and pointed to the ground. Nan looked down. Below, the land spread out like a tablecloth, the geometric plots of cultivation showing clearly. Neat, tidy and predictable. But over to her left she could see the wound in the earth that was the Badlands. She glanced back at Jesse and smiled at him, her complaint forgotten.

This time, when the wings tipped and the little plane plummeted toward the ground, she didn't grab for the false safety of the seat and strut. Instead, she trusted the pilot, as he had suggested.

That attitude freed her! She flew with the plane and pilot, sensing that somehow she had become one with them both. The land below became wild and majestic, full of form and subtle color. She leaned out, tears filling her eyes in spite of the goggles he had given her to wear. It was all so beautiful in a strange exotic way. Like flying over the moon. Or one of her fantasy worlds. She almost expected to see an army of warriors mounted on gigantic reptiles appear atop one of the rises of land. Her hair broke loose from the ponytail band and whipped around her face. Filled with high emotion, she gave a yell of pure pleasure.

Jesse heard her and knew he'd been part of something special. He felt a closeness to her that transcended physical needs. This was greater than sex, though sex certainly was part of it, he decided. With Nan, it would have to be. The longer he knew her, the more the aura of sensuality she carried so unknowingly worked its spell on him. It didn't matter anymore that she would be moving on eventually. Didn't matter that she was only half in the real world and the other half in her own dreams. He was hooked and hooked good!

He had figured that out this past week all by himself. Now as he watched her hair flying wildly around her head, forming a blond halo, he thought how exciting it would be to have that halo on his pillow. He promised himself that would happen before too much longer.

It had to, or he was liable to go crazy!

She wanted him, too. He was sure of that. She had made it perfectly clear last weekend. Her teasing had been light and playful, certainly. But he'd sensed the volcano underneath. She was a woman capable of high passion in spite of her loose grip on reality at times. He watched her as she leaned out the window again to stare at the landscape passing below. Her lips were parted with wonder at what she was seeing.

High passion.

He had to make her his!

Yeah, sure he did. Jesse eased the stick over, guiding the plane in a gentle arch. Did he sound like a scene from a bad romantic movie or what? Nan liked him well enough to go out, but her kisses the other night hadn't indicated any real interest in sex. She'd been playing and teasing and that was all. *Face it,* he told himself. *You are inventing your own reality. Doing just what you claim to despise in others. Let's have a little reality check, Jesse,* he thought as he flew the plane down to glide through a canyon. *Keep it simple, keep it clean. That way, you won't screw up again.*

But, God, did he want her!

Nan glanced back as they soared skyward once more. He was giving her a show she'd never forget, and she wanted to thank him from the bottom of her heart. It was difficult to tell with the goggles and earphones, but she thought he looked tense. Odd. She would have expected him to be having a heck of a good time. She was! She smiled, then turned back to the front.

After a few more minutes, they left the Badlands and headed north, or so she guessed from the position of the sun. He flew low now, skimming the land. She relaxed even more and enjoyed the feeling of speed and the sensation of flying. Never, in her dreams and fantasies, had she felt as good as this—wild and free, yet safe and secure.

All because Jesse Rivers was at the controls. She closed her eyes. She dreamed, not sleeping, but not entirely awake, either.

Jesse reached forward and tapped his passenger on the head. He was ready to start the descent to land on the road by his father's wheat fields, and he didn't want her to be dozing. She sat up abruptly, grabbing at the sides of the plane and confirming his suspicion that she had drifted off to sleep. Well, he'd asked her to trust him, hadn't he? Falling asleep in an open cockpit was about as close to total trust as she could get.

He wondered, however, what she had been dreaming about.

Nan gave him a little wave of her hand to let him know she was back in the world of the wakeful. She did not turn around. She thought he might have been able to see the erotic dream still burning on her face. He might have been able to see he had a starring role in the fantasy. She stared down at the rapidly approaching ground.

He was obviously aiming at the dirt road running along the edge of a plowed field. A pickup truck was driving on it, dust kicking up behind as it paced the plane. She looked more closely and saw Jimmy leaning out the passenger window, waving up at them. So, Jesse really was taking her home.

They landed with a few bumps. Nan started to unfasten her belt as soon as she saw the propeller stop. Jesse was already on the ground, setting the wheel chocks. He gave her a hand down. "How did you like it?" he asked.

"Wonderful!" She raised her hands over her head. "I had no idea! No wonder you love your job so much. To be so free and fly like a bird every day . . ."

"It isn't the same when you're doing a job," he said, smiling. "This was fun. That's work. It's structured and ordinary."

"Yes, but . . ." She turned and touched the plane. "The potential's always there."

"Yes, it is." He touched her tangled hair. "It's always there."

"Yo, Jesse! Nan!" Jimmy called to them. The pickup had come to a halt behind the plane.

Jesse took her arm. "Hope you're hungry," he said. "And not on any diet. Mom's going to take one look at you and figure it's her God-given duty to put ten pounds on you today. Ready?"

"You think I'm too skinny?"

"No." He was trying not to laugh. "But my momma will. You wait and see."

Nan met Ned Rivers, Jesse's father, at the pickup truck. The elder Rivers was taller than either of his sons and had thinning blond hair. His face was tanned and his eyes a bright, far-seeing blue. He smiled without showing his teeth, but she saw warmth in his expression. "You're welcome here," he said, taking her hand and briefly holding rather than shaking it. "I'm more than mighty pleased with what you've done for my boys."

Nan blinked. "Thanks," she said. "But I've done nothing special. Jimmy's a good worker and... and Jesse's a good friend."

"Um-hmm." Ned Rivers made no more comment. On the way in to the house, he said little, Jesse said nothing at all and Jimmy chattered like a magpie.

Nan, squeezed into the seat between the brothers, tried to pay attention. It wasn't easy with Jesse's body pressed against her side and his arm across her shoulder over the back of the seat. Jimmy was talking mostly about his friends, kids Nan didn't even know, and by the time they passed the tree-shaded entrance to the farmhouse, she realized she hadn't absorbed very much. All she could think about was being alone with Jesse. She had little hope that would happen today, however.

"So, who're you going to ask to the prom?" Ned asked his second son, his question keeping with the subject of Jimmy's social life. "That Andersen girl?"

"Yeah," Jimmy replied. "I guess."

"You don't sound real enthusiastic," Jesse said, breaking his silence. "Prom's a big deal for you kids. You ought to take a girl you really like." His hand shifted off the seat to Nan's shoulder. His palm was warm enough to feel hot.

"Who'd you take, Jesse?" his father asked. "Remember?"

"No."

Nan glanced over. Jesse was frowning. Scowling, really. Either he actually didn't remember, or he didn't want to. Before she could edge the subject on, however, they reached the main house.

It was more or less what Nan had pictured. Two stories with a white frame and dark blue shutters, it was flanked by huge old trees. A full-length front porch added to the feeling that this was a real home. Across the grassy yard was another, more modest house. Jesse's sister's place, Nan guessed. They all got out of the truck. Nan heard a screen door slam.

"Jesse!" A short, dark-haired woman came running down the steps. She wore an apron over a cotton dress and plain, low-heeled shoes. When she came close to hug her son, Nan saw she wore no makeup and didn't need any. Her round face had a smooth, white complexion with high, natural color on her cheeks and lips. She turned to Nan and smiled happily.

"Thanks for getting this big lug home for Sunday dinner," she said. "I'm Julia Rivers." She gave Nan a hug, too.

That set the tone for the rest of the time. Love and warmth radiated throughout the Rivers household. The focus, Nan could tell, was the energetic, cheerful, forthright

Julia. Just before they all ate, Jesse's sister, Jane, and her husband, Steve, came over. Jane was obviously a Rivers. She had a sturdy build and her mother's round face. Her hair was a lighter brown, but her eyes just as blue as the rest of her family. Jesse was the only green-eyed one.

"Jimmy says your business is booming," Jane said after they had settled down at the table. There was already enough food on it to feed a small army, and Julia was bustling in and out of the kitchen, carrying more. Everyone else sat, waiting. This was Julia's show alone. She had actually not heard Nan's offer to help, Nan realized.

"It's going well," she said, watching the mother. This was clearly the high point of Julia's week, and she was glorying in it. "I couldn't ask for a better helper than Jim, either," Nan added.

"Thanks." Jimmy grinned and turned slightly pink at the tips of his ears.

The conversation halted as Julia slid into her seat at the far end of the table. The family bowed heads and held hands while Ned prayed. While it was happening, Nan wondered if the electricity she felt running from Jesse's hand to hers was being passed around to the rest. When the prayer was over, she looked up and saw he was watching her. The tingle in her hand and arm continued for some time.

He had little to say during the meal, answering only when asked a direct question. He was not being surly or bad-tempered, though. Just very quiet, as if he was thinking hard about something. After a while, she noticed, the others ignored him, allowing him the privacy he seemed to need. His silence was hardly a problem. Between Jimmy and his mother, there was gossip and chatting aplenty. Several times, Nan laughed until tears came into her eyes.

When the meal was finally over, Julia accepted help. Nan carried dishes into the kitchen, afraid she was waddling, rather than walking, because she had eaten so much.

"You're going to church in town," Julia said as she ran a sinkful of hot water. "Have you heard my boy sing yet?"

"Yes, I have." Nan carried over a stack of dishes. "He's very good."

Julia sighed. "I wanted him to study music, but he wouldn't have it. Had to go off flying with Charlie Deaver." She sighed and smiled. "They don't listen, you know. They just go on and do what they want."

"He's happy." Nan set down the dishes and went back to get a platter. "I think that's all I'd want for my children."

"Do you have any?" Julia looked at her. "I know you were married."

Nan felt heat on her face. "No, we didn't get around to children. There were too many problems right from the start. We were much too young, anyway."

"Never too young for kids." Julia started scrubbing pots and pans. "But you can sure get too old in a hurry."

"Maybe." Nan bolted from the room, anxious to avoid any further discussion of that or related subjects. It was like being at her own home with her mother gently ranting at her about marriage and kids.

Jane was in the dining room, clearing off the linen. "Mom getting on you already?" she asked, smiling. "She figures Jesse brought you home for inspection as bride material."

"Good grief! He didn't warn me. Where did he get to?"

"They're all out walking the fields, speaking wisely as men do about the weather, the dirt, the crop. You know, farm stuff."

Nan regarded the other woman. "You sound like you don't buy into this wholeheartedly. Am I wrong?"

"Oh, I'm in for the count," Jane said, her expression pleasant, but serious. "I married Steven Lindberg, knowing he was a farmer like my dad. Knowing it was in his blood and he'd never be happy at anything else. But I enrolled in nursing school last year, and I'm almost done with my associate degree."

"That's great!"

"It is, and isn't, according to who you talk to." Jane looked a little weary, and Nan realized that she was close to tears. "I'm getting unbelievable pressure from everyone to start a family. I want to, but I don't. Not yet."

"Then don't. It's as simple as . . ."

"No, it's not." Jane smiled. "I admire you, Nan. You seem to have it all figured out. For me, it's just a mess." She pushed her bangs back from her forehead. "But I will work it out, myself. I can't be like Mom, with only the farm and family to live and work for. But I can't be like you, either. I have Steve, and I want his children."

"Eventually."

"That's right!"

"More power to you, then," Nan declared. They smiled at each other. Understanding, and accepting.

WHEN JESSE CAME BACK to the house, he was full of anxiety. He hadn't planned on leaving Nan alone for his mother to work on her. Jane could buffer, sure, but she wouldn't be a whole lot of help if Mom really got on her high horse about marriage and family being the ultimate role for a woman. Nan was tough, but Mom could be like a steamroller when it came to her opinion.

He ought to know. She'd rolled over him once or twice. Much as he loved her, there were times when he just had to stay away to keep from getting flattened. No telling what shape Nan was in by now.

But when he entered the dining room, he heard the sound of spirited discussion coming from the kitchen. Jane, who was standing at the sideboard, polishing silver before putting it away, gave him a big smile.

"Your new lady is more than a match for Mom," she said. "She turned tail for a minute, then went back to the fray. I can't tell who's ahead anymore."

Relief swept through him. "She not exactly my lady, sis, but I'm glad to hear she's not bleeding yet. Mom's got a sharp tongue, as you well know. Nan's armor must be thick."

"Maybe. But she's not burning her bra, either." Jane laughed. "It's funny. They don't think they agree, but if you listen, they aren't really so far apart. A lot of it's just the way they say it. Listen."

"No, thanks. I've got to get back while there's still daylight. Would you mind going in and getting Nan out of there?"

"Not on your life!" Jane turned back to the silverware. "Good luck."

Jesse muttered to himself and went into the kitchen. The two women were winding down, and he managed to extract Nan without much trouble. Goodbyes were exchanged, and Steve drove them out to the plane. He promised to have Jimmy into town before ten and then hung around until the two took off, giving Jesse no chance to find out how Nan felt about his family. He had to wait and wonder. As they flew through the early evening sky, he found he was wondering about a lot of things.

"Your mother should have been a lawyer," Nan informed him after they landed back at his airstrip. "She's got a mind like a steel trap. And what energy! Wore me out just watching her."

"I know the feeling," Jesse said as he landed the plane. He continued talking as he went over to check the big Cessna for the next day's trip. "I should have warned you what you were getting in to. I didn't mean to leave you alone, but Dad wanted to talk."

"I hardly needed warning. What did your father want? Is anything wrong?"

Jesse looked up. She was regarding him with some concern on her face. Why should she care? "No, nothing's wrong. Thanks for asking. He just wanted to touch some bases. It's been a while since we talked."

"Work?"

"What?"

"Work been keeping you away? Your mother said this was the first time since Easter you'd been around for a meal. She sounded sad about that."

"Yeah." He slammed the cargo door. "Work. It eats up a lot of time."

Nan studied his back. The set of his broad shoulders showed great tension all of a sudden. He was lying. And she was pretty sure why. He was the eldest child, and he hadn't married yet. Hadn't produced grandchildren. Julia was putting pressure on Jane now, but she hadn't given up on Jesse. And he had brought Nan home....

"Jesse, what do you think of me?" she asked. "Why did you take me to your home?"

He straightened, banging his head on the wing. Rubbing his injury, he turned and looked at her. "I don't know," he said. "Any problems with that?"

"No problem with an honest answer." She stepped back, putting her windbreaker on over her sweater. "Well, I had fun. Thanks for everything." She started to leave.

"Nan!"

"Yes?"

"You're going home?"

"Tomorrow's a workday." She shrugged. "I thought I'd get some rest for a change."

He regarded her for a moment. "I don't want to say good-night to you yet."

A pulse started beating pleasantly in her throat, and there was a sudden sensation low in her abdomen that had nothing to do with the big meal she had eaten. "What do you want, then, Jesse?" she asked, lowering the windbreaker.

He said nothing in reply, but keeping his gaze locked on her, he went over and pushed a button on the wall. The doors of the hangar closed with a metallic clatter. When it was silent again, he spoke.

"I want you, Nan," he said. "I hadn't intended to be so blunt about it, but I just can't let you walk out of here tonight without letting you know how I feel." He folded his arms and leaned against the wall. "I can't seem to stop thinking about you, and I go a little crazy when I try."

"I want you, too, Jesse." She let her jacket fall to the floor. "My place or yours?"

He pushed off the wall and started toward her. "Have you ever made love in an airplane, Nan Black?"

She shook her head, unable to answer otherwise. The sensation in her midsection had settled lower and was turning into a full-fledged sexual arousal. She was sure she had never seen a sexier man than Jesse Rivers as he walked to her across the bare cement floor of his hangar.

"Well, there is a first time for everything," he said, putting his hands on the small of her back. His touch radiated heat, spreading warmth across her skin. "Interested?"

"I... Do we get to stay on the ground?" His eyes were filling her universe, and a sweet weakness was taking the strength from her body. "I mean, you don't plan to fly, do you?"

"Not this time." He moved his head until their lips were a millimeter apart. "At least the plane won't take off. I don't know about me." His mouth came closer.

Nan rested her hands on his hips, hooking her thumbs in his belt loops. "I feel like I'm having the best fantasy of my life," she said. "Only this is much crazier than anything I could dream up."

"No dream, Nan." He kissed her gently, his lips only slightly parted. She felt the heat of his breath. "Want to wake up?"

"Yes!" She pressed to him, reaching up to wrap her arms around his neck. Their lips met again, this time with a pressure that was close to pain. His tongue danced in her mouth, tasting, teasing, taking. She relaxed against him, letting her body form to his, feeling soft and hot and yielding and so ready for love she thought she might faint with the anticipation of pleasure. For one fleeting moment she wondered what was happening to her. It was as if she had really entered one of her own fantasies. Real-life Nan had never wanted a man so much!

Jesse ran his hand down the back of her body and picked her up in his arms. She was like a cat—silken and boneless, yet strong and warm, all sinew and softness. He carried her over to the plane and set her down while he opened the door. She slid along his side, her hands already working at the buttons on his shirt. He was ready to burst and prayed he could maintain control for a decent length of time.

"There's a sleeping bag in here," he said, helping her up into the cargo hold. "I keep it on hand for times when I—"

"Let's go up front." Her eyes were wide and bright, shining with desire in the gloomy light. "The pilot's seat!"

"It's cramped." He was having trouble breathing because the beating of his heart seemed to take up all the room in his chest. "We won't have much room."

"Who needs room?" She grabbed the front of his open shirt and pulled his mouth down to hers. "All I need is you. Jesse Rivers. The sooner, the better!"

He kissed her, feeling the fire in her igniting him further. He slipped his hands under her sweater and cupped her breasts, feeling the fullness of them and the hard points of her nipples. Her skin was like silk. If she wanted it to be in the pilot's chair, that's where they would go! "Come on," he said, releasing her for a second. "But watch your head. Low ceiling."

"Go on, Jesse." She pulled off her sweater, revealing the flesh he had just caressed and the simple cotton bra that covered her. "I'll be there in a minute."

He went, unable to disobey.

Nan stripped as quickly as she could. Her fingers trembled, and she was scarcely able to think clearly. All she could do was follow her passion and pray it was the right thing to do. She shook her hair loose and went to him.

When she climbed around to sit on his knees, Jesse looked like a man who couldn't believe what was happening to him. His eyes were a deeper green than she had ever seen, and the lids were heavy with unspent desire. "You've pulled me into one of your fantasies," he whispered, tangling his fingers in her hair. "I have to be dreaming!"

"Me, too." She ran her hands over his bare chest and down his stomach to the top of his jeans. He was more muscular than she had thought, and a pattern of soft hair decorated his chest and belly. While he explored her with his hands and lips, she undid the jeans.

She paused to look at him. Leaning back against the instrument panel, she whispered, "You're beautiful! Beautiful!"

"Ordinarily," he replied, his tone so husky it was almost a growl, "I would say that was my line. But since so far nothing about making love with you has been ordinary, I'll just say, 'thanks, so're you.'" His eyes said a great deal more than that.

Nan listened to the unspoken words. She moved against him, rejoicing in the sensation of his skin next to hers. His hands moved on her, driving her further and further toward ecstasy. When she knew she could wait no longer, she rose up and took him deep inside. And then...

Jesse threw back his head and clenched his teeth. She was no volcano; she was a cataclysm! She gripped him with arms and legs of silk steel, her voice crying out her passion and pleasure in his ear. And inside, she writhed around him like a hot, wet satin python, rippling and twisting, drawing at his very life force in her loving greed! Under his hands, her skin grew damp, then wet. Her teeth tore at his shoulder, then her mouth moved to his. He grabbed a handful of her hair and clamped down on her pulsating hips with his arm.

And then Jesse let himself go.

CHAPTER TEN

NAN FELT HIM FALL over the edge into his release. His body seemed to turn to solid steel, hot and hungry, just for her. New tremors rocked her body as she responded, and when he finally cried out his passion, she was calling his name breathlessly. He held her with an iron grip, as if he wanted to fuse their bodies together forever.

They were motionless for a long time, holding each other tightly, then gradually relaxing into the dream state of spent desire. She rested her head on his shoulder and listened to his breathing, felt the beat of his strong heart beneath her hand, felt the throb of him still inside her. Nan had never known this kind of physical union, hadn't even imagined it.

Jesse was the first to recover enough to speak. "I will never fly in this plane again without thinking about you," he said, stroking the tangled, damp hair at the nape of her neck. "What did you do to me?"

"It . . . it was a team effort," she said, kissing his collarbone. "Quite a good one, actually."

"Um." He ran his hand down her bare back. "You are so beautiful. I thought I had an idea what you'd look like naked, but I was far off the mark."

Nan sat back, laughing. "You mean to tell me you've been fantasizing about me?"

"Well." His grin was sheepish. "Maybe a little. But the reality is so much better than any imaginary event." He looked around. "Besides, I'd never have thought of this. Very creative."

"Strictly a bed-and-nighttime lover?"

"I'm open to suggestions."

She kissed him on the lips, lightly. "Well, here's a suggestion I really don't want to make. We'd better get going. Monday's always a nightmare for me with folks bringing in the weekend rentals."

His expression darkened. "How can you think about work at a time like this? Nan, I want—"

"What, Jesse?" She felt a cold draft on her skin. "We made love. It was wonderful, but life goes on." She eased away from him and noticed he wore a protective device. "Hey, when did you get that on?"

"I'm not an irresponsible lover," he said, not looking at her while he rearranged his clothing. "You were a bit too carried away to think, so I—"

"*I* was carried away? Jesse, I thought we were both overwhelmed. Guess I was wrong." She slid off him and headed back for her clothes. Why did she feel so angry? Was she more angry because he'd obviously planned to make love to her or because he'd implied that she was the one who had been out of control? Tears stung her eyes, and her body still throbbed and tingled from his loving. She felt wounded, torn in two pieces.

"I was overwhelmed, damn it!" He was buttoning his shirt as he came down the aisle, hunching over to keep from hitting his head. "But I don't lose all sense at a time like that."

"Well, sorry." She sat down and dragged on her tennis shoes. "I don't, either. It just so happens I'm on the pill."

"Oh." He turned from her and jumped out onto the hangar floor.

"What's that supposed to mean? 'Oh.'" She followed him, picking up her jacket as she passed it. "What kind of tone is that?"

"I didn't mean anything." He still didn't look directly at her. He pushed the button on the wall and the doors clanked open. "I shouldn't have been surprised, I suppose."

"That I protect myself? Or that I'm ready any time for a lover?" The warm afterglow of love had faded entirely, and Nan was furious. "You figure you're just one of the many? Is that it?"

"No, I—"

"Well, just think whatever you want, Mr. Rivers. Good night!" She took a few steps out into the darkness and turned about. "Goodbye!" she snapped.

"Nan!" Jesse went after her, catching up to her a few yards from the hangar. He grabbed her shoulders and spun her around. "Wait a minute. Listen to me!"

"Why?" She fought to free herself, but he held her firmly. "I know you, Rivers. I've known guys like you all my life. A woman is either a saint or a sinner. We just had sex. And now I fit in the last category."

"No, you are wrong!" He let go, unwilling to control the situation by force. "Listen to me. I can't help my feelings, but I can deal with them. Can you?"

"Wh-what do you mean?"

"Nan, what happened to us in there was special. You'd go along with that, wouldn't you?"

She nodded, puzzled, wondering what he was leading up to.

"My emotions are right up on the surface. I am jealous of every man who's ever looked twice at you, much less the ones you've gone to bed with. Can't you accept that?"

"I . . . I don't know."

He moved close again and touched her cheek. "What happened in there, Nan? I'm almost thirty years old, and I've never felt that way making love to a woman before. I...I admit I'm a little scared. Don't step on my face while I'm down, please."

"Oh, Jesse." She turned her head and kissed his palm. "I'm scared, too. Startled, at least. What're we going to do now?"

He smiled and drew her into his arms. "If I wasn't sure it'd kill us, I'd suggest we try that aloft. But loving you is far too distracting for a pilot's safety."

"You don't love me, Jesse. You wanted me." Her eyes burned, and she buried her face in the warm fabric of his shirt.

"Don't tell me what I feel," he said softly, running his hand over her hair. "And I won't go telling you what you feel. Fair enough?"

"I guess."

They kissed again, but this time both sensed the reservation in the caress. Whatever had occurred between them was gone. Nan felt spent and empty. Cold and alone, though the night was relatively warm, and his arms were definitely designed to give a solid sense of security and comfort. When he led her over to her car, she knew it would be some time before they were able to feel safe with each other again.

If they ever would.

SHE MADE IT A PRIORITY the next week to keep her mind on business, rather than fantasy. She didn't even allow herself to daydream at night before falling asleep, a practice that usually brought her much enjoyment. Now, all it did was rerun her memories of lovemaking with Jesse. All it did was bring back the ecstasy and the pain. She did not need that!

Even though he reminded her of his brother, Jimmy was a welcome distraction. She gave him a crash course on keeping books and was gratified at how quickly he grasped the essentials of accounting. He was a natural business-man, she told him.

"But Dad wants me to go to agricultural school," he said, when she suggested he consider a business college. "He says Steve's gonna need my help on the farm in a few years."

"He might. And you still might help. But it's your deci-sion, isn't it?"

Jimmy looked grim. "Not if it ain't my money. Jesse wanted to go to college once. But Dad couldn't see clear to paying for what he called a waste-of-time education."

"I see."

"So Jesse left and went into the army. I sure don't want to do that, myself."

"There are scholarships. Loans. Maybe Jesse would pay."

Jimmy laughed, his tone bitter. "Jesse and me ain't get-ting along so good right now. I don't think he'd pay my way to a candy store. He's been like a bear with a sore head this week. Growling around all the time he's home."

Nan found that more interesting than she cared to admit to herself. It was also interesting that Jesse managed to stay away from town for most of the next two weeks. When she had materials delivered, Jimmy brought them over. Jesse had finally agreed to let him drive the truck when he was gone, much to Jimmy's delight. Jimmy told her Jesse had taken some special jobs involving out-of-state travel.

So he was not around when she officially joined his church.

She and Walker and Sue had talked about it, and Inge volunteered to be her sponsor. After the short ceremony that made it a reality, Nan was almost able to forget her hurt. Jesse didn't want her, but plenty of other people were willing to be her friends and welcome her to the church family. When she asked how she could contribute above and beyond her regular offerings and attendance, she was immediately invited to join one of the lay committees that ran the institution. Nan chose Finance. No one thought to mention the name of the head of that committee to her.

JESSE SAT ALONE in the meeting room, looking over the treasurer's report, waiting for everyone else to gather to hear the bad news. Ed Mack had tendered his resignation, and it was plain to see it came several months too late. The books were in a mess. It would take a financial wizard to sort them out. Jesse knew he didn't have time and wasn't sure he had the skill. Nor was he sure who on his committee would be able to give up time from their own affairs to straighten out the church's tangle.

"Evenin', Jesse." Warren Moffitt, the town's one pharmacist, wandered in and sat down. "Busy week?"

"Yeah." Jesse set down the report. "You got anything for a headache, Warren? A real big one?"

"Ed's report?" Warren eyed the paper. "Bad news?"

"The worst." Jesse scrubbed his face with his hands. Two more committee members came in, a teacher and her sister, who was a nurse at the clinic. "Miss Ryan, you or Tess here got any idea about bookkeeping?"

"No, Jesse." The elder Ryan sister smiled at her former pupil. "We just know how to spend it, not keep track of it."

"Great." Jesse watched the last member of his committee, Lars Handley, the town police chief, settle into his chair. "We may have to farm this out to a professional accountant, since none of us can handle it. But I really hate to spend the church's money that way."

"Well, maybe our new member can help," Lars said, his deep voice a friendly rumble. "She'll be along directly. Had a little trouble out by her shop earlier, but she told me she hadn't forgot the meeting." The big man seemed to be having trouble controlling laughter.

"New member?"

"Hi, everybody. Sorry to be late." Nan Black came in, bringing with her a very unpleasant perfume. "And sorry about the smell. I tried bathing in tomato juice, but it didn't help much."

Jesse stared. The smell was the only unpleasant thing about her. She looked scrubbed and radiant. Her cheeks were bright with high color and her hair stood out around her face like an electric halo. All the desire he had managed to keep underground in his mind since last seeing her came rushing back. "What the h— What happened?" he asked, finding his voice.

"A skunk." Nan sat down. "Good evening, Jesse." She had positioned herself at the far end of the table, away from everyone, but right where he had to look at her every time he raised his eyes.

"Some joker let a skunk loose in her store early this evening," Lars explained. "Either that or it wandered in. Nan here thinks it was deliberate, but I don't know."

"This isn't the time or place," she snapped, fire showing in her blue eyes. Jesse pitied Lars. "Let's pay attention to church business and deal with my problems later!" She glared at Jesse, as if the whole thing was his fault.

He sat back and explained the situation. "Ed did the best job he could," he said in conclusion. "But we all know the strain he's under with his wife so sick, and he's been failing in health himself lately. The books reflect that in a big way. So I'm asking for ideas, help, suggestions, anything."

Everyone began talking at once. Nan's voice cut through. "Let me see the report," she said, holding out her hand. Silence fell as he passed it down to her. "I can do this," she said crisply, after studying the pages for a few minutes. "I sure won't be able to open the shop until the stink airs out. I might as well tackle this mess."

"That's very generous of you," Jesse said carefully. "But are you sure you can handle it?" It was possible she just wanted something to do while her problem...evaporated. He was uneasy about her attitude, too. She seemed strangely cold and pugnacious.

She glared down at him from her seat at the end of the table. "I seem to be the only volunteer with accounting experience, Jesse. I'm what you've got. *All* you've got."

He shifted in his seat. She was closer to the truth than he liked to admit. "Well, I..."

"Go for it, Rivers," Moffitt said. "Take a chance on the lady. She sounds sure enough of herself."

Jesse raised his hands. "Okay, Nan. The job is yours. I'll go over to Ed's place for the books and bring them by sometime this week. When—"

"Now." She stood up. "Tonight. I'll follow you over, since I doubt you'd want to be close to me, given the circumstances." Her expression showed she wasn't thinking only of the smell that clung to her. "I'm so mad, I need something to take my mind away from that...skunk!"

But when they got outside, Jesse saw she had left her lights on. "You better let your battery recharge," he said. "Come on. I don't have a keen sense of smell. Destroyed it with smoking for so many years. I'll drive you over to Ed's and then home. You can pick up the car tomorrow."

"You're going to regret this."

"Probably. Come on, anyway." They got into his truck and he found out she was right. Beautiful as she was, desirable as he found her, she did smell terrible. And she was clearly still madder than a wet hen over it. Jesse tried to control himself, but couldn't. Halfway to Ed's place, he started to laugh.

"It's not funny!" she snarled.

"I know it's not, but..." He choked on laughter and aroma. "I wish I could have seen your face when it sprayed you."

"You're warped. Sick! It didn't spray me. Not directly. The poor thing was as frightened as I was. Thank goodness no one else was in the store." She sighed. "If I wasn't such a soft touch for animals, I'd not be stinking like this. I tried to shoo it out and ended up smelling like a rose gone bad...."

Jesse sputtered, trying not to laugh. He hummed a few bars of "My Wild Irish Rose." At the same time, a feeling of great affection for her washed through him. She was mad, but she was also being a real sport about it. And for her to volunteer to do the books was...

"I know that snake Neilson set it loose in the storeroom," she said. "It practically has his signature on it. It's just like something he'd think to do."

"What did you say?" Jesse slammed on the brakes, and the pickup fishtailed. Nan grabbed for the dashboard. "How do you know Neilson?" he asked. "What's going on I don't know about?"

"N-nothing." She saw an anger in his face that frightened her. "Forget it."

"The hell! You said Neilson did it. That means he must have bothered you before. What haven't you told me, Nan?"

"It's not your concern."

"It is!" Jesse gripped the wheel. "You don't know the man. He's crazy."

"Everyone seems to agree on that point." She reached over and touched his hand. "Let it go, Jesse. Like I said, it's not your concern this time."

He started driving again. "So, you heard about the fracas over Charlie?"

"And the restraining order. Don't fret. I can handle guys like Neilson. I already did, once."

He made no reply. Studying his profile, Nan decided he was either sulking or deep in thought. She wasn't sure which she preferred to be the reality. Either way, what she felt was only gloom.

TWO DAYS LATER, the sun started to come back up in Nan's life. The books weren't as bad as everyone seemed to think. It took her hours, but she finally figured out the old man's method of accounting, and from there, it was a piece of cake. Jesse, however, was impressed.

"You've really pulled our chestnuts from the fire," he said, studying the spreadsheets she had brought out to his office at the airfield. "I can see what you did, but not how you did it."

She shrugged, pleased at his praise. "I just thought like Mr. Mack. Once I saw his system, it was all downhill from there."

"Well, thanks." He sat quietly for a moment, looking at her. "I guess I owe you an apology," he said. His hand beat a slow rhythm on the arm of his desk chair.

"Why?"

He didn't answer right away, but continued to watch her. Nan had expected some tension, given what had happened between them the last time she was at the airfield. But this didn't seem to have anything to do with sex. In fact, except for appreciating how very masculine he looked in his black T-shirt and jeans, she wasn't the least bit turned on.

Then he smiled. Her heart jumped and started to ache so gently, she wasn't sure it was happening.

"I'll tell you why, Nan. I misjudged you in some ways. Made some poor assumptions. Just like you did to me. You do have a skill for figures. I've been paying attention to Jimmy when he talks about work, and I can see he's learning the ropes from you. No fluff, just hard business facts. This is the final piece of evidence." He patted her report. "You are no lightweight. So I apologize."

"For thinking...?"

"You might be an airhead. You aren't."

She didn't know how to react. "You...you mean we made love while you still thought I was a dumb blonde!"

"I never said I thought you were dumb. Just...less than practical. Too much of a dreamer to be a good business-woman."

"You're a jerk, Jesse Rivers." She stood and collected her papers. "Know that?"

He leaned back and spread his arms wide. "Yeah, I know. Come here, Nan."

She did. Dropping the papers and briefcase, she went over and sat on his lap. "I can't stay long," she said. "I have to open today. The skunk is now no more than a memory, thanks to the friend you recommended and his cleaning company."

"And I have to get skyward myself in a few minutes," he said, burying his hand in her hair. "But that doesn't mean I can't capture the moment." Having said that, he captured her mouth with his.

Nan relaxed into the kiss. Sitting here on his lap with the early morning sun in the window warming her back seemed the most natural pleasurable thing in the world. His caress was sensuous, but not demanding. It was the kiss of a lover who chose for the moment to be a friend as well. The ache that had started in her heart turned hot and spread over the rest of her body, but it was not a fire that had to be quenched right now.

It could wait, and so could she. She surely had that much self-control.

Jesse felt his body begin to stir in response to the delightful pressure of her weight on his thighs and the delicious taste of her mouth on his. The hell with schedules, he thought. He ran his hand down her back and across her leg to her knees. Applying gentle pressure, he started to push them apart.

"Whoa, Hoss," she whispered, blowing the words into his ear and setting his sexual nerves aglow like burning coals. "Don't do that or we'll never get on with the day." She eased away from his hand.

"What day is it?" He looked up at her and saw that although she was smiling teasingly, her pulse rate was up. He could see it beating in the soft part of her throat. "What year is it?"

"The year I intend to knock my parent company out of its socks." She slid off him, standing and dusting the seat of her pants with both hands, as if trying to slap the touch of him away. "And I won't accomplish that by staying here any longer." She went over and gathered up her belongings. "I accept your apology. How about a late dinner at my place tonight?"

There it was. The typical Nan Black response, Jesse realized. An honest, open invitation to continue at a time and place when they would both be free to relax and let things happen. She was no package of false promises, offering and never delivering. But the delivery had to be at the mercy of her primary plans.

"I can't," he said. "I'm not coming back tonight." He had been, but now he wouldn't. "I'm staying over in Omaha. Business."

"Oh." She brushed her fingers through her hair, rearranging it to resemble the style she'd worn when she came in. "Well, then. I guess I'll see you when I see you."

"I'll call." He didn't move from the chair. If he did, he knew he'd take her in his arms and not let her go, no matter how fiercely she protested that she needed to get to her store. The hell with her store!

"All right," she said, smiling at him. He thought he saw her lower lip tremble, but decided it was only his imagination. "Have a safe flight, Jesse."

After she left, he sat, staring at the empty chair across the desk where she had sat and explained carefully how she had straightened out the church books. He was jealous, he realized. Stupidly, insanely jealous. And it had nothing to do with another man or any man she had ever known. He didn't give a damn about her past lovers. He was jealous of her brain! Worse, he was jealous of her drive for success. That lover he couldn't compete with. He was defeated before he started.

Beat that! He got up, his muscles feeling weak and shaky. He reached for his flight plan papers and saw his hand was trembling. He needed her. Just like Charlie needed drink.

No! He wasn't going to let her do this to him. He'd never have believed he could get this way about a woman. Someday, maybe, when there was that special woman in his life—one he was planning to marry, maybe—he'd want to be this crazy about her. But not Nan!

Scowling, he tossed the papers into his old briefcase. He wasn't going to allow himself to be addicted to her. No way. He'd find a cure somehow, somewhere. He thought about a woman he knew down in Nebraska, but dismissed that idea immediately. He was going to have to find the strength within himself, not from anyone else.

For good measure, he added a package of cigars to his baggage, just in case.

"Nan, are you going to be busy this Saturday?" Jimmy Rivers and two of his buddies stood in front of the counter, looking at her hopefully.

Puzzled, she shook her head. "I don't know. I have the store open until ten, usually, but..."

"Could you maybe close early?" This, from the red-haired boy on Jimmy's right. "Just this once, ma'am?"

"Please, Nan," Jimmy begged. "Or if you won't, could you let me find someone to watch the place? I'll even pay!"

"What's this all about?" She leaned on the counter and regarded the boys. The redhead she knew as Turtle, Jimmy's best friend. The other kid was Fred something. "Why the desperation I sense in you guys?"

"We need chaperons!" they chorused.

"What?"

"We're the chaperon committee for the prom," Jimmy explained. "If we can't get two more responsible adults to come to the dance, we're sunk. I thought maybe you and Jesse would—"

"Whoa. Have you spoken to him about this?"

"Not yet." Turtle grinned, revealing braces. "But it's a sure bet he won't miss a chance to go out with—"

"Shut up, Turtle!" Jimmy poked his buddy with his elbow. "Jesse's chaperoned every dance every year since I've been in junior high school. I can count on him, even though we haven't talked about it yet. How about you?"

Nan considered. "This seems a little late to be asking, but, yes, I'll do it. I can shut down early just for one Saturday. What's my job?"

"Yes!" Turtle reached up and pulled down a fist. "I knew she'd do it!"

"We thought Jesse'd bring that lady he's dating over in Sioux Falls. Or one of the ones over in Casper," Fred volunteered. "But Jimmy says—"

"Shut up!" Jimmy looked at his friends angrily. "You guys sure got big mouths!"

Nan remained silent. *You wait,* she thought, *and you learn.*

JESSE DIDN'T CALL the next day or the next. She figured he had put her far down on his list, a list she had discovered included an impressive number of lady friends, if gossip could be credited. Well, why not? He was an eligible bachelor in a land where marriage seemed to be the ultimate aim of many young women. She remembered growing up in a small, rural town. She knew what it was like. He hadn't learned to be such a skilled lover by keeping his hands off the local lovelies. That was for sure. Hadn't he been prepared for sex before she had even thought about it that night? It just made sense that he had a romantic life she knew nothing about.

What didn't make sense was how she felt about that. She was furious and jealous when she thought of him being with anyone else the way he had been with her last Sunday night.

That was not how she wanted to be, however! It was wrong and unsuited to the person she had hoped she was becoming—a strong, independent woman who needed no one but herself to succeed and find happiness in life. *That* was who she was!

Except when she thought of Jesse.

Friday morning, Sue came in, laden with children. "It's my day to baby-sit," she said. "We're on our way to the park for some fresh air, but I thought I'd pick up a movie for later."

Nan ushered her over to the kiddie shelves and showed her the new selections. "You still have five videos left on your twenty-for-twenty-dollars card," she said. "Choose away."

"I understand you're going to be a lion tamer Saturday night," Sue said. "You know, there are quite a few parents in town who are eternally grateful to you for volunteering so they don't have to."

"Oh, my gosh!" Nan slapped her hand to her forehead. "The prom! I forgot all about it!" She had forgotten, she scolded herself, because Jesse hadn't called. He was supposed to be her date, or had she misunderstood the boys?

No, wait. They hadn't said he would take her. They had just said they needed two adults. Nan felt a burning of humiliation in her face. She had only agreed to be one of those adults.

"Nan, what's wrong?" Sue touched her arm. "You look like you're about to cry!"

"No. I...I just realized I don't have anything to wear. At least nothing that won't look like I'm going to a board meeting, rather than a teenage dance. I'm going to feel old anyway. Isn't that silly?"

"Not at all." Sue looked thoughtful for a moment. Then her expression lit with mischief. "I think I may know someone with an answer to your dilemma."

CHAPTER ELEVEN

JESSE PULLED UP and parked behind the high school. The lot was full to overflowing, and he knew he was lucky to find a place within a mile. Every kid who could wangle, wheedle or bully his way to get a car for tonight had done so. Jimmy had double-dated with Turtle, who had his father's Chevy. Jesse, for a variety of reasons, had arrived alone in his truck. Alone and angry. No, he decided, trying to get calm. Not angry. Upset. He didn't want to be here alone. He wanted to be here with Nan.

It wasn't as if he hadn't tried to get in touch with her, because he had, damn it. He got out and dropped the keys into the pocket of his monkey suit.

The tuxedo fit like a cast-iron shroud. He hated the thing, but knew it was appropriate. The waist was fine, but the jacket was tight across his shoulders, upper arms and chest. Tough. He'd had to drag it out and wear it. All the kids had rented or borrowed formal outfits, and he knew Jimmy would be embarrassed and disgusted if his brother showed up in a regular Sunday suit. Besides, before he had tried unsuccessfully to reach her, he had been looking forward to Nan's reaction to seeing him all decked out like this. Acting like a damned peacock, he was.

He had called and called. She had never been home. He hadn't left any messages on her answering machine until yesterday afternoon and evening, figuring he could get her eventually. But she hadn't responded to the messages, either.

She was unavailable to him, it seemed. He pulled at the stiff collar and adjusted his cummerbund.

Well, fine. He hadn't planned to ask her to this thing, anyway. When Jimmy told him she'd agreed to chaperon, he assumed she would understand they would go as a pair. But she hadn't. So what?

Jesse started walking toward the building. He was a little late. The flight had taken longer than he had planned. It was already after nine, and he could hear the sound of dance music. The spring night air was cool, but with all those hot young bodies, undoubtedly the temperature in the lunchroom was high. The windows had all been opened. Although the sound was different, the beat was the same as when he had attended the spring prom as a sixteen-year-old, all those years ago. Jesse paused.

Memories flooded into his mind. His date that year had been Mary Beth Styles. She was long married now, with four or five kids of her own. He hadn't been in love with her, but she was a senior and he was only a sophomore, so taking her to the prom had been a big social coup for him. Out for the evening with an older woman! He remembered how awkward and how proud he had felt. How terrified, wondering if he ought to try to have sex with her. If she expected it of him. He smiled at himself. Thank God he wasn't that young anymore. That unsure about sex and everything else.

If he had been able to talk to Nan, he would have made this a very special date for the two of them, and there would have been no hesitation about having sex with her. He had been able to think of little else since leaving her the other morning, in spite of his good intentions. Now, he just didn't know what to expect. Jesse hunched his shoulders, jammed his hands into his pockets and made his way to the dance. At the door of the lunchroom, he stopped.

As usual, the large room had been transformed by busy, youthful hands into a fairyland. Stepping through the silvery streamers veiling the entrance was like stepping into another world. He blinked, adjusting his sight to the alternate gloom and brightness. Pulsating strobes cut through the air, and the band was brightly spotlighted, but the corners were shadowed. Deliberately, he knew. Patrolling them with tact and discretion was part of his job as chaperon. He smiled again, remembering, and moved past the doorway into the room.

He saw Nan Black immediately.

She wasn't surrounded by an admiring cluster of males, although she should have been. She was a vision of loveliness and desirable womanhood to him, and he couldn't imagine one red-blooded male who wouldn't be moved in the same way. Her dress was black lace over a silvery material and reflected the style of the 1950s. Her hair, on the other hand, was pulled high and back and clustered in curls and ringlets that fell in a charming disarray reminiscent of the Old South. Her bare shoulders seemed to glow with an inner light, and he was sure he could smell the fragrance of her perfume clear across the noisy, crowded room. She was talking to Genny Weaver and two other teachers Jesse knew. He went over to them, unable to resist going to her any more than a moth could have resisted a flame.

"Hello, Jesse." Nan turned and smiled at him. Her gaze slid over him, and he wasn't quite sure what to make of her expression. "Don't you look nice tonight," she said, her voice raised to be heard over the music.

"Thanks." He felt his face growing warm. "I swear this is the last time I let myself get roped into wearing one of these straitjackets," he said, running a finger around the front of his collar again. "Only times a man ought to have to get this dressed up is when he gets married and when he's buried."

"Why, Jesse Rivers," one of the other women said. "You make them sound like the same thing."

"Maybe he intended to," Nan commented, her eyebrows raised. "Did you have a good trip?"

He took her elbow. "I got back into town an hour ago. Let's chaperon, Ms. Black," he said softly, leaning close so she could hear. He nodded to the others. "Ladies, excuse us."

Nan felt their curious gazes on her bare back as he led her away toward a darker section of the room where the sound of the band wasn't so deafening. "Jesse, I wasn't through visiting. I—"

"Where have you been?" He let go of her arm and put his hand on the small of her back. The dress was low-cut enough for his thumb to rest on soft, warm skin. She smelled better than he had imagined she would. The curls dancing at the nape of her neck teased his eyes and tempted his fingers to touch. "I tried to call."

"I've been with my... dressmaker. I didn't have anything to wear for tonight. Inge took me on as a special project. Time was limited, and I just stayed at her place last night. You could have called me at the store."

"I did. The line was always busy, and then, no one answered. Like I said, I just got into town, and I had no chance to chase you down. Nan, I was supposed to bring you here. Didn't Jimmy tell you?"

"Jimmy only asked if I would chaperon. He said you were, also, but not that I was to plan on coming with you."

"Well, he should have!"

Nan stopped and turned to face him. He looked gorgeous, no, splendid in the tuxedo, but she was still upset with him. If he'd planned on taking her, he could have said so days ago when they were together. "I don't take you for granted, Jesse. I don't assume anything where you're concerned. I rode over with Turtle and Jim and their dates, and I'll ride home—"

"With me." He put his finger under her chin. "Nan, I'm not taking you for granted, either. Check your answering machine, and you'll know I'm telling the truth. I called at least a dozen times last night."

She looked at him, and believed. Something new shone in his eyes, and although she wasn't sure what it was, she found she responded to it. "I should have called you when I agreed to this," she said. "I just didn't. And Inge and I were having so much fun fixing this old dress to fit me...."

"Dance with me, Nan." He moved closer. "Inge may be a genius with a needle and thread, but you could be wearing a flour sack and still look beautiful tonight." His hand slid to her waist in back. "So we messed up in our communications. That shouldn't stop us from enjoying the evening."

"I suppose not." Her hand nestled into his palm. "But don't forget, we're also supposed to keep the kids from enjoying themselves in the wrong ways."

"I won't." He drew her to him. The lace on her dress rustled softly as she pressed close. He smelled her warm flesh, as well as her perfume. Her head tilted back, and he saw the soft line of her neck and shoulders and bosom.

Then it happened. She looked at him with her eyes open and guileless and her lips parted, as if for a kiss, and Jesse Rivers fell in love with her.

Love hit him like a fist to his heart. He heard himself gasp, and his grip on her hand and waist tightened. If he held her tightly enough, she could never get away. Never leave, never cause him pain...

"Jesse, what's the matter?" She lifted her hand from his shoulder and touched his face. "You look so pale all of a sudden."

He managed a smile. "Indigestion, I guess. I bolted down a sandwich for dinner."

"You're sure you're okay?" Again the touch. It made him quiver deep inside. As if the tips of her fingers were lighting tiny fires all along his nerves.

"I'm fine." *You idiot,* he thought. What a sap! Dozens, no, hundreds of women he might choose from and he had to go and fall for this one! This woman, with her plans and her dreams that didn't include a man like him.

"Hey, Jesse, Nan! You two planning on dancing like that?" Jimmy appeared beside them, his date with him. The girl was sweating and clutching his hand. Perspiration poured down Jimmy's face, too. Both young people were out of breath. "No close dancing tonight!" Jimmy said.

"Well, we'll see about that." Jesse recovered and grinned. "Evening, Betty," he said to the girl, thankful for the distraction. "You look mighty pretty tonight." Betty Andersen blushed.

Nan was worried. He had suddenly looked very strange. Sick, almost. Indigestion was one thing, but she remembered the symptoms could sometimes mask a heart problem. Jesse smoked, or at least he had. He had a stressful job. That made him a candidate.

He seemed to be fine now, however. She greeted Jimmy's date again, pleased to see her young friend was having a good time. She knew he hadn't been overly enthusiastic about taking this girl to the dance. She was too familiar, too old a friend, Jimmy had confided, for her to be a romantic date. Nan had teased him about watching too many romantic movies and had warned him that the sky didn't usually fall in on a person in love. Usually, in real life, it just crept up on you and happened without fanfare. Jimmy didn't seem convinced, but he took the teasing in good spirits.

"I'm going to have a word with the band," Jesse announced. "I want some slow stuff for a change. You wait here. I'll be right back." He squeezed Nan's hand and was gone.

"What's with him?" Jimmy watched his brother make his way through the sea of gyrating couples to the bandstand. "He usually likes fast dancing. Can go all night without resting."

"I don't think he's feeling too well." Nan watched him talking to the band leader, a thin young man with hair longer than her own. "He's acting funny."

"Jimmy says he's been doing that ever since you came to town," Betty informed her. "Jimmy thinks—"

"Let's dance, Betty!" Jimmy jerked her away from Nan. The music had started again, and they melted into the crowd.

Which now moved to a slow, sensuous number. Jesse came back and took her into his arms again. "I requested only one of these," he said. "I don't want to stir up the teen libido any more than necessary." He moved her skillfully around in time to the beat. "I remember what it was like!"

"And now you have total control, of course," she said, smiling at him. His hand was at her waist, but she could tell he wanted to move it lower by the way his fingers kept shifting position and by the heat of his palm.

"Total control," he agreed, showing his teeth. "Of course." Their bodies danced together in perfect rhythm. "I am an adult, aren't I?"

Nan registered his claim in her mind and began to make plans for later on in the night.

They danced, and she stopped thinking clearly. Though she had already known the delight of seeing his naked body, his form encased in the tuxedo was a fresh turn-on. His broad shoulders seemed even more muscular under the jacket, and the feel of the material against her skin brought new sensations to her nerves. The room was hot, and he was getting warmer. His heat radiated out through his clothes. Though they moved slowly, perspiration was beading his forehead, and the dampness brought out the scent of his skin and after-shave. Nan breathed him in, wishing they were all alone, so she could do much, much more.

Jesse held her as close as he dared. His hands were trembling with the need to touch her intimately. The music poured into him, and he took the rhythm of the love song into his body, giving it to her as they danced. Her hair was soft as a breath against his cheek, and all he could smell now was the fragrance of her skin. She moved as if she actually were part of him. Nothing marred the sensation of oneness. It was as if they had been dancing together for a lifetime.

Jimmy watched his older brother. This was it! This time, for sure. Jesse had to be in love with Nan. He'd never seen him like this with any other lady. He was happy for Jesse, yet at the same time, seized with an intense feeling of jealousy. Not for Nan, of course, but for a woman of his own. Someone he could hold and love like that. He glanced at Betty. No. Not her. She was too much like a buddy to be the girl of his dreams. But, she was pretty tonight and she did have blond hair....

His thoughts were interrupted by the sound of voices rising in argument. The music slowed and died. Jimmy stood on tiptoe to see what the commotion was about.

Then he saw his brother again. Now, love had nothing to do with the expression on Jesse's face.

Nan had felt him suddenly tense. One moment he had been holding her in a lover's embrace. The next he was pushing her behind him, his fists balled and knuckles whitened.

"Lewd entertainment! Lewd music! Lewd behavior!" The voices chanted the words. She looked and saw a small band of adults, mostly male, marching toward her. The kids parted and gave them passage. Douglas Neilson was at the head of the group. He pointed to her when they mouthed the word *entertainment*. One of the strobe lights spotted him, turning his face red, then blue, then a garish yellow. She felt frozen in place.

The overhead lights blazed on. Genny Weaver's voice boomed out over the PA system. "You people are not invited! Leave the premises at once, or I'll call the police! This is a school function."

"Lewd behavior!" The little mob took a turn around the bandstand, ignoring the principal's command. The musicians all looked horribly embarrassed. One guitar player looked as if he were going to cry.

Jesse took a step forward. Nan grabbed his arm. "Don't do it," she whispered. "Let Genny handle this. She's capable!"

"I know. I just..."

She could feel his muscles trembling with controlled rage. "Jesse..."

"Lewd entertainment! Evil in our midst!" Neilson broke from the group and stuck his wagging finger in her face. "Evil woman!" He sneered at her.

Jesse lurched at him. Nan dragged on his arm, relieved beyond measure when she saw Jimmy on the other. She heard the murmur of excitement and fear from the crowd of teenagers and knew she had to stop this now.

So she laughed. Loudly, freely. She shot a glance at Jimmy, who still had his brother in a modified hammerlock, and jumped up on the stage. The chanting slowed and stopped. She took the microphone from the band singer. "Okay, people," she yelled. "Bunny hop!" She waved at the band. "Everybody!"

By the time Neilson and his flock realized what she was up to, the entire lunchroom-ballroom was filled with a snaking file of bunny-hopping, screaming teens. No chant in the world could be heard over the din. She grinned in triumph. Then the pleasure was snatched from her. She saw the little man give her a look of pure hate just as two brawny male teachers offered their services as escorts to the parking lot. The venom in his expression chilled her to her core.

Jesse eased himself out of Jimmy's hands. "You can let me go, brother," he said. "I've got it under control now." He turned around and looked at the boy. "Thanks," he said. "You thought fast and acted right. Better than I did."

"Sure, Jesse." Jimmy's blush of pride was visible even in the dim light. "You taught me, remember."

Jesse wanted to ruffle Jimmy's hair and give him a hug. Instead, he put out his hand. They shook like men, like equals.

Then Jesse looked up at Nan.

She was still watching the exit of the intruders. The band leader had taken over the mike and was exhorting the kids to dance and sing, and she had stepped back. Her eyes gleamed, and he wasn't sure it was from triumph. Tears were more likely, judging from the vulnerable look on her face. His heart ached for her, though he was proud of the way she had taken over and controlled the situation.

More than he had done. He had been ready to use force rather than his brains. A gut reaction, seeing her threatened. If he had any doubts about his feelings for her, they were gone now. He'd been ready to behave like a wild animal protecting his mate. If she knew that, the danger to him was likely to be worse than if he had busted Neilson's jaw!

On the other hand...wasn't it even more cowardly not to tell her? Jesse walked around behind the bandstand. He should tell her, he thought. Be honest with her. She was waiting for him and grasped his hand tightly as he helped her down from the stand.

"Good work," he said, guiding her around to the side of the room. "You stopped a small crisis in its tracks. Quick thinking, Nan. It could have been nasty if he'd kept on yelling. Made the evening a bust for the kids. They all sure owe you one!"

"Thanks." Nan shuddered and forced herself not to step into Jesse's protective embrace. She wanted his arms around her, but knew he would provide only a false security, a fleeting comfort. It wasn't right to ask him to give her what she must learn to get for herself. Her courage and strength must come only from herself, or it would eventually turn on her and fail. She'd already learned that the hard way.

So she just smiled at him. "Quite a show, huh?" she said, as lightly as she could. "I wasn't even sure they knew the bunny hop. Lucky for me, it's a classic." She spoke quickly, hoping the tremor in her voice wouldn't be noticeable.

"You okay?" He had a strange look in his eyes. "I thought you might be...I mean, it looked like you were crying, Nan. If Neilson's upset you, I'll..."

"Nonsense." She blinked, angry at the betraying weakness of her tears. "I wouldn't cry over a little thing like that. Just watering a bit from the glare. The spotlight up there's murder on the eyes." She put her hand on his arm. "Never mind me, how about you? Are you all right? You looked like you were going after Neilson with both barrels there for a second."

"Yeah, I was. Good thing Jimmy's learned how to hang on to me when I get rowdy." His grin was lopsided, but genuine. "Feel like dancing again?"

"Sure." The band had stopped the line dance and was back to playing raucous rock. It wasn't what she wanted to dance to. She wanted there to be more slow music, so she could have an excuse to melt into Jesse's embrace, to feel that security, that lovely oneness they had enjoyed for a few minutes before the intrusion. She wanted that all for herself!

But the night wasn't for her, she reminded herself. It was for the kids. *Act happy,* she thought. *Do it!* She grinned and threw up one arm, grabbing Jesse's hand with the other. Giving a yell, she pulled him back into the gyrating, youthful crowd and started to boogie.

Her energy infected him like a shot of adrenaline. Before he could consider her quick recovery, he found he was matching her wild moves with some of his own. They danced, and he almost forgot his worries. The music was not his favorite style, but the band played it well, and he couldn't help his natural response to the beat. Jesse let himself relax and begin to have fun once more. The other matters, he thought, could wait until later. Later, when he was better prepared emotionally to deal with them. And so they danced, hard and fast.

They did chaperon duty, as well. Between dances, when Genny Weaver came up to Nan to thank her for helping defuse the Neilson situation, Jesse patrolled the hallways with Tom Davis, the football coach and history teacher. They routed one group of booze guzzlers from behind some lockers and suggested to several young couples grappling in dark corners that they take their energies out in the light on the dance floor.

"That's some lady you've got, Rivers," Tom said to him while they checked out the parking lot for further problems. "If I wasn't a happily married guy, I'd give you some competition."

"I got all I can handle." Jesse squinted up at the full moon. "She's married to her career. Happily, as well, it seems."

"Bull." Tom gave him a slap on the back. "Ain't a woman alive would give up a chance at a good man for any career."

Jesse didn't feel like arguing the point. Tom had lived all his life within a few hundred miles of Hennington, even when he went to college. He didn't have the experience to realize a woman like Nan was quite capable of giving up anything she wanted in order to get what it was she really needed. That thought clung to him as he made his way back inside.

Nan noted his gloomy expression when he returned, and assumed rousting teenagers from their youthful follies didn't agree with Jesse. "You weren't designed to be a policeman," she said. "You're a natural lawbreaker, yourself. A real wild one."

"Oh, really?" He smiled, his dark mood forgotten in the light of her beauty and teasing comment. "Why do you say that?"

"I'm not sure." She put a hand on his chest. "Just that you seem to have more of the Old West outlaw in you than the lawman."

"Fantasy, again?"

"Mind?" She put her other hand on his shoulder.

"Not when it comes from you." He slipped his arms around her, letting his hands drift a few inches downward from her waist. "The wilder the fantasies you have about me, the happier I'm liable to be, I think."

She felt his hands, felt herself growing more aroused. "I don't have any doubts, Jesse Rivers. I can make you very happy," she murmured. Music began to pound again, and she pulled him back out onto the dance floor. Her passionate feelings became submerged in the exuberance of the dance movements.

Forty minutes later, midnight struck and the prom was over for another year. The band signed off with one last slow number, and the lights were turned down low. The atmosphere was thick with romance. But it was the sweet romance of the young. Imitating many of the girls, Nan placed her arms around Jesse's neck and moved in as close as she could. She had intended to be funny, copying the style of the kids, but he reacted by embracing her with arms that bound her to him so tightly they might as well have been glued together.

"I want you tonight," he whispered, breathing his words directly into her ear. "Your terms, Nan. Whatever you say. But I want you!"

Nothing sweetly romantic about the need in his voice! She was hearing a very adult male making himself vulnerable to her femaleness. He *needed* her. Her heart started to pound with a beat that had nothing to do with the exertions of the dancing. She sensed the deep seriousness of his statement. Whatever she said? That was what they would do? Her terms?

She didn't have any. What was he thinking of? Terms? She was happy to offer her love freely to him without terms, without strings. Wasn't that the kind of love men wanted, anyway? She felt a sudden agitation within herself and decided she didn't want to know what he meant.

She wouldn't let him tell her, either! It was almost a sure bet that he was caught up in some emotional memory or possibly a reaction to the near-confrontation with Neilson.

He might even be imagining he felt things she knew he couldn't be feeling. He might think he was feeling true love, and she knew that just wasn't the case. Not between her and Jesse, however much the desire that had burned them both. She wouldn't let him make a mistake tonight by saying or doing something that he would regret in the morning.

But she did want him, too. Wanted him very much. There had to be a way . . . a way to distract him and let him just do what he felt. . . . What he *really* felt, not just thought he felt.

Jesse couldn't tell what effect his words had on her. She didn't stiffen and pull away, as he'd expected she would if his overture was unwelcome. Instead, she seemed to grow more pliant, more molded to his body, warmer and softer. More desirable. But when the dance was over and he looked into her eyes, he saw only amusement there.

Was she laughing at his passion for her?

He still wasn't sure when they said good-night to the other chaperons. Jimmy and Turtle and their dates were members of the cleanup committee, and as such, were doomed to return early in the morning to help restore the lunchroom to its plain, everyday state. So Jesse knew his brother would be home in bed as soon as possible. He could stay out all night himself, and not worry about the example he was setting for Jimmy. He took Nan's wrap, a shimmery, silver-colored wool shawl, and settled it around her bare shoulders, then led her outside.

The night was soft and warm, with just a hint of chill in the air. Overhead, the stars shone and the full moon beamed. The light seemed to flow over her hair and skin, giving her an ethereal appearance. In the dark ball gown, she really did look like a princess, he thought. All she needed was a diamond crown.

And what was he? The commoner, yearning after the unattainable lady? This was crazy! The way he was starting to think was just plain nuts!

"My terms?" she asked, startling him by speaking. "Whatever I want? Was that the way you put it?"

Jesse looked and saw she still looked as if laughter was bubbling around inside her head. It scared him to death.

It also turned him on in ways he'd never experienced before.

"That's what I said," he said. "What have you got in mind?"

She had to think about it only a moment. Then she knew what to do, what to say. She smiled at him, and felt the night and the magic of her feelings stir in her heart.

CHAPTER TWELVE

"WHERE," NAN ASKED, "is the most romantic place you can think of to make love?"

"Oh, I don't know." Jesse knew the kind of emotional anticipation he was feeling was dangerous in this situation. Not even Nan Black could satisfy that craving. It would be impossible, since it involved needs way beyond what she could or would fulfill. He put on a solemn expression with no difficulty, playing her game, but playing his feelings as well. "I guess bed is out, since it's too normal."

"I would say that depended on the bed and the participants." She had a definitely devilish gleam in her eyes. "And what's considered normal."

They were by his truck now. Jesse leaned against it and touched her cheek with one finger. "What do you consider to be normal?" he asked. For certain, the level of desire he was feeling now was more than he was used to, normally. Her skin was so soft, she could be made of moonlight. His mind was spinning a little, making him dizzy.

"Normal," she said, laying her hand on his bow tie, "is what works for you and me." She moved her hand and the tie came undone, spilling in two black lines down the front of his white shirt. She moved again, and he felt the stud at the top of the shirt come loose.

"I see," he said, the words catching in his throat. His mouth was dry, suddenly, and he was having trouble swallowing.

She picked open another stud. Nan could see his pulse beating hard in his neck. She kissed it, gently licking the skin before she pulled away. Jesse groaned, and put his hands on her shoulders. His palms felt hot.

"I think we'd better get inside," he said. "This street's a little too public for what we're doing."

"Yeah?" She released another stud. "I thought this was to be on my terms." Another stud. Another. She tugged his shirttail free of the cummerbund. Touched his chest with cool fingers. Kissed him just below his breastbone where the skin was soft and his heartbeat pulsed.

"Nan!" He captured her wrists with one hand. "Cut it out!" He glanced around. They were alone for the moment, though cars were still driving out of the school parking lot. "Somebody's going to drive by and see us."

"So?" She jerked at his cummerbund, turning the thing around and unhooking it with nimble fingers. The snaps on the suspenders went next. "I'm not embarrassed to have people know I want you. Are you?" She looked at him with big-eyed innocence. The sides of her mouth twitched. She licked her lips.

And unfastened his pants.

Jesse yowled and grabbed her. Throwing her over his shoulder, he tossed her into the truck. Only when he had gone around and gotten in on the driver's side, did he see she was shaking with laughter. Laughing so heartily, in fact, that tears rolled down her face.

He shut the door and zipped his pants. "Funny," he said. "Really funny."

"Oh, it was!" She wiped her eyes. "If only you could have seen your face when I undid your britches!"

"I was *in* my face, remember. And in the britches, thanks very much." He shifted the cummerbund around into the correct position, adjusting it with deliberate motions. "Safer to be in a chastity belt, with you around."

"Oh, Jesse. I just couldn't resist. Did I offend your dignity?" She wasn't laughing now, but she was still having trouble keeping a straight face.

"Yes."

Nan leaned over and looked at him carefully. He was holding the pose of an indignant male, but he was smiling. She had accomplished her aim of keeping things hot, but not serious. And it had been tremendous fun and extremely exciting. If he hadn't stopped her, no telling what she might have done! "Forgive me?" she asked softly. "I promise to make it up to you."

He turned and raised an eyebrow.

"Really." She slid her hand into his open shirt. He said nothing, but leaned forward and started the engine.

They made love in her bed that night. She was more than as good as her word. After the emotions, excitement and tension of the evening, Jesse found loving her was like sinking into a warm, soft place where peace mingled deliciously with passion. He had thought he was primed for wild, crazy sex like they had enjoyed in the airplane. But what she offered him tonight was infinitely better and what he really needed, he found. She wrapped him with love and drew him into herself so thoroughly, he actually had moments when he wasn't sure who he was.

It was a world of ecstasy beyond the physical realm. Far beyond. And Jesse knew he was lost in it.

Long after he had fallen into a deep sleep with his arms around her and his head pillowed on her breasts, Nan lay awake. Something was happening here that was beginning to scare her. She wasn't new to love and emotional involvement. She had been married; she had had a lover. Both were men she had cared for and thought she loved at the time.

But it had never been like this. No man had ever made love with her like Jesse Rivers. With him, she experienced a kind of rapture that reached down and touched her far more deeply than she liked. When he did that, he could control her. Maybe make her love him . . .

He had said the words tonight. She didn't think he would remember, but she had heard him cry out her name and that he loved her. Passion's truth, probably. Not to be acknowledged or remembered in the light of the coming morning. But it added to the reasons why she was frightened.

She could not fall in love! Not now! Jesse stirred and his lips moved against the side of her breast. His hand curled next to her face on the pillow. Tears welled in her eyes as she stroked his hair. Soft and curly, it only *looked* tough and wiry like strands of real bronze. Like Jesse. So tough. So...tender. A strong man with a center of vulnerability she didn't dare touch.

Unless she already had. That thought terrified her even more than worrying about falling for him herself. It was one thing to let herself get hurt, quite another to do it to someone else. It was a long time and nearly dawn before she fell asleep, her conscience still trembling with imagined guilt.

When Jesse woke, he felt wonderful. Nan was deep in slumber, and her breathing indicated she was nowhere near waking. He rose carefully, making sure not to disturb her. Though her face was relaxed, she had an aura of exhaustion about her delicate features. She looked beautiful, but tired. She needed more sleep, he decided.

It was early. He pulled on his pants and went into the kitchen. Sunlight streamed in the window over the sink, and while he set coffee in the microwave to heat, he looked out at her backyard. Spring was here now in full force. The leaves were tiny, but green and growing. Daffodils had already bloomed and were starting to wilt. They ought to be cut back.

But she was only renting this house, he thought as he got his coffee. She wouldn't think of tending the yard as if it were her own. She didn't have time, anyway. He turned away from the window. The smell of the hot coffee didn't cover the musky scent of sex that he carried on his skin. He needed a shower, but was still reluctant to bother her. The noise of the water would surely wake her, and she obviously needed more rest. More time in her dreams. Time was not her friend; it was her boss. She was in a hurry, on the fast track. Yard work was for those who were not.

Like him.

Jesse went over to the kitchen table and sat down. He was in love with her, no denying it now. Especially not after last night. But it wasn't going to do him one bit of good. They might as well be from different planets. She wasn't about to stay in a little place like Hennington, and he wasn't about to leave it. He drank the hot liquid.

Gloom settled over his mind slowly. Waking up next to Nan Black was great. Staying awake, thinking about her wasn't. The coffee settled into his stomach, making him feel slightly queasy. He needed . . .

He needed a shower and breakfast. He looked at his wrist and realized his watch was by her bed. He'd just sneak in and gather up his belongings and head home. He tossed the rest of the coffee into the sink and went into the bedroom.

He got there just in time for the phone to start shrilling. Without thinking, he grabbed it. He said his name by reflex.

"Hello, Jesse Rivers," cooed a female voice. "Is Nan there? Or, I should ask, can she speak? I'll be happy to go on talking to you, sweet thing, if she can't."

"Who's it?" Nan was sitting up, her eyes half-shut.

"Just a moment." Jesse put his hand over the mouth-piece. "It's for you," he said. "Some woman. Sounds like long distance. Can you take it?"

She held out her hand. He put the receiver in it and turned to get his stuff.

Nan rubbed her hand across her eyes and said hello.

"Nan, darling! This is Denise. From Fantasies. Are you able to talk?"

"Hi, Denise." Nan blinked. "Why are you calling me on Sunday morning?" The public relations director for the firm was known to be somewhat eccentric in her dealings with the managers, but this was odd. She and Denise were friends. If she was calling off hours, it might be bad news or a warning. Nan tensed. "I can talk freely," she added.

"Who was that who answered, darling? He sounds delicious! Sorry if I interrupted anything vitally important."

Nan looked around the room. Jesse wasn't there. "You didn't interrupt. I was sleeping. Denise, get to the point, will you?"

"Sleeping? Oh, darn. I'm in New York, love. I forgot. It's only seven there. I'm still thinking California time. If I were there, of course, it would be an hour later where you are. Or is it two hours? Never mind. So, you aren't living like a nun out in the hinterlands after all? Is this Jesse one of a kind, or are there more?"

"Denise!" Nan swung her legs off the bed. "What's this about?"

"Oh, nothing. Just that you've been named most successful new manager for Family Film Fantasies this quarter. I got the news last evening and decided to surprise you today rather than waiting until tomorrow and maybe losing the chance to some low-level gnome in personnel."

"Denise! You don't mean it!" Nan stood up, dragging the tangled sheet with her. "I actually logged in more business than anyone else? I can't believe it!"

"Neither can anyone else. But remember, you have absolutely no local competition. You're out there all alone. And you have been innovative, taking advantage of that."

"That does make a difference." Nan sobered, nodding. "I am the only game in town."

"Speaking of games. Is that Mr. Rivers as smooth as he sounds? Choice? Or is he just the only game in town, male-wise?"

"I . . . I don't know. I mean . . . he's the only one I've had time to get to know. I've been working. . . ."

"It shows. Well, darling. Get back to him and have fun. Take it easy today. You deserve it. At the rate you're going, you'll be jerked out of obscurity soon. Once you hit the big time, you won't have Sundays off anymore. Not if you really want it all. Do you still want it all, Nan?"

"I do!" She clutched the sheet to her chest. "I . . . this is really encouraging, Denise. Thanks for calling to tell me."

"My pleasure. Darling, I owe you, remember. You're the one who helped me see what a drag that man, Mark, was on my psyche. Since I sent him packing, I've been happier than I can ever remember! And my work-production rate! My career is as hot as yours is going to be. Thank God we're not competing! It could be bloody."

"Nonsense. We're friends."

"True. You are the most sensible woman I know, Nan. You're the only one I know who really doesn't let some idiot man turn her head away from the direction she wants to go. I truly admire you. You're going far!"

"Thanks," Nan said weakly. She sat back down on the bed. "And thanks again for the call. I'll be in touch."

After she finally got Denise to hang up, she called Jesse's name. He didn't answer. Nan got up and put on her bathrobe and went looking for him.

Jesse was gone. His truck was not out front. She almost went back to the phone and called him. But Denise's praise rang in her ears, and so Nan just went back to bed. As soon as she lay down, her eyes closed. She was escaping, she knew as she drifted into dreams. Avoiding. But right now, that was all she had the willpower for. She'd skip church today. Tomorrow, she would talk to him.…

BUT THE NEXT MORNING she slept late, the result of drowsing all day Sunday and being unable to get back into real sleep until well after midnight. After rushing around, she made it to the store just in time to open. Her phone was ringing. She grabbed at it, but got a hollow burr. The caller had hung up.

Annoyed, she went over to the front door and pulled the drop box back from the slot. She noticed a number of the films had fallen out of their cases and that increased her anger. The drop box was there for the customers' convenience, but to just throw the videos in was abusing her merchandise. There were some red streaks on some of the boxes, too. Pizza sauce, probably. She decided to put up a sign, warning people to handle the films more gently. She heard the front door open as she reached in. "Be with you in a minute," she said, hearing Sue Petersen sing out her name. Her hand touched something soft and damp.

Then she started screaming. Screaming until the world turned dark.

"IT WAS JUST a dead snake," Walker told Jesse. They were sitting in Nan's living room on her couch. Sue was in the bedroom with Nan. "But she went nuts when she saw it. Guess she's kind of scared of the things."

"I guess so." Jesse had pressed his hands together to keep the rage he felt from making them tremble. "I wonder who could have known that?"

"Nobody had to know it would hit her so hard, Jesse." Walker gripped his arm. "Snake's a symbol, nothing more."

"Symbol of evil, you mean."

"Yes. Sometimes. Also of healing. The physicians' caduceus has two snakes intertwined on it."

"Doug Neilson put it there." Jesse's back teeth ground together.

"You don't know that. This was prom weekend. The kids are still pulling pranks. The snake was road-killed. Anybody could've—"

"Anybody didn't! And you know it as well as I do, Walker. That bastard is harassing her. Are you going to just brush it off? Stand by and watch? Well, I'm not!" He glared down at his hands.

"What're you going to do, Jesse?" Nan's voice brought his head up. She and Sue had come out of the bedroom while he was yelling. She looked pale, but composed. She gave him a small smile. "We can't prove anything. You'll only hurt yourself if you try."

He stood up, his anger inexplicably twisting and turning on her. "That's my business, if I do, isn't it?"

"Not if it involves me in any way." She moved closer to him, her chin up and eyes darkening.

"Hold it!" Walker got between them and put his hands on their shoulders. "If you two want to fight, do it on your own time. Sue and I have better things to do than listen to you bicker."

"Jesse," Sue said, "leave it alone. I told Walker not to call you in on this. It isn't your problem."

For a terrifying moment, Jesse considered making public confession of his feelings for Nan, but his pride won out over his emotions. "Sure," he said. "It's not my problem. But my kid brother works at her place. Suppose Neilson had put a live-and-kicking rattler in that box? What then?"

Nan put her hands up to her face and she turned several shades paler. "I hadn't thought about that. Oh, my God!"

Walker looked upset, too. "I doubt it would come to that kind of behavior, even if Douglas is involved. He's not an evil man, just fanatical about his beliefs."

"Bull!" Jesse confronted his old friend. "I won't hide from the truth, Walker. He's out-of-his-mind mad because Nan made a fool of him again. What is an evil man? Huh? Isn't it someone who can't see he isn't the center of the universe? Can't see that another person, particularly a woman, has a right to think what she wants? That snake deal was a purely malicious act."

The minister sat down and folded his hands. "You've made a good point," he said sadly. "If it is Douglas Neilson who's behind this, I am partly to blame. I have made no attempt to interact with him as a fellow Christian."

"But it doesn't make any difference with people like that." Sue sat down beside her husband. "Darling, you learned that lesson yourself years ago, remember?" She put her arms around his neck.

"I know." Walker smiled and encircled her waist. "You win some, you lose some. It's not my job to set the world straight. No one can do everything perfectly right." He recited the words like a memorized litany.

"Good." Sue snuggled closer. "You do remember."

"I suggest we step into the kitchen," Jesse said to Nan. "When they get like this, there's no point in hanging around and getting embarrassed." He put his hand on her back and guided her around the corner. "I have a proposal for you," he added.

She turned, almost more frightened by that word than she had been when she picked up the dead snake. "What proposal?"

"Security."

He was close, his face only inches away from hers. The word itself, his warmth, the look in his eyes, all combined to make her want to melt into his arms, to ask him to care for her, solve her problems, be her strength. Give her security...

In short, to give up.

"What do you mean?" she asked, turning from him. "Since you fixed the back door, all my entrances are secure. I can't afford to hire a watchman at night. This kind of thing happens. Not much I can do about it, given the situation. We don't have any proof, and it might actually not be the man we suspect." She folded her arms and stared out the kitchen window, waiting.

Jesse regarded the stiff set of her shoulders. "You're right," he said, resisting the need to touch her. "But, like I said, Jimmy's working there, and I have an interest in your...his safety. I'm going to be there every morning when you open."

Nan whirled around. "You can't! You have your own business to run. You aren't even in town most of the time."

"I'll arrange—"

"No, you won't! This is not your problem, Jesse Rivers!" She felt a strange weakness come over her. "It's not even mine for long," she said. She turned around again so he wouldn't see the tears. Tears she couldn't even explain to herself. "Not anymore."

"What do you mean?"

"That phone call. Yesterday morning. Remember?"

"I remember."

"Well, it was from an old friend. She said my business has done so well, I've been recognized as the best manager of a new operation for the quarter."

"So?"

"So? What? No congratulations?" She looked at him now, not caring that his image was shimmering through her tears.

"All right. Congratulations. But what does it mean where your safety is concerned?"

"It means I won't have a reason to worry in a few months. I'll be promoted out and up, if everything goes according to schedule. Neilson can rant and rave all he wants. Stick any garbage he desires in my drop box. The fact that business is good means he's having no impact on what matters. And I'll be out of his reach soon."

"I see." Jesse felt the bottom drop out of his world. "Well, I guess you don't need me, after all. See you around."

"Jesse, wait." She saw in his face what her news meant to him. She felt sick suddenly. She reached out her arms, but he was gone. She heard the front door slam and a minute later, the squall of truck tires.

"Nan?" Sue appeared in the doorway. "Are you all right?" she asked.

Nan nodded. She was getting exactly what she wanted, wasn't she? Why shouldn't she be all right? "I'm crying just out of reflex," she lied. "Means nothing, really."

"If you need to talk . . ."

"I know." She went over and hugged Sue. "You and Walker are my friends. I can't thank you enough for being there this morning. I don't know what I would have done alone. Silly of me to faint like that, but snakes just freak me out. I did need your help."

"Most of us are like that," Walker said, coming up behind his wife. "We need one another more than we know." He put a hand on Sue's shoulder. "I think I'll take a little ride outside of town, honey. Check up on one of my flock. Mind?"

Sue laid her cheek on his hand. "No. Nan will give me a lift back to the house, I'm sure."

"Of course. I've got to get back to the store now, anyway."

She drove Sue home, studiously avoiding any conversational topic that would include Jesse Rivers's precipitate exit from her house. It was obvious Walker had gone after him to find out what was wrong. She could tell Sue was itching to ask, but her friend's sense of propriety kept her nicely silent. She did tell her about the phone call from Denise, however.

"That's terrific!" Sue responded. "Do you get some kind of bonus, then?"

"Just ups my status," Nan said. She kept quiet about moving away. It was bad enough saying it to Jesse and seeing his undisguised reaction. "Makes the big boys and girls take notice."

"That's good, I guess."

"Yeah, I guess."

When Nan returned to the store, she found a good deal of her usual enthusiasm was gone. No wonder, she told herself. She'd had several emotional upsets today. Silly to be so afraid of a dead snake. But for a horrible moment, she had thought it was alive. She shuddered as she passed the empty box. No one else was in the store. Time to get hold of herself, she thought. Past time, really.

She pretended nothing had happened. That was the best way to deal with the situation. Ignore the nasty reality of the present and concentrate on the possibilities in the future.

Jesse would probably call it escapism. She called it focusing. It had worked before. It would work again.

No matter what Mr. Rivers thought.

The phone rang again, and she grabbed for it. She nearly dropped the receiver when the caller identified himself as one of the senior vice presidents of the Fantasy company. Denise had been wrong—this was no low-level gnome.

But as she listened to him, little alarm bells began going off inside her head. Amid hints of promotion and goodies to come, the man kept emphasizing her phenomenal profit record in contrast with the other stores around the country. If she was the best they had, was this a good sign or a bad one? Sure, she was doing well, but the best? It didn't make sense.

Still, she thought after hanging up, it was better than being last.

Jimmy came in at three-fifteen. "Heard about the snake," he said, looking at her closely. "You okay?"

"Fine." Nan stacked the computer printout sheets of the last week's business on the counter. "But there's been a suspicious lack of customers today. Do you suppose the word got around I was harboring reptiles?" She let her lips turn in a smile she didn't feel.

Jimmy grinned. "I guess you are okay, if you're joking about it," he said. "Jesse left me a note. Didn't sound like he thought so."

"Jesse sees and thinks what he wants." She turned back to the computer. "It doesn't always jibe with what is actually so."

Jimmy said nothing for a moment. Then he said, "Yes, ma'am," and went to work.

After an hour, the phone rang again. Nan took it, feeling her heartbeat increasing. Hoping it was Jesse. It wasn't. The caller was the business editor of the state's largest newspaper, asking if he could send a reporter to do a story on her and her business. The news of her success was worth public notice, he said. Nan agreed to the interview. The publicity would help her attain her goals.

She told Jimmy. "That's great," he said. "But what happens when you get so good you have to move up?"

"I move out." She saw something in his eyes similar to what she had seen in Jesse's this morning. "Hey, I have to. If you want to get ahead in this business, you can't be limited to one location. It's just the way it is."

"But you and Jesse..." He trailed the words off, looking away.

"Jesse and I what?" Nan leaned forward on the counter. "Jim, I like your brother. Like him a lot, in fact. But I don't want to give anyone the wrong idea. I'll be here just as long as necessary, and no longer."

The boy stared at her, his expression growing sullen, hurt. "You're scared of old man Neilson?"

"No!" She slapped the counter. "And that's enough talk! You've got work. Please get to it!" Her heart ached, but she couldn't have him looking at her any longer with that wounded face. It reminded her too much of his brother's angry one. Anger she knew he used to cover pain.

Jimmy set himself to his job, determined not to let her see his tears. When he'd asked Jesse about her, Jesse had snarled and hadn't answered. Now he understood why. Disappointment and hurt joined to form a solid lump in his chest. He had been so sure they were in love!

He'd been stupid. *That* was for sure. But not as stupid as Jesse!

He was never going to let himself get the way he'd seen his brother this afternoon. So hurt inside he was almost crazy with the agony. Jimmy hid behind the shelves, sorting film boxes. He didn't want to look at Nan now. Not while he was thinking about Jesse's pain.

What was really dumb about the whole thing was he was sure they were lying. She said she wanted to go. Jesse said the sooner she left, the better. But Jimmy had seen them on Saturday night. He knew Jesse had spent the night with her. Jesse was no saint, but he didn't do that casually. Not around home, anyway. If he'd made love with Nan, then it had meant something to him.

Guess it didn't mean the same to her. Jimmy dropped a box with a clatter. He squatted to pick it up. A hand settled on his shoulder.

"I'm sorry, Jim," Nan said, her eyes full of tears. "I...I was wrong to yell. You've done nothing to deserve my bad temper." She held out her hands. "Friends?"

Jimmy stood. "Jesse..." he began, wondering how to tell her his hurt was nothing compared to his brother's.

"No, leave Jesse out of this." She had a hard look in her eyes now. "This is between you and me." She blinked and a tear fell down her face, belying the hardness.

Then Jimmy *knew*. She was in love, too. She just hadn't the guts or brains to admit it yet. He put out his hand and took hers. "Okay, Nan. We're still friends." She started to cry hard. Jimmy stood rooted to his place as she ran into the storeroom.

He thought about following, but the sound of the front door opening stopped him. If she was crying, he'd have to stand at the counter. He owed her that. He came around the side of the shelves, wondering why he was so pleased she had broken down and started bawling. It wasn't the kind of thing he liked a girl or a woman to do. Usually it made him real uncomfortable.

He spotted the newcomers. An older guy and a girl. People he didn't know. Strangers in town. Jimmy put on his best smile and said, "Hi, there, folks. Can I help you find something?" The girl turned, smiled back.

And Jimmy Rivers lost his heart.

CHAPTER THIRTEEN

NAN FINALLY REGAINED control and returned to the front
of the store. Her intention was to reassure Jimmy she was
fine. In other words, to lie. To her astonishment, Jimmy
wasn't lurking and sulking. He was engaged in deep conversation with a teenage girl, a blonde of considerable
beauty. Nan smiled in spite of her emotional pain. Jimmy
seemed entranced.

"Hello," she said, noticing a strange man standing near
the teenagers. He was watching the girl. "May I help you?"
she asked.

He turned and she experienced an odd mixture of reac-
tions. He was handsome, distinguished even, with gray hair
and dark, penetrating eyes. Dressed in an old tweed sport
coat and khaki trousers, he looked like a casting director's
dream of an academic type—perhaps a professor. His smile
was wide and showed a considerable expanse of white, perfect teeth. But Nan was reliving her reaction to the snake
that afternoon. She held the counter to hide the shudder
running up her spine.

"I'm just here with my daughter," he said, moving over
to stand near Nan. "I'm David Conners," he said, his voice
smooth and reassuring. "We've moved here for the summer." He held out his hand.

Nan took it. She was being silly, she scolded herself. His
hand felt warm and dry, softer than the men's hands around
here that she was used to shaking. There was nothing at all

weird or sinister about him. "Welcome to Hennington, then," she said. "I'm Nan Black. This is my shop. Look around. Help yourself to a movie. First rental's on the house."

"That's most kind—"

"Nan!" Jimmy came over, leading the girl by the hand. "This's Angel. Angel, Nan."

Angel smiled shyly and extended a small hand. "Hi," she said, almost whispering the word. Nan saw that Jimmy couldn't take his eyes off her. Understandable, since the child was so pretty; she could be called adorable, Nan thought. Only, when she touched Angel, the snake sensation resurfaced again.

"Nice to meet you, Angel," Nan said, forcing her wild imagination back into a dark corner of her mind. This was crazy! She was obviously experiencing a delayed reaction to the shock and taking it out on these poor innocent people! She would make an effort to be extra pleasant, she resolved.

"You're in town for the summer?" she asked, addressing both of the Connerses. "Why?"

David Conners smiled again, flashing teeth. "I write Westerns," he said. "Under a pseudonym, I confess, and my agent would hang me from the rafters if I told you my pen name. No publicity, you understand. At least not until the publisher's ready to release the book. But I am here to research and write." He put his arm around his daughter. "Angel's my executive secretary," he stated. "Best there is, too!" Angel blushed and glanced at the floor, then up at Jimmy.

Nan controlled herself. The urge to be sarcastic was almost overwhelming. If this little Barbie doll ever did a lick of quality hard work, she would be quite surprised. "I'm sure she is," she said evenly. Then she felt ashamed. She was judging the girl on appearance only. Not fair, Nan!

"Um, Nan." Jimmy was grinning uncontrollably, and the tips of his ears were bright red. "Since Angel won't be helping her dad until he's got his research done, and since school won't be out for a few more weeks, I thought maybe she could work here." He came perilously close to winking. "You know, help keep things going okay during the day until I can get here."

She nearly said no without thinking. The idea of little Angel around all day gave her something close to the creeps. But she hesitated. "I'll have to give that some thought, Jim," she said. "My budget..."

"Oh, I don't want money," Angel said. Her big blue eyes were wide with sincerity. "I'd just like something to do, Ms. Black. And Jimmy says this is a great place to meet people. Please?"

"Now, Angel," her father said. "Don't bother the lady. We'll find plenty for you to do, honey."

Angel didn't look at her father. "I just love movies," she said softly. "Especially old ones."

Nan sighed. "I guess it couldn't hurt to have some extra hands around. But before you get excited," she warned, seeing the light in the girl's face, "I have to let you know there might be some... difficulties."

"I can handle it!" Angel glanced up at Jimmy, rather than looking at Nan.

"My little girl's tougher than she appears," David said. "Don't you worry about her. She can be a big help for you."

"You don't understand." Nan told them about the snake and the problems with Neilson's group. "I just don't know if you want to land in the middle of a controversy, that's all. I don't believe there's any actual danger, of course, or I wouldn't let Jim work here." Jimmy sputtered a little, but didn't say anything.

Neither of the newcomers seemed disturbed by her story. "Folks like that just enjoy kickin' up dust now and then," David said, his attempt at Western slang obviously deliberate and sounding forced. "We won't worry about them. Come on, Ms. Black. Since you've given us a free one, why don't you help me pick out something we'd really like? Something we haven't seen. Jimmy can show Angel around, if you don't object."

"Of course not." Nan came out from behind the counter, feeling a little as if she'd been maneuvered, but attributing the sensation to an overactive imagination. They were nice people. Reasonable. And Jimmy Rivers did seem fascinated with the girl. It wouldn't hurt to be accommodating, she decided.

JESSE MADE UP his mind. Talking with Walker this afternoon had helped, but this was his own idea. His alone. If he was to act like any kind of man at all, he had to tell her how he felt. It didn't matter if she told him to get lost. She should know. There were plenty of things he didn't like about her, but that didn't stop the fact that he loved her. He really did.

Love was a funny thing, he thought, turning his truck around the corner of the street that led to her store. Did a lot of things to a man, including sometimes making him a coward. Afraid of his own feelings, even more scared of the feelings of his woman. Soft, romantic music was playing on the car stereo. Jesse felt mellow and sure of himself, confident what he was about to do was the right thing. Clean and honest! That was the way to be!

He pulled into one of the parking spaces in front of her place. He knew Jimmy'd be there, but he planned to ask her to step into the storeroom for a private talk. Only one other car, a sedan with a New Jersey license plate. Strange. What would an early-season tourist be doing in a video rental store? The local motels weren't set up for VCRs, he didn't think. No matter. Jesse got out of the truck and dropped the keys into his pocket.

His nerve almost failed him when he walked through the door. She was standing alone in the middle of the big room, the dying sunlight staining her pale hair to a darker reddish gold. For a second, he thought she was looking at him without really seeing him. Emotion etched her features, the inner tension in her showing clearly on her face. Her eyes were huge, giving her a haunted appearance. Her cheekbones seemed more prominent than when he had first met her, and he realized she had lost weight. The tight jeans that had clung to her curves a few weeks ago were now loose. She focused on him, and the anxiety vanished, replaced by such a look of welcome, he hardly believed what he was seeing. She was soft and warm, not angular and icy.

"Nan," he said, keeping his voice as gentle as possible. "I have to talk to you."

She came to him, almost put her arms out, he thought. She was going to, but stopped. Thought about it, rather than acting on her feelings. She threw up an invisible wall when she was a foot from him. "Hello, Jesse," she said, her smile brittle, shutting him out. "I don't suppose you've come to rent a video."

"No, I haven't." Anger smoldered in his mind, but he tried to listen only to his heart. "Can we—" He stopped speaking at the sight of the strange man who stepped out from behind the shelves. He held two movie cartridges in his hand and had a big smile on his face that he directed right at Nan's back.

He was also a good-looking son of a bitch!

"Never mind," Jesse said. "I see you're busy. Came in just to catch Jimmy."

"Oh." She sounded weak. "Well, he's showing Angel around right now. If you want to wait..."

"No." He stuck his hand into his pocket and pulled out the keys. "Just tell him I was..."

"Hey, Jesse!" Jimmy came barreling out of the storeroom. A pretty little blonde trailed behind him. "Want you to meet somebody."

"I think you should," Nan said softly. She didn't look directly into his yes, but cut her gaze around to the gray-haired guy. Jesse simmered.

"This is Angel," Jimmy announced, waving his hand until the girl came to stand by his side. She looked down at the carpet, but her mouth was turned in a little smile. "Angel Conners," Jimmy went on. "That's her dad. This is my brother, Jesse Rivers."

"David Conners," the other man said, stepping forward and offering his hand. "You men both local boys, eh?" he asked.

Jesse shook the hand. "Yeah. That your car out front?" He didn't like the man at all, and now he knew it didn't have anything to do with jealousy. Nan didn't look any happier than he was with the newcomer. He was reacting to her negative vibes, he realized with some relief. Picking up on her feelings.

But Jimmy? Well, Jimmy was another story. Jesse watched him out of the corner of his eye while he spoke with Conners. Instant love! The kid was practically drooling over the girl!

"We're from back East," David Conners said, making it a confession. "I'm a Western writer. Out here doing research. Getting the local flavor, you might say."

"Mr. Conners will be here all summer," Nan said, still avoiding Jesse's eyes. "Angel has volunteered to help me for free." She smiled at the girl, but Jesse was sure he could see a shadow on the expression. "At least for a little while until school gets out. Then, if things are going well, we might renegotiate."

Jesse said that was nice and listened for a little while longer, while everyone was nice to one another without saying a single thing worth a damn. Jimmy, in particular, was acting and talking like an idiot. Then Jesse decided he'd had it. "Nan," he said, not even paying attention to what he was interrupting, "I need to talk to you. Now."

"I..." She looked at him. Her eyes were those of a confused, possibly frightened, person. "I...don't..." She couldn't seem to get a coherent thought out.

"Oh, my goodness," Conners exclaimed, raising his wrist and studying his watch. "It's way after your closing time, Ms. Black. Angel and I have to be going."

"I can show you around town," Jimmy volunteered. "It's not far for me to walk home from the motel."

"Why, son, we'd be delighted, wouldn't we, Angel?" Conners slapped the boy's back in a friendly fashion. "How about getting an ice cream or something."

It took Jimmy less than a second to agree. The Connerses gushed goodbye, then Jesse and Nan were alone.

"I didn't expect to see you," she said, turning away from him and going over to close the blinds on the large front windows. "You left in rather a bad mood this morning."

"I had reason."

She leaned against the wall. "Jesse, don't."

"Don't what?" He walked toward her. "What don't you want from me? I'd kind of like to know."

She turned her gaze on him, and it was like looking into the winter sky. "You know what I don't want," she said. "I don't want involvement that will have to be broken when I leave. Simple as that."

"Simple?" He stopped. "You really don't want me, do you?" he asked, his voice flat. "Man, have I been a prize fool!"

She shook her head, and he saw tears. "No, it isn't you who's been the fool. It was my fault. I should never have—"

"Never what?" His muscles all felt tight enough to snap. "Never had sex with me? Sure as hell wasn't making love. For you, anyway. I see that now."

"Think what you want." She seemed to sag in place. "I can't take back anything we've done or regret anything. I just don't want to hurt you."

"Well, thanks a lot, ma'am." He forced back the fury he felt rising. This wasn't the way he'd wanted it to be, but here it was anyway. "Because you have. You see, Nan, I love you. It's not what I want, it's what is. I can't change it just to make you feel all right. I thought you ought to know." He turned and left, glad he had kept the keys out in his hand. If he'd had to take time to dig for them in his pocket, he might have somehow betrayed the depths of his pain to her.

And that was the last thing he ever intended to do!

Nan stayed frozen until she heard the grind of gears from his truck. That galvanized her. She raced out of the store, not bothering to lock up, and flung herself at his vehicle. She beat on the closed window of the passenger side with her fist. "Open up, Jesse!" she yelled. "You can't run away from me."

He glared at her. "I'm not running away," he called, loud enough for her to hear him clearly. "I'm just leaving. Stand aside!"

"No!" She gripped the door handle. It was locked.

"Suit yourself." He leaned forward and turned up the music. She heard Bach beating the air. Then he spun the wheel hard, and the handle was jerked out of her grasp. Without thinking of the possible consequences, Nan grabbed at the truck bed as the vehicle moved past at an increasingly fast rate. She tensed and jumped, landing on her back in the bottom of the bed.

She lay there for a minute, getting her breath. Night had fallen, though there was still a low dusting of purple along the edge of the western horizon. Above her, the stars winked as if they were laughing at her undignified situation. Nan sat up.

Through a narrow window in back of the cab, she could see his head. He was looking forward, clearly unaware he had a passenger. She scooted up to the glass and hammered on it with her hand.

Jesse just managed to avoid driving halfway up a telephone pole. He regained control of the truck with some difficulty and screeched to a halt in the middle of Main Street. His heart pounding with terror for her safety, he jumped out and looked in the back for Nan. If she'd been thrown out and injured, or worse, he would never be able to live with himself!

She was lying on her back, sightless blue eyes staring up at the night sky. Jesse leaped into the truck and bent over her. "Nan? Oh, God! Nan!" He touched her cheek with a hand that shook violently.

Her eyes focused. On him. "Breath...knocked...out of me." She smiled tentatively. "Nice driving, Ace." She reached up and encircled his neck with her arms. "Jesse, do you really love me?"

"Yeah." He sank down. "Dumb of me, isn't it?" His body covered hers, and he buried his hands in her wildly tangled hair. His pride didn't matter now. All that counted was that she was safe. He hadn't hurt her! He kissed the side of her throat.

"Probably is," she agreed, softly. Tears filled her eyes. "I know I wouldn't have recommended it." He kissed her lips, and she felt something inside start to melt. His tenderness, his strength, his . . .

"Hey, Jesse. Evening, Nan. You two planning on setting up housekeeping here downtown?" The harsh beam of a flashlight made her squint suddenly. Police Chief Handley's gravelly voice chuckled.

"Lars?" Jesse sat up. "We . . . uh, we were just . . ."

Lars Handley turned off his flashlight. He didn't really need it, Nan realized. Headlights from several cars illuminated the scene to make it resemble a movie set.

Which was what it must look like. She remembered exactly where they were, and groaned in embarrassment. Jesse's truck had skewed around to block both lanes of the street. No traffic had been coming when they had halted. There was plenty now! All the passengers getting an eyeful as she and her lover rose from the depths of the truck bed. She knew she looked as if she'd just been through an erotic fire storm. Jesse didn't look much different.

But he maintained his dignity. "We skidded," he said, standing up and helping her to her feet. Her muscles nearly failed her, but his strong arm kept her upright. "Nan was riding in the back. I checked on her, and I guess we got a little carried away. Sorry."

"Just move the truck, Jesse." Lars waved his arm, signaling the small crowd that the show was over. "I don't need no explanation." He stepped back as they climbed down. "Can't figure how a man could skid on a bone-dry street, though," he added under his breath. Nan looked at him and saw he was having a hard time restraining laughter.

Someone honked a horn. "When's the wedding, Jesse?" a voice yelled. The tone was jovial.

Nan felt a rush of blood to her face. Jesse didn't look at her. He just waved in a friendly fashion to the heckler and opened the passenger door for her. She got in meekly, rolling down the window as she settled.

Jesse got in behind the wheel. He glanced at her, but said nothing. As he started the engine, something hit the windshield on Nan's side. She cringed and threw up her hands in instinctive defense. Through the open window, she heard the word "Jezebel!" cut the night air. The tone of the cry was full of hate!

Jesse was out of the truck before she could recover. With the blade of his palm, he scraped the clod of mud off the window, leaving a dark streak that looked like blood. Then he stood on the front bumper of his truck.

"Who did this?" he called out, his voice shaking with anger. "What coward insults by mud and lies?" He raised his filthy hand. Mud drooled out of his palm and onto the street. "Who did it?" he asked again. "Answer up for yourself!"

No one answered. Nan was sure she could have heard a pin drop. The headlights spotted him like a star on a stage. His hair was haloed by the light and looked like the bronze curls on a Greek god. His body, clad in his usual black T-shirt and jeans, looked carved out of solid dark marble, his muscles clearly defined. He turned his head, and she saw his profile, strong, noble, classic....

Something that had started a few minutes earlier when they were alone in the back of the truck came a bit closer to the surface of her awareness. She had to work to catch her breath.

"Skunks, snakes and mud," Jesse announced, whipping his hand down so that the dirt was flung away from his palm. "This sort of message says only that the sender gets dirty and stinks!" He glared out at the headlights for a moment more, then stepped down. Nan watched as he moved around to the side of the truck holding his mud-streaked hand aloft.

It was like watching a skilled dancer. He got in and turned the key with his clean hand. The engine purred. "Do you have a tissue?" he asked, his tone calm. "I still have junk on my hand, and I'd rather not get the wheel all dirty."

She searched around and came up with a rag. Handing it to him, she let her fingers linger on his, let him see what she was feeling inside. He looked at her, a little surprised at what he read in her face, judging from the expression in his eyes. Then he scrubbed away the last of the mud and tossed the rag on the floor. "Let's get the heck out of here," he said.

"Let's go home and make love," she said. Suddenly she wanted him badly. So much, in fact, that she found she had no negative emotional reaction to the mudslinging. Only a positive one to his defense of her and his challenge to the invisible enemy. Her heart had swelled with pride at his behavior, and it still felt larger than normal. Large enough to include feelings for him she never thought she would ever have for a real-life hero. The kind of wild exuberance that embraced the entire person and all he stood for. Feelings that went far beyond mere sensual need. "Jesse, I—"

"Don't, Nan." He pulled away from the scene slowly. One brave soul honked a horn. No one else said or did anything. "Your emotions are all fired up right now. You won't mean what you say."

"How can you . . . ?"

"I just don't want to hear words from you you'll be taking away with you when you leave." He sounded so sad, she felt a lump grow in her own throat.

But he was right. Nan looked down at her hands, clasped together tightly in her lap. They were fists, aimed at herself. It would be doubly cruel to say she shared his affections now. Not only would it sound like a shallow parroting of his confession, but she'd twist the knife every time she talked about her ambitions and hopes. "Take me back to the store, then," she said, her voice a mere whisper. "My station wagon's parked in the back."

He was quiet for a moment. "I didn't say I didn't want to make love," he said finally. "You're like a drug I have to have, Nan." He put his hand on her fists, covering them both with his big palm. Warmth raced through her from the touch. "Don't feel bad, though. It isn't as if you can help it. I love you for who you are, and nothing you can do will ever change that."

"I didn't get the impression you liked me much, today," she managed to say.

He laughed, low and bitterly. "To love is not necessarily to like. I don't think I was ever madder at a living soul. But I'm over that now."

"Walker talked to you?"

"Walker's a good friend. A brother, really." He put his hand back on the wheel. She felt a chill go through her without the contact. "He came out to the office while I was still ready to spit bullets. We did talk. But it was my decision to tell you how I felt. Only mine." He stepped on the brake and the truck slowed to a halt.

Nan looked up. She had been so engrossed in his words, she had failed to notice their destination. They were parked in front of his house.

Jesse unfastened his seat belt. "I've been in love before," he said, staring out at the night. "Thought I was, anyway. Wanted women aplenty. But I've never known a person who got under my skin like you have."

"I had no intention—"

"Of course, you didn't." He folded his arms across his chest. "I don't blame you for my feelings, like I said." He turned and looked at her. "But if for one second I thought you might feel the same about me, be assured I'd fight to my last breath to keep you."

Nan gazed at him without saying a word. She was so close to saying she shared his love that it terrified her. She had no doubt he would do exactly as he said. To tell him about her emotions would be to let him take hold of her soul.

And she didn't think Jesse Rivers would ever let go once he'd decided on keeping her.

So she lied. "It's just that I do want you. But I can't stay here at your house with you tonight," she told him, her fingers picking at a loose thread on the seat. "Jimmy . . ."

"Jimmy's a good excuse," Jesse said, nodding slowly. His hand slid over the back of the seat to her neck. Gently, softly as a breath of wind, he stroked the side of her throat. "He'll do as an excuse for you for a few more weeks until he goes back to the farm."

"Goes back?" She wanted to move away from his touch but couldn't make her muscles obey. "What do you mean?"

"He goes back right when school gets out. Dad needs him to help out." His hand moved, and now he was kneading the back of her neck where the knots of tension had settled. He chuckled, the sound low and very, very sexy. "After getting an eyeful of that little New Jersey Angel, I doubt he's going to go quietly, though."

Unwilling to give in to the sensual lassitude slipping over her, Nan sat tall. "Will you stand with him, if he wants to refuse?"

Jesse put his big hands on her shoulders, turning her so her back was to him. "Why take on his problems, Nan? You have enough of your own. You're so tense you feel like 'you're made of wood." He ran his hands down the sides of her spine, digging his thumbs into that sensitive area and bringing warmth to her whole body. In spite of herself, she groaned in pleasure and arched like a cat. "You've got enough troubles of your own," he whispered, his lips now near her ear. "Don't you know that?"

She didn't know anything. Not right now. His hands slipped around her waist, slipped under her shirt to touch her bare skin, and she felt fire running through her. "Jesse," she whispered. It was the last word she uttered before his mouth closed over hers.

A few minutes later, they were in his bed, making passionate, desperate love, and if Jimmy Rivers's entire high school class had walked in on them, she wouldn't have noticed.

MANY HOURS LATER, Nan woke. She was wrapped up in sheets and Jesse. She was on her back, and he lay partly on top of her. He was sound asleep, his big body relaxed, but still sexual. Moonlight showed her the masculine curve and slope of his back down to his muscular rear. She ran her hand over his skin, surprised as always how soft it was in contrast to the oaklike strength of his muscles. He stirred slightly at her caress, and she felt the pressure of his sex against her thigh. She was greatly tempted to wake him and return to the high plains of ecstasy they had enjoyed hours before.

She did not, however. Easing carefully from under him, she got up. She dressed, telling herself she was thinking of Jimmy. If she emerged from Jesse's room in the morning, the boy would not only get the wrong impression about her intentions toward Jesse, he would get an improper message about the morality of their relationship. If he was really interested in his new friend, Angel Conners, this was not the time to let him think sleeping together was okay. She glossed over the fact that the boy was not naive and undoubtedly had already figured out she and Jesse were lovers. It was one thing to do it; quite another to flaunt it, she told herself.

Besides, Jimmy wasn't the only one whom she wanted to have a realistic view of their lovemaking. Jesse must never suspect how she was beginning to feel about him. She tiptoed through the dark house to the front door and let herself out into the night as soundlessly as possible. He had given her fair warning, and she took it to heart. If he thought she loved him, she would be in for a real fight!

Nan looked at the house for a moment, thinking about him asleep in there. Would he wake soon and reach out for her, only to find the bed empty? How would he feel?

Did she really care? Admit it, she did. She scuffed the side of her tennis shoe on the ground and started walking to the main part of town. The night was shot, but she ought to go close up the shop and get her car. Even if she wasn't likely to get any more sleep, she did need something to eat and to take a hot shower.

She walked swiftly, her head bent in thought, not noticing her surroundings much. Just stepping over an occasional crack in a sidewalk here or around a small obstacle there. She was almost to the shop when she glanced up.

The lights were off. Nan went tense all over. She had left the place in a wild tearing rush, going after Jesse. She had closed the blinds, but hadn't hit the light switch back in the storeroom. Had Jimmy come back and restored the proper order?

Or was someone inside who didn't belong?

She crouched and ran across the parking lot. It was empty. She flattened herself against the building and eased over to the front door. Carefully, gingerly, she tested it. Locked!

Nan felt ice filling her insides. Jimmy *must* have done this. It was the only explanation. But she couldn't be sure, and her instincts were screaming at her that all was not well. Telling herself she was being foolish, nevertheless she continued moving quietly around the building to the rear.

Her station wagon was the only vehicle parked there. All looked in order, and she began to relax. She had been operating once again out of an overactive imagination. Just the sort of thing that would make Jesse—

The back door was open.

Nan blinked, making sure she was seeing reality. Only a fraction of an inch was off, but she knew that since Jesse had fixed it, the door fit the jamb like a glove. He did exact work. She moved silently over to the door and pushed. It opened half a foot, then a foot. She slipped inside.

Now, she could hear something. A clattering sound she knew was the noise of video boxes hitting the floor. Then a loud crash. A shelf! Nan lost her temper and her fear. She ran forward, yelling her rage. She hit the light switch as she swung into the main room and the area flooded with bright light. A masked figure stood in the middle of the floor, staring at her through the holes in a ski mask. But that wasn't what stopped her dead in her tracks.

What stopped her was the sight of her own gun in the hands of the intruder. Her gun. It was pointed right between her eyes!

CHAPTER FOURTEEN

NAN THREW HERSELF to the floor, counting on the bulk of the counter to protect her from the first shot. It came, but instead of the thud of a bullet hitting wood, she heard a horrendous shattering sound that seemed to go on forever. She cowered even closer to the floor, covering her head with her hands and wishing with all her being she had stayed in bed next to Jesse, regardless of the consequences. Noise battered her ears and fear assaulted her mind.

Then there was only silence and the sound of her heartbeat and rapid breathing.

Nan eased herself up. The gunman was gone. So was the big plate-glass front window of the store. Her fear shifted again to rage. He had literally blown his way out! Shot the window rather than her. Any relief she felt was engulfed by her fury at the destruction of her property. Swearing aloud and shaking with anger, she stood erect and walked stiffly out from behind the counter.

The store was a wreck. Whoever it was had managed to break open and ruin a number of the videos. Tape was spread about on the floor along with some intact boxes and others with the covers ripped and shredded. A complete shelf was overturned. In the middle of the mess was her revolver. She picked it up. One chamber was empty. She held out the weapon and emptied the remaining five cartridges into her palm. Cupping them, she stared at the shiny brass. Slowly, the full realization of what might have happened hit her. Tears came then, and the brass blurred. She scarcely heard the yowl of the siren or Lars Handley's voice calling out her name.

JESSE'S BOOTS SCRUNCHED on the fragments of shattered glass from the front window. Lars had called him, waking him from a sound sleep. Nan hadn't wanted him notified, the policeman had said, but he thought Jesse'd want to know.

Damn right! He wanted to know everything!

The bullet had blasted the glass outward onto the parking lot, where it lay like ice on the black asphalt and glittered in the pale red of dawn. He shoved open the door, his muscles aching to be doing far worse to the creep who had done this to her. Nan, seated on the floor, surrounded by a pile of ruined videos, looked up and saw him.

She said nothing. Her expression was blank. He felt almost invisible to her for a second.

"You could have been killed," he said, hearing the tremor of deep emotion in his voice. "You should have stayed with me." Lars Handley and an officer, who were doing cop things just around the corner of one of the shelves, looked over at him, then went back to their business. Jesse didn't care who heard him. "You walked in on a robber with a gun, Nan," he said. "What kind of damn fool thing to do was that?"

She looked at him, eyes cold as the ice the shattered glass resembled. "I didn't know he'd taken my gun. This is my place. What was I supposed to do? Turn tail and run? Go get my big guy to protect me?" She might as well have slapped him outright, so thick was the sarcasm in her tone. He thought he heard an undercurrent of tears, but nothing outward about her betrayed it.

Jesse felt heat in his face. "You shouldn't have left in the middle of the night like that. If you'd woken me up, I would have driven you—"

"And then what, Jesse?" She stood up, her eyes hot now with anger. "You would have taken the gun from him? Or maybe taken a bullet instead?"

"Better me than—"

"What? Better you than me!" She was almost screaming now. "What sort of antiquated, macho claptrap is that?" She struck a pose. " 'Stand aside, li'l lady. I'll take the hot lead fer ya.' Is that what you're thinking?"

Lars came over to her, put his hand on her shoulder. "Take it easy, Nan. You had a shock. It ain't Jesse's fault. He ain't the bad guy here."

The words seemed to work. She sagged a little, her anger leaving like air out of a balloon. Jesse's heart ached to go to her, hold her, comfort her. But he stayed where he was, sure that if he moved, she would misunderstand his actions. Now was not the time for embracing her, and he knew it deep in his soul.

And maybe, just maybe, he would be wrong to comfort her, in spite of his good intentions. Maybe this pain was necessary for her. Something she had to face alone. Whatever the case, he did right to hold back, judging from her next move.

She smiled at him weakly and with tears now streaking her cheeks. "I know," she said, wiping her hand over her face. "I'm sorry, Jesse. I'm lashing out now. You happened to get in the way." The glacier in her eyes had gone, leaving only a blue emptiness.

He jammed his hands into his jeans pockets, so she couldn't see how much he was shaking, how desperately he wanted to enfold her and comfort her. "I understand," he said gently. "Did you see who it was?" he asked, his voice dropping into a growl.

"She saw the guy but he wore a mask," Lars said, giving Jesse a hard look. "She didn't know who it was. Like I told you on the phone, she ain't hurt, and if you go jumping to conclusions about who done this, I'll toss you in the clink myself."

"I won't conclude a thing, Lars," Jesse promised. But that didn't mean he wouldn't do something, once he was sure of the culprit.

Nan saw it in his face. "My parent company has insurance to cover this, Jesse," she stated, all business and in control again. "It won't cost me a dime. Just some aggravation." She looked around, disgust and regret in her eyes. "For certain, I won't be letting anyone else work here now. It's just too dangerous. Jimmy will—"

"Jimmy'll stay on," Jesse said firmly. "And so will that little girl. Because this place will have around-the-clock guards. They'll be safer here than they would be at home."

Lars's frown mirrored Nan's. He beat her to speaking. "You ain't thinking vigilante, Jesse?" he asked. "'Cause if you are..."

"Oh, come on! Give me a little slack, will you?" Jesse took his hands from his pockets and planted them on his hips. "I am not trying to be John Wayne, no matter what some folks seem to think! I'm just suggesting a security guard. The bastard who trashed this place didn't have a gun when he came in, or he wouldn't have used Nan's to blast the window. Finding it near the cash register was just a stroke of luck for him. He wasn't out to hurt her, or he'd have..." He couldn't verbalize the thought. But Nan nodded, agreeing.

"That's true." She paused, and the color on her face deepened into a full blush. "And if I hadn't been...

distracted by personal business, I wouldn't have forgotten my safety measures so thoroughly that I left the door open. No one could have entered with my locks and security-alarm system activated.''

"But they did." Jesse moved closer to her. "Did they get much from the cash register?"

"That's what's strange. Not a penny. I had several hundred dollars in the till that I hadn't taken out because of being in a hurry. All that was taken was the revolver." She glanced at it where it lay on the counter. "I messed up any prints by picking it up myself. I wasn't even thinking."

"I'm getting prints all over the place, but prints wouldn't mean much, anyhow," Lars said. "Few folks in town would be in any register, and I'd have to have probable cause to get prints off any suspect. Right now, I ain't got any."

"Suspects or probable cause?"

"Neither one," the policeman admitted. "Least not in one package."

"How about—"

"Jesse, it wasn't Neilson." Nan read his thought before he could express it. "Even with the mask, I would have recognized him by his body. This man was leaner, taller. Not someone I know at all."

"Neilson could've hired him."

"Jesse," Lars said, turning back to where the officer was dusting the overturned shelf with a dark powder, "you got Doug Neilson on the brain. Give it a rest, man. He ain't smart enough to do this." The policeman glanced at Nan. "Why don't you take her home?"

"I can't go home," Nan protested. "I have to stay until the insurance appraisal's done." She squared her shoulders and stuck out her chin. This time, however, her glare was reserved for Lars.

Jesse felt an urge to grin in spite of his feelings of anger and frustration. Lars hadn't seen this side of Nan before, and he was in for a fight, Jesse could tell. Nan drew in a deep breath and prepared to do battle.

The upshot of the confrontation was that Nan went home alone for a quick breakfast, a shower and change of clothing. She planned on returning to the store as soon as possible. It was a good idea to be alone, she realized, given the mood she was in. Her emotions were in turmoil and unreliable. And it wasn't all because of the break-in and vandalism, or the close call she had experienced.

She regretted her show of temper with Jesse. The events had not been his fault. But he had provided the distraction that had led to her carelessness. The fault was hers for allowing him to get to her like that.

It was this that she really had to think about.

But while she took her shower, all she could see was the skull face that the ski mask had made of the intruder's face, and all she could hear was the terrible sound of breaking glass as the crack of the gunshot echoed in her mind. When she emerged to towel herself dry, she was shaking like a leaf in the wind. Nan closed her eyes, drew the bath towel up to her chin and wished Jesse were there to hold her.

The shrilling of the telephone brought her back to reality. The reporter who had wanted an interview about the success of her business was on the line. The news about the break-in had come to him via an informant who monitored police bands. Now, he wanted a scoop on the vandalism and, as he put it, the grass-roots sentiment against the rental of pornographic materials in a small Dakota town.

She straightened him out. "I do not rent movies with even an R rating," she explained, keeping calm with an effort. "Who told you I stocked porn?"

"It . . . I can't reveal sources, Ms. Black. You understand that."

"I understand libel, Mr. Sanders," she replied sweetly. "So does my company. I doubt they will take kindly to their top salesperson being accused of carrying materials not approved by the company policy."

After that, Mr. Sanders was much more cooperative. She hung up, certain that the article he would write would be favorable. She could certainly use it, she thought. Sales record or not, this kind of problem wasn't likely to endear her to the higher-ups in Fantasies. Reluctantly she decided to make her report to the company by telephone as soon as the office in California opened.

To her astonishment, the executive vice president who took her call told her they were behind her all the way. She wasn't to worry about the inventory—new material would be on its way within the hour. She was to be commended, the woman told her, for her fighting attitude and aggressive sales initiatives.

Nan hung up, relieved but puzzled. She told herself not to worry where there was no problem, but it didn't make sense for the company to take her news with such calmness. If she'd been in charge there, she thought, she'd sure have been upset!

But she wasn't in charge. She was just responsible for her own operation. Dressing for hard, messy cleanup work, she returned to her store, determined to take care of the mess as quickly as she could.

During the morning, she discovered the break-in had become breakfast-table news in Hennington. No need for newspapers or radio around here, she thought as people called or wandered by to check on the damage. She also learned how polarized the community had become on the issue of her movies. The positive side was more noticeable at first.

She had more than enough support. Many of her new friends, particularly members of the church congregation, came by before going to their own jobs or about their daily chores. One and all, they offered sympathy, and a number offered to help. Sue and Walker came over early, their concern for her safety obvious.

"You can't stay here at night by yourself anymore," Walker said sternly. "I can't believe someone would do this. Not here in Hennington!" He stared at the shattered window, an expression of pain and disappointment on his lean face. This whole business was getting to him, Nan realized. Sue looked almost as concerned about her husband as she did about Nan.

"Walker," Nan said, putting her hand on the minister's shoulder, "I don't think it was anyone from town. I'm pretty observant, and I didn't recognize the guy. It certainly wasn't Douglas Neilson. I'd recognize his potbelly a mile away." She grinned, hoping to coax a little lightness into his face.

But Walker stayed somber. Later, after he had left, Sue confided he was exhibiting his old tendency to take on the burdens of the world. "And don't tell me he doesn't have a right to take on yours," she said to Nan.

"I was just about to," Nan admitted. "Between Jesse's macho—"

"That's another thing." Sue frowned. "I know you don't need to be scolded right now. But you're reacting all wrong, you know. There's a big difference between macho behavior and the actions of a person who cares for another person."

Nan blushed so hard the tips of her ears burned. "He came by to see you both, I take it?"

"On his way to arrange for some help for you," Sue said. "Nan don't turn him away. Not unless you're sure you don't love him, too. I know it really isn't my business, but I think you are my friend, and friends speak honestly with each other."

Tears welled in Nan's eyes. She glanced around the store. A retired carpenter was clearing the frame for the front window. Another church member was sweeping up the glass debris outside. Inge was seated behind the counter, patiently rewinding the tapes that could possibly be salvaged. "I don't know how much I love Jesse, Sue. But I can't let him hurt himself over me. It wouldn't be right."

"I don't think you have much choice in the matter," Sue said quietly.

The insurance appraiser arrived then, so Nan was unable to continue the conversation. Just as well, she thought, as she showed the woman around the store, pointing out the damage. She was hardly able to deal with the subject of Jesse in her own mind, much less aloud to Sue, who was a friend of them both!

"You seem to have already marshaled your repair crew," the insurance appraiser said, once the tour was over. "That'll look good on the report." She made some notes on her clipboard.

"Just friends," Nan said. "They marshaled themselves. I didn't do a thing."

"Wonderful! Now, how about additional security?" She eyed Nan through narrowed lids. "You're going to need to show preventive measures, so this sort of event doesn't happen again."

Nan started to answer, to explain she was planning on setting up a cot in the storeroom and sleeping in the building until the perpetrator was caught. A sudden silence from all the workers kept her from speaking. She turned to see what had drawn everyone's attention. Jesse Rivers walked through the front door.

He looked like a figure from a Clint Eastwood movie—the one where the actor appears backlighted on the horizon just before meting out blazing justice to the bad guys. A cannon-size shotgun rested in the crook of Jesse's arm. He had on his leather jacket, jeans and black T-shirt and aviator sunglasses. Nan heard the appraiser draw in her breath.

"*That's* my security," Nan said. The words just came, and she couldn't keep from saying them. "Any questions?" The other woman just made a note on the clipboard and then scurried away. Her eyes were big as saucers as she eased past Jesse and hurried out of the building.

Jesse took off his glasses and slid them into his pocket. "Morning, everybody," he said mildly. "Nan, you got a minute? I need to talk to you."

"Sure." She motioned for him to come behind the counter. "Let's go into the storeroom," she suggested. "You seem to have a dampening effect on folks, carrying that thing like that." She pointed at the shotgun.

He just grinned. Inge waved at him, smiling as if he were on his way up front in church to sing. The rest of the people went back to their self-appointed tasks. Nan felt a little out of touch with reality as she led him back to the storeroom and closed the door.

"About the gun," she said, turning to face him. "I can't—"

"Ease up, Nan," Jesse said, breaking the shotgun open and taking out a shell. "It's just loaded with salt pellets. Won't kill anybody, but it'll get their attention fast."

"Still, I don't think..."

"Don't worry, it's not for you." He set the empty gun down and took her face in his hands. "Listen to me for a minute. You're tough and you're smart. No need to go proving that to anyone, least of all to me. But you can't be everywhere. If that break-in wasn't engineered by Neilson, but by someone else with bad intentions toward you and your business, then you've got real troubles. At least Neilson is a known devil. This other guy is not. You need help."

She felt relief flow as a sweet weakness through her veins. She wanted to cry, to bury her face against his chest, to feel the strength of his arms around her. "I...I know," she said, barely managing to stand her ground. "What do you suggest?"

Jesse relaxed. She was going to listen. If he had to patrol her place by himself without her knowledge, he would. But if she would accept his plan, others would be helped as well as herself. "I've lined up three guys," he said. "They'll take eight-hour shifts here in the back room, guarding you and the building without anyone else seeing or knowing. Even if your enemies do get wind of them, they'll be a deterrent. Can't lose, either way."

"Jesse, that's impossible. I can't—"

"Hush, love." He lifted his hands to her hair. It tumbled loose and soft over his fingers. "It's not going to cost a penny out of your pocket. Or mine. These are men who want to help. For free."

"Why?" Her hands sought him without consulting her mind or will. Beneath the thin material of his shirt, she could feel his warm skin and solid muscles.

"Because," he said. "They're my friends." He kissed her, touching her lips gently with his, filling her senses with the taste and smell of him.

And Nan knew she was in love with him. Never mind her plans, her dreams, her logic. Nothing mattered but Jesse. Nothing mattered but the intensity of the emotions she felt for him. She was a fool, and she was lost.

But she had to keep it to herself for now.

She managed to listen quietly as he explained about his buddies. "Mike Dap is an old Marine sergeant," he said, releasing her and looking as if nothing special had happened during the kiss. "He lives up in North Dakota, but he's real happy to come down here. Says the fishing's better this time of year. Fred Press is from my army days, too. He's in a wheelchair, but that doesn't stop him much. And then, Charlie..."

"Jesse, are you sure?"

"Charlie's the best man on the team. Don't let the way he looks these days fool you. He's sober as a judge, not just dry. And he's willing to take the graveyard shift."

Nan put aside her newfound feelings, and thought. "I'll have to meet with all of them," she said. "Get the ground rules straight."

"Of course."

"Jesse, I..."

"What?"

"Um, I just wondered why you weren't taking a shift." She heard herself laugh nervously. "I mean, when I saw you walking in the place, looking like Charles Bronson, I..."

"Who?"

She laughed again, this time for real. "Oh, never mind. I'll show you a movie of his sometime."

"You'll have plenty of opportunity for that," Jesse said. He took his glasses out of his pocket. "I didn't take a shift at the store, because from now on you've got a personal bodyguard. If you want me to sleep on your couch, that's fine, but I'm sticking to you like a burr. While you're working you'll be covered by the others, but the nights are mine." He slid the glasses on before she could see his eyes and read their expression. And he was out the back door before she could think of a thing to say in response.

"Nan?" Inge called her. "Nan, dear. There's a gentleman out here who wants to talk to you."

Nan shook herself free of Jesse's spell and went out front. David Conners waited at the counter. He had the movie she had loaned him the evening before. "Hear you had some problems last night," he commented.

"It should be obvious," she said, taking the video. "Some jerk tried to play O.K. Corral in my store."

Conners's friendly smile turned wry. "I guess you aren't in a very good mood. I understand." He turned and started to leave.

"I'm sorry." Nan opened the gate and caught up with him. "Come on, I'd like you to meet some people." She took him around and introduced him to her friends. Inge greeted him with studied coolness, however, which surprised Nan. When Conners had departed, she asked the other woman about it.

"He's a slippery sort, seems to me," Inge said. She smoothed a wrinkled tape with her small, wrinkled hand. "That's all."

"What's that supposed to mean."

"Oh, nothing." Inge didn't look directly at her. "But when you're an old woman, you learn to watch. Most folks won't notice you. He didn't. But I saw how he looked at you when you weren't looking at him. Nasty, I think. He's slippery, Nan. I don't like him."

Nan didn't dismiss Inge's intuitive analysis out of hand, but she was soon too busy to give it much more thought. While her supporters had gathered to her side early in the day, by lunchtime she was painfully aware of the others and their opinions of her business. It started with phone calls, reviling her anonymously and declaring the break-in was only what she deserved. Then a little group, mostly women, gathered outside and glared at the people who were helping her. They also handed out poorly written pamphlets, explaining why her videos were the work of the devil. Occasionally, a car drove by, honking its horn derisively.

She solved the problem of the phone first by not answering and then by unplugging the unit when the strident ringing got to her nerves. The pamphlet people were persuaded to move away from the front door, but reconvened out on the sidewalk, which was public property. As for the honking, well, Nan figured, that was just an annoying manifestation of the same freedoms she was fighting to preserve. Just because she didn't like it, didn't make it wrong.

Jimmy showed up right after three. He seemed remarkably unconcerned about the damage. He sauntered in the front door, his eyes scanning the big plywood board set up in the broken window frame. Most of Nan's volunteer helpers had finished their tasks and gone. Inge remained, as did Sue, who was sitting in a corner with her two oldest girls, repairing the torn covers of the boxes. Jimmy didn't even seem to see Sue. His first question was "Where's Angel?"

Nan was working at the computer. "I have no idea," she told him. "Would you mind—"

She didn't get to finish her request. "I'll go find her," Jimmy said, turning around. "She said she'd meet me here."

"Hold it!" Nan stood up. "You're supposed to start work now. You have a responsibility to me, and I need you here. You can't just run off and find your friend because it suits you. I'm sure she has a good reason for not showing up."

Jimmy turned back, and she saw rebellion written all over his face. For a moment, she thought he was going to defy her and leave. Then he slipped from rebellion into sullenness. "Okay," he said. "What do you want me to do?"

It was the first time since she had completed his training that he had ever asked. Before, he had seen the tasks and taken them on without being told. Nan felt betrayed. This hurt much worse than the insults of strangers and ill-wishers!

But, she reminded herself, he was only a kid, entitled to mistakes and bad moods just like anyone else. Calmly, but coolly, she pointed out that Sue could use some assistance. Jimmy nodded and slouched over to the corner. Nan saw Sue's expression and knew the other woman understood the situation. She figured she owed Sue and Walker about a lifetime of free rentals by now, and the account was still growing!

A few hours later, Sue and her kids had left and Inge had gone home. Nan was alone with Jimmy. Every time some-one came through the front door, he looked as if he was going to leave his skin. Every time it turned out not to be Angel, he dropped deeper into a pit of gloom. By seven, he was a veritable basket case.

"I'm going to close early tonight, Jim," Nan told him. "I expect people are going to stay away after dark for a while. I know I would. You go on and look for your friend, if you want."

"Naw." He stared down at the floor. "She told me she'd meet me here. She must not want to see me, after all."

"What is this!" Nan reached up and spun him around to face her. "Defeatism? From a Rivers?"

"Well, you're dumping Jesse, aren't you? When you leave, anyway. She ain't from here. She won't stay, either. Why should I bother?"

Nan pulled away from him. She couldn't say anything. So much had happened since last night, when he'd asked her almost the same question. Then, she hadn't known she loved his big brother. "Don't compare me and Angel," she finally said. "You're both so young. It isn't the same."

"Sure." Jimmy shrugged, unconvinced, unhappy.

The front door opened. "Hi, Jimmy! Sorry I'm so late."
Angel Conners drifted in, a warm smile on her delicately
featured face. "Daddy said there was trouble here today,
and he didn't want me to come." She closed on the boy and
put her arm through his. "But I came anyway." She turned
the smile on Nan. "Hi, Ms. Black."

"Hello, Angel." Nan watched Jimmy metamorphose
from a defeated kid into a stalwart youth. "Jim, if Angel's
father doesn't want her here, maybe you'd better—"

"Oh, it's okay." Angel looked up at Jimmy. "Daddy's
working. He won't even know I'm gone. What should we do
tonight, Jimmy? I've missed you today."

Jimmy just grinned and made a gurgling sound. Nan was
about to suggest that checking with Daddy, working or not,
was the best way to go about matters. But the front door
opened again, and she forgot about Angel and her father.

CHAPTER FIFTEEN

THEY LOOKED like characters in a scene from a Western movie. Four tough men, battered by life but still kicking back. Jesse, of course, was the hero. Compellingly handsome. A little less battered than the other three, but equally tough. "Evening, Nan," he said. "Jimmy." He only nodded at Angel.

"Hello," Nan said, studying the trio with him. She remembered Charlie, who was looking much better than she recalled. He was thin and stringy, but tanned to a healthy color and his eyes were bright. The other man who walked in was built like a bull with shoulders twice the size of Charlie's. His white, close-cropped hair indicated this was the ex-Marine, Mike something. The third man, who was in a wheelchair, had thick ropes of muscles on both arms and a smile that melted her. "Hi, guys," she added, liking them all immediately, in spite of her prejudices about Charlie's weakness.

Jesse introduced the men—Charlie Deaver, Mike Dap and Fred Press. She expressed her gratitude, but found they weren't interested in that. "We're here for the fun of it," Fred informed her. "Chance to get together with old friends and do Jesse a favor. You, too, since you're Jesse's special—"

"Jimmy," Jesse said abruptly, interrupting Fred's personal comment, "there's a bunch of stuff out in the back of the truck. Mind bringing it in for us?"

"Um." Jimmy glanced at Angel, who was smiling sweetly at everyone. "Um, sure. But afterward could we borrow the truck for a little while tonight? I mean, are you going to need it, or..."

"Let the kid have the truck, Jesse," Mike Dap said. "We can all ride in my Land Rover. Much more comfortable than your old heap, anyhow. Who's your friend, Jimmy?"

Nan watched and listened as Jimmy awkwardly introduced Angel to the men. She understood Jimmy's heightened self-consciousness only too well. When Jesse walked in, her heart had started to beat a hundred miles an hour and was still speeding along. She could scarcely take her eyes off him. He looked tired, as if he'd had a hard day. Probably hadn't gotten a shower. He certainly hadn't gotten around to shaving. But to her, he looked magnificent. Utterly male. Utterly desirable. The man she loved. The man she was going to have to leave, eventually, no matter how much it hurt both of them. She tried pushing the thought away, but it continued to bob up like a bad apple in the back of her mind.

Eventually, things were arranged. Jimmy and Angel left, given the loan of the truck for a few hours. Guard duty was divided. Mike was to take the first shift, with Charlie on graveyard and Fred during the day hours. The men set up a comfortable area in the back, complete with hot plate, cot, lounging chair and TV. Nan attached a VCR to the set and announced they were free to help themselves to movies.

"But there ain't no skin flicks," Charlie said sadly. He winked at Nan to assure her he was joking.

"That's right," she said primly, going along with him. "Only wholesome family fare. But you're all welcome to sample whatever you want."

"Good enough for me," Fred stated. The others all agreed.

It was almost midnight by the time Nan and Jesse pulled into her driveway. They were in her station wagon. Jimmy and Angel had not returned the truck by the time they left Jesse's house, where the men were bunking while they stayed in town.

"I'm worried," Jesse admitted. "And mad. He knows I'll skin him for being out so late on a school night." He sat back in his seat, not bothering to unfasten his seat belt yet.

"For goodness' sake, cool down. It's a school night, sure, but how much goes on the last week of school, anyhow?" Nan held out the car keys. "Want to go hunting for him?"

"No."

"Then quit fussing. Your buddies will give him a hard enough time when he finally does show up. Jimmy's in for one heck of a ribbing from them, I'll bet."

"It's still bothering me. He hardly knows that girl."

"Jesse, Mr. Conners knows my name. He knows yours. If he's worried, wouldn't he call? It seems more logical to me for the father of the girl to be concerned than the brother of the boy."

"I trust Jimmy. He's got values. Been taught 'em since he could crawl."

"Well, then?"

"I don't know the girl."

"Jesse, it's been a long day. I'm tired enough to fall asleep right here. If you want to stay up, playing anxious parent, fine. But I—"

"Nan."

Something in the tone of his voice told her to pay attention, that things had suddenly changed direction. "Yes?" she asked.

"Why haven't you been screaming bloody murder about my moving in with you?" He faced her now, his eyes gleaming in the moonlight. Most of his face was in shadow, however. He looked sexy and dangerous. "It isn't like you to take this . . . invasion quietly."

"How do you know what's like me and what isn't?"

He shut his eyes slightly, and she knew he was smiling. "Experience," he said.

"Well." She rubbed the line of upholstery that separated their seats. "I guess I haven't complained because I don't mind this invasion, as you call it. I realize you care about me."

"I love you."

"You say you love me, and—"

"I do, damn it!" He unfastened his seat belt and opened his door. He was around to her side before she could do the same.

He opened her door. "We've done enough talking. Get out of the car, and I'll show you just how much I love you," he said. He held out his hand, and she placed her palm against his.

He was as good as his word.

FOR THE NEXT FEW WEEKS, time seemed to stand still for Nan in a hazy, happy, sensual way. Nothing went wrong, and in a special, indefinable way, life seemed to be better than she had ever known it. Better, for sure, than she had expected it to be during her time in Hennington.

Jimmy, much chastened by his brother's wrath over staying out until the wee hours that first night with Angel, was a model of good behavior. The blistering lecture Jesse had delivered did nothing to dim his ardor over his newfound romance, and he spoke of the girl with almost every other word. Angel was, he declared to anyone who cared to listen, an angel. Perfect in every way, including her standards of morality. She was shy, sweet and pure, he said. Although Jesse said he found it singularly difficult to believe,

Jimmy stoutly maintained that the night of the late, late date, they had never even held hands. Just talked until time got away from them.

"You're a bit of a hypocrite," Nan informed him when Jesse stormed around her kitchen, complaining. "Here we are, living in sin, as open as you please. And you're griping about Jimmy's romantic activities, which he calmly denies even happened. You must be feeling guilty. I don't see how you can justify your suspicions otherwise."

"You don't?" He gazed at her until she felt sweet heat all over. "He is my little brother, after all," Jesse added, holding out his arms to her. "And I don't feel one bit guilty about loving you!"

That closed that discussion for the time being.

Jimmy also managed to talk his dad into giving up his help for the summer and allowing him to continue living in town. Nan put him on at the store full-time, with full-time pay and benefits. In spite of his absorption with Angel, he was still the best assistant she had ever had. And his presence added to her sense of security.

All harassment of her business ceased overnight. It was as if nothing had ever happened. Except for her storeroom guards and the board over the window, she had little reason to remember the terror and rage she had felt that night. No one called to shriek invectives at her. No pious patrol handed out fliers in front of the store. She didn't see hide nor hair of Douglas Neilson or any of his flock, even though she used to run into them in town regularly before the break-in.

Best of all, as far as she was concerned, no more snakes appeared in the drop box in the morning and no skunks were left to stink up the place.

The company was as good as its word at replacing her stock. The only thing that made her feel uneasy was the frequency with which she found traces of scratched-out names of other stores on the plastic cases. The posters, too, had been stamped with the names of stores in other, more populous parts of the country. She wasn't getting fresh stuff, but rather the leavings of other businesses. That was okay, since she wasn't so proud that she minded seconds, but she thought it was a little strange.

She reported her security arrangements and received verbal praise, especially since it wasn't costing the company anything. They promised to pay for a new front window soon, as well. The article written by the reporter, Pete Sanders, came out, and it was very favorable. In fact, it went a little too far for Nan's taste, espousing her cause along with that of firms that offered less than savory material. But she didn't feel she should complain. Good press was good press, no matter what kind of company it put her in.

The good press did seem to be paying off, too. Her business got better every week. She had anticipated a drop-off once school was out, figuring both kids and adults would be busy with summer work and taking advantage of the long days to be outdoors. But families were starting to come in from the outlying regions and asking to rent videos for up to a week at a time. She made special arrangements for out-of-towners, since it was clearly not convenient for them to abide by the one-day rental system. This was against company policy, but she cleared it and was given the go-ahead. Nan began to keep a small notebook of ideas she had that were counter to standard practice but would work better for her.

Her friendship with Sue and Walker deepened daily. Now, when Sue came in with Tommy, the little boy would wriggle and fuss until Nan held him. The girls, too, especially Callie, who clearly remembered her rescue from "Billy's daddy," seemed to like hanging around her at the store, at church, at the Petersen home or anywhere else they all happened to be at the same time.

Which, given the size of Hennington, included most places. Nan found she didn't miss the big cities with their crowds and chaos and problems. Granted, she had her own set of problems due to the narrowness of some minds around here, but still, all things considered, her life was...better. She had more energy, more fun and far less stress.

Strangely, this lack of stress included her relationship with Jesse. She had expected the tension between them to increase after he moved in. Instead, she found she was quite comfortable living with him. She was also pleasantly surprised that no one seemed especially offended by their living together without being married. No one spoke of it, of course, but to Nan's way of thinking, that was a plus, a polite way of avoiding an embarrassing subject. Living together wasn't without its tensions, of course, but they were good ones, the results of their desire for each other and their friendly differences of opinion about almost everything from squeezing toothpaste to reading the morning paper. The sorts of tensions, she realized, a married couple would have and would work on.

If there was a dark spot on her horizon, it involved the knowledge that this idyllic time would one day come to an end. That there would be no marriage. And that would be of her doing. This was a dark demon she chose not to face, however. Plenty of time for that in the future, she told herself, trying not to think how much she sounded like a weak version of Scarlett O'Hara.

Though it caused him to have to make adjustments in his business arrangements, Jesse managed to be home almost every night with her. When he wasn't, she knew her home was patrolled by one or more of the Terrible Three, as she had come to call Mike, Charlie and Fred. She now counted the men among her growing circle of friends, too, and was beginning to understand Jesse's loyalty to Charlie. The ex-pilot had a delightfully wry sense of humor and a rapier-sharp wit. He was also a genius with machinery and could fix anything. She found she easily relied on him when Jesse was gone. But most of the time Jesse was with her.

They spent time together on weekends, too. With Jimmy working full-time and Angel assisting him, Nan could take off more frequently. She began to get involved in his crazy hobby of aerobatics.

She started going to the small fairs held on Sunday afternoons in nearby counties. Jesse would fly, and she would meet him there. At first, she stayed in a state of constant anxiety, sometimes bordering on terror, as he performed his seemingly death-defying maneuvers. But gradually she got used to them and learned how meticulously careful he was. This alleviated much of her concern.

They spoke of this one night while sitting outside in the dark, watching the stars twinkle in the sky. Jesse had brought over lawn chairs from his house and set them up in her backyard for such occasions.

"My sky-jinks don't bother you anymore, do they?" he said, squeezing her hand where it rested under his on the arm of the lawn chair. "At least you don't look so white and scared lately when you come up to the plane after I land."

"They scare me," she admitted, feeling lazy and sleepy and a little sexy. "But I trust you. You know what you're doing. I don't. Simple as that."

"Nice to hear." He used the side of his thumb to caress the top of her hand. "But, you know, I'm not going to keep on doing the tricky stuff competitively much longer."

"Why not?" She came alert. Something in the tone of his voice prompted her to pay attention.

He shrugged. She felt the movement of his shoulders all the way down to his hand. "I'm not getting any younger," he said. "It takes a young man to concentrate hard enough on details to be really sure of himself doing some of that stuff. I'll be thirty in a few months."

"So?"

"So I don't want to push my luck. The reflexes necessary for tight competition won't stay with me forever. I've got other things to do besides try beating the odds until I run out of sky. Other people to think of besides myself. Hope so, anyway."

She knew what he was trying to talk about. Tears burned her eyes. "Jesse, I . . ."

He was quiet. She could feel the tension of sorrow in the air all around them.

"I . . . wish . . ."

"What, Nan?" He lifted her hand and pressed it against his forehead. "If I could figure out what it was you really wished for, don't think I wouldn't move heaven and earth to give it to you, because I would. I'd deliver it to your heart, special delivery!"

"Oh, Jesse," she moaned, the tears flowing freely down her face. "Don't do this! It's blackmail!" She tried to pull her hand away, but he held on tightly.

"No, it's not. I can't keep you here like I can hold you physically right now. I know better than to try."

"If only there was a way," she said, controlling the tears with an effort. "But I'd stifle here eventually, just like I did in Wyoming. Come to resent you for keeping me here. I can't do that to you, even if I could do it to myself."

He was quiet for a while longer. Then: "Well, I guess there's not much point in borrowing trouble from the future, is there? We've got it good right now. That ought to be enough." He reached out and pulled her into his lap.

Nan went to him willingly, but in her heart, she was still weeping. Why, now that she had found him, was Jesse in the one sort of place in the whole world she had sworn she would never live?

And had she really been sure about that vow?

Jesse was sure she had meant it. He was sure his love wouldn't change her mind about leaving. He had too much pride to beg or blackmail her emotionally; he knew she was vulnerable right now, but wouldn't always be that way. When the time came for her to make a choice, he wanted her to make it freely. It was no more than he would ask for himself, after all.

Although she hadn't said the words to him, he was sure by now she was in love with him in her way. Problem was, he thought later that night as he lay, sleepless, beside her, that love meant different things to each of them. To Nan Black, he mused, watching the pale silk of her hair shine in the moonlight, love would always be tightly linked with fantasy. Romantic fantasy, a dream that would never match life in the real world. Romance was great, but love needed deeper roots. She might not have it in her to ever put them down.

That made every minute he had with her now all the more precious. Made them all the more bittersweet, since he had no idea when they would end. His heart aching with a pain he saw no way to heal, Jesse rolled onto his side and put his arm protectively over the only woman he knew he would ever love in this special way.

So June segued quietly into July. The company did not replace the broken window, though they continued promising. Nan kept in touch with key people at Fantasies, but daily she grew more concerned for the future of the company. Even Denise was giving her mixed signals, and if she couldn't count on the straight truth from a personal friend, she knew she couldn't accept what the rest were telling her. Gradually, she came to grips with the reality of her situation. If she was to be able to see through the smoke, she was going to have to go to the fire.

But the fire was in California, and Nan found the idea of leaving Hennington to go there now almost made her ill. Remembering what it had been like to live and work there, compared to her life at present, caused her emotions to shift into instant conflict. She became tense across her shoulders just thinking about facing rush-hour freeway traffic or dealing with unreasonable, hostile customers every day.

How different it was here! She drove to work each morning after leaving Jesse's loving arms. The drive took her about five minutes if she didn't hurry. Quite a bit different from a two-or three-hour commute! She was busy enough each day, but able to spend time visiting with friends who wandered in the store to gossip. Sundays she went to church with her man, and afterward they spent time together. Life was full and sweet.

So she tried to put her worries aside. Dipping into a cash reserve, she had the window replaced out of her own pocket. Fond as she had become of her security trio, she pulled the plug on their guard duty. Nothing had happened, and she was certain by now that the incident with the gun had frightened off anyone who wished her ill. Mike and Fred went home, swearing they would return in an instant if there was any renewal of trouble. Charlie hung around, but moved back to Devil's Hole rather than sleeping over at Jesse's. That left Jimmy alone, but Jesse said nothing about moving out and going home.

Jimmy was clearly living in a wonderful dreamworld. David Conners put no social limits on his daughter, and she spent all her time with Jimmy. Nan believed the boy when he said that nothing sexual was happening between them. There was a sweet air of innocence about them.

Angel, she decided, was lovely beyond measure, but not too bright. Her one, indispensable talent lay in making Jimmy feel important and giving him a willing ear when he talked. Which was most of the time. She was, Nan recognized, a dream of a girlfriend for a teenage boy—insubstantial, beautiful though asexual, but satisfying in a dreamlike way. No threat, no challenge. Jimmy wasn't really ready for either from a woman, so Angel fitted his needs perfectly.

But if Angel and Jimmy weren't a problem, Nan's future was. She knew she had to come to grips with it soon. To be fair to herself, of course, but more important to be fair to Jesse. She owed him a clear view of his own tomorrows.

On the Fourth of July, she finally made up her mind. The day was fiercely hot—the sun a bright furnace overhead. Hennington made the holiday an annual civic event, she discovered. A large, open field at the edge of town had been set aside for a community festival, including fireworks late in the evening. A volunteer band played patriotic music with more fervor than skill, and the field was full of kids playing games and engaging in competition under the supervision of various adults.

She and Jesse were sharing a picnic with the Petersens and Inge. Fried chicken, hard-boiled eggs, potato salad, coleslaw, baked beans and a staggering variety of baked goodies covered the checked cloth. They had found a shady place near the edge of the clearing by a row of cottonwoods. Behind the trees, a pencil-thin creek gurgled along with the last of winter's generous moisture. Jesse and Walker had set up a folding table and some chairs, but Nan sat on the ground with the kids, eating food sprinkled with a bit of grass and dirt. It all added spice to the homey, delicious fare, she thought.

After lunch, Tommy fell asleep in her lap. His small hands and face were streaked with sticky patches of food and dirt and his red hair stuck to his tanned skin as he grew sweaty while he slept. Sue offered to remove her messy offspring, but Nan shook her head. "I'd hate to wake him right now," she said quietly. "He's so peaceful."

"Won't be, if he wakes," Callie said, rolling her eyes to heaven. "He's a real stinker when he wakes up and he's all hot and sweaty. Like he is now."

"I can imagine." Jesse gently brushed Tommy's hair back from his damp forehead. His eyelashes made silky little crescents on his chubby cheeks.

"Speaking of sweaty," Sue said, pointing out at the center of the field where her husband and Jesse were supervising a potato-sack race, "I hope no one has a heart attack out there."

"The paramedics are ready, just in case." Nan indicated the far side of the field where the young men who made up the fire department fireworks team were lounging, asleep in the shade of their truck. "Not to worry."

Besides, she thought, fitness was clearly not one of Walker's problems. He was lean and moved astonishingly fast for a man in a sedentary profession. As for Jesse...

Jesse had turned a deep bronze color since the beginning of summer. His hair had lightened from exposure to the sun and was highlighted with gold streaks. Unlike Walker, who had wisely worn shorts because of the heat, he was in jeans. But he had shed his shirt. Nan felt a shock of jealousy that his magnificent torso was bared for other women besides herself to see. Sweat had turned his skin to a glistening sheath for his muscles, and as she sat in the shade and watched him run and laugh with the teenagers and children in the sack race, she knew she could never want another man as she wanted him.

She looked down at the sleeping child in her lap. She looked over at Sue, reading quietly to her three girls, and at Inge, napping in her lounge chair.

Suddenly, she was back in time. She was a child, sitting by her own mother, watching the pages of a book turn, hearing her beloved grandmother snore gently and hearing the hearty shouts of her father and other young husbands at play. It was a Labor Day picnic, and they were engaged in touch football instead of potato sack races, but she remembered looking up and seeing her mother's expression as she watched the men. Watched *her* man.

"Oh!" Nan said, sitting erect and nearly dumping Tommy from her lap. He stirred and frowned, but didn't waken.

"What's wrong?" Callie asked. "Bee bite you?"

Nan smiled at the girl, noticed her solemn, thoughtful expression and wondered if someday, in some sunlit meadow, Callie would have the same mental experience while watching her own lover cavort with his friends. "No," she said, speaking carefully, so the child would hear every word. "I think love did."

Callie frowned, shrugged and turned away. Nan smiled and looked back out at the field. She was a different person now than she had been just moments ago.

Jesse declared one of the Danson kids to be the sack-race winner and went over to the fire truck to sluice down the sweat that soaked him. The water from the hose was luke-warm and smelled like plastic. But it was wet, and he was sure he smelled a little better himself after the dousing. Nan wasn't particularly squeamish about earthy odors, but he was still a little self-conscious with her. Dripping, he headed over to their group, knowing the sun would dry him quickly enough.

He let out a groan as he flopped on the grass beside her. "Whew, I must be way out of shape," he declared. "Those little kids ran me ragged."

"You look in pretty fair shape to me," she said softly.

Something in her tone made him look at her. She was beautiful, he thought. No, more. She was...

She had no makeup on at all, not even a trace of lipstick. Her long hair was pulled back in a ponytail, but wisps and strands had come loose and were clinging to the damp skin on her face and neck. She wore a white tank top, which was now stained with food and sweat, and khaki shorts with big pockets. Her feet were bare, sandals set to one side. Tommy slumbered messily in her lap. She was...

She was smiling at him with a new expression. Something he hadn't seen from her before. Jesse sat up. "What's on your mind?" he asked.

She continued to regard him with that new look. Her skin was lightly tanned from Sunday afternoons spent outdoors watching him zoom around the summer sky. Tiny little laugh lines webbed out from the corners of her eyes. Her delicately drawn eyebrows had lightened to a pale champagne color, and the fine hair right at the edge of her scalp had been bleached to white. She reached over and touched him. His skin seemed to electrify where her fingers rested.

"I have to go to California," she said.

Jesse felt his insides ice. "When?"

"Soon." She didn't look upset at all. "I've been meaning to do it. Should have done it a while ago. But I just couldn't bring myself to. I know I should have talked to you, but I didn't feel it was anything you should have to worry about."

"What wasn't?" The ice was gone now. In its place was a burning sensation. Frustration and anger. And fear.

"My company." She looked down as Tommy stirred, brushing a soothing hand over his head. "I think it might be going belly-up."

Jesse's own stomach twisted. "As in out of business?" He watched her touch Tommy and realized how he yearned for her to be caressing *their* child. How unlikely that ever was to be.

"Yes." She gazed at him, her blue eyes showing him only serenity. The strange, woman look of inner peace. "I think so. At least, that's how I'm reading the signs I keep getting. But I have to go there to make sure."

"I see." He clasped his hands over his knees and looked away from her. "And why did you decide to tell me all this just now?"

"Because," she said, in a calm voice, "just now was when I realized I love you enough to want to spend the rest of my life with you."

CHAPTER SIXTEEN

A WEEK LATER, Jesse still wasn't sure Nan had meant what she'd said. Her declaration of love had dropped onto him like a bombshell, stunning him into silence. Because she had said it in such a public circumstance, he hadn't pursued the subject at the time. And later it was like pulling teeth to get her to address it. She confirmed her love by her actions, over and over, but he couldn't get her to talk, to explain. It was killing him not to know what had prompted her change in attitude. She seemed unable, not just unwilling, to talk about her intentions, now that she had admitted her feelings.

He didn't doubt her sincerity. That wasn't what was bothering him. He needed to know whether she could focus on a future in the real world and leave both her past and her dreams behind. Her love might be real enough, but until she could accept without reservation the kind of life he could offer, she might be capable of destroying them both with her unfulfilled dreams. Dreams, he thought, had a way of eroding reality unless they were solidly tied to it. Unless they took into account the drab, ordinary aspects of life and love as well as the romantic.

"I told you how I felt," she said, as he drove her to Rapid City to catch the plane to Los Angeles. "Isn't that clear enough?"

He wanted to tell her it wasn't. Instead he said, "I just wish you'd let me fly you. No need for you to spend the money on a commercial fare."

"We've been through that," Nan replied calmly. "This is something I have to do by myself, and you've sacrificed enough of your work time to me, anyway. You need to get back to business."

Jesse gripped the steering wheel. She had told him last night to move back to his own home while she was gone. She'd done it lovingly, sensibly, but nevertheless, he was being kicked out. It just didn't figure. Not if she loved him. Not unless this was her way of setting him down gently. Not unless she meant to set aside even her own feelings for her ambitions. "Business as usual?" he said, feeling confused and angry.

Nan heard the odd tone in his voice. He was upset she was leaving. Well, she couldn't help that. Before she could truly open her heart and commit herself to him, she had to know if she would be able to abandon her old dreams. If she couldn't, if she was making the mistake of confusing an unusually deep infatuation with lasting love, then they would both pay dearly down the line. She was determined not to let that happen! "Be patient," she said, putting her hand on his thigh. "I'll be back as soon as I can. We can talk then."

Jesse felt the hot, electric current her touch always brought start to course through him. "I don't understand why we have to wait. Why we can't talk now?"

"Don't." She withdrew her hand. "Don't do this, Jesse. Please. Try to be reasonable."

"Nan, I love you so much it hurts! I can't be reasonable."

"You're going to have to be," she said. Then she was silent.

Glancing at her profile, he thought she looked as if she were carved from fine stone. Beautiful, cold and hard. She had abandoned her casual Hennington look and was decked out in High Business. Her hair was pulled back into a French twist that gave her added stature and made her look a year or two older. Her makeup was painted perfection. The glimmer in her eyes, he decided, was just from the bright summer sunlight. It couldn't possibly be tears.

They didn't speak for the remainder of the trip to the airport. At the gate, Jesse found he wanted to say so much the words backed up in him like floodwaters at a dam, and he could only mutter a brief farewell.

"You take care," he said, wishing he could explain to her exactly what he meant by that. That he wanted her safe and happy, that he wanted her back with him more than he wanted to breathe! But that even more, he wanted to see her with her dreams intact. Not stripped away, but solid and real for both of them. She didn't say anything, but she kissed him and looked at him for a long time before turning and walking down the carpeted tunnel to the big plane. Her feet, in medium heels, moved with purpose. Her briefcase swung at her side. She did not look back.

Jesse didn't look back, either. He looked ahead at the long years, and found they would be terribly empty without her. Without her as he had come to know and love her in Hennington, not as she was right now. This woman who had just left him was almost a stranger. He watched her, however, his eyes burning, until the plane disappeared into the sky.

A WEEK LATER, still in California, Nan struggled with every word in the letter she was writing. All around her at the motel swimming pool, people were playing. She hardly noticed as she wrote.

Dear Mother,

So much has happened since the last time we talked, even more since last I wrote. The company I worked for is going out of business, leaving me literally high and dry out in the middle of South Dakota. However, this is good news, I believe.

I believe I have made a major readjustment to my goals in life. I now think I understand what you and Dad have enjoyed for so many years. What I lived with when I was a child, but never understood or appreciated. What I guess I was looking for in my first marriage. Real love! I have found a man I know I will love all my life. This time, I *know!* He isn't perfect, and the kind of life he can offer me is exactly what I *didn't* want when I started out on my own. But he is wonderful, and I have some ideas about how to make life with him work for both of us. I only hope he'll be able to accept my dreams as his own, just as I want to take on his as mine. Wish me luck, Mom. This guy is tough, and I'll need all the help I can get. You might try praying, too.

Love...

She stared at the page for a long time before signing her name, folding the paper and inserting it in an addressed envelope. The next letter she had to write was to Jesse. She had tried calling him all week, only to get a curt message on his answering service and no response to her pleas for contact.

Jimmy had called, reporting on Angel, the video store and his brother in that order. Jesse, Jimmy told her, was out of town with Charlie on a competitive aerobatic tour. Gone for two weeks, he said. Gone and out of touch. Jesse was mad, Jimmy told her, because she'd gone off to California and he wasn't sure she'd be back. Nan had protested that was nonsense, but Jimmy said that was what Jesse had indicated.

"Ms. Black? Nan Black?"

Nan looked up. A thin young man she recognized as the day clerk in the motel front office was standing in front of her. "Yes?" she said, taking off her glasses.

"There's a long distance phone call for you. They say it's an emergency."

JESSE HEARD her come into the room. He knew it was Nan because his heart started to beat strongly, and he felt more alive than he had since they had hauled him out of the wreckage of his plane. She touched his hand, and the love that shot all through him made him cry out, call her name.

"Shh," she said, the tears audible in her voice. "I'm right here, Jesse. And I won't go away. Not to California. Not anywhere without you! Not anymore. Never again!"

Jesse believed her. He clutched at her fingers, and then his pain-battered body pulled him back down into deep, healing sleep.

Nan sat by him, holding his hand, watching him as he slept. He was badly hurt, the doctor had told her. But it was all temporary, including the blindness. He was one lucky guy, all the hospital staff who had been involved with his initial treatment agreed. His plane had stalled and crashed just as he was taking it into an upward path, but while it was still quite close to the ground. So the height and speed were low. A few seconds more either way, and she would be helping his family plan his funeral instead of sitting by the bed of her lover.

But he *was* alive! And she was more sure than ever about her feelings for him. The dreams she had fought so hard to attain were merely wisps of fantasy when it came to the dream he offered. Love for life!

"Hey, Nan." The door to Jesse's room shut. She hadn't heard Charlie even come in. It was Charlie who had called her with the terrible news. Called her first, he had said, even before Jesse's family.

She turned. "Hello, Charlie. I got here as soon as I could. Thanks for calling me. I could tell how upset you were."

The ex-pilot sighed and slouched against the wall. "I got to admit to you I was calling with one of my A.A. buddies standing right by me, making sure I didn't detour into the airport lounge for a little liquid support. Closest I've come in a long time to losing my sobriety. I kept seeing that little plane rise up and stall. Kept seeing... Well, you know. I just wanted to blot it out."

"I believe I understand."

Charlie stared at her for a while. "Maybe you do, after all," he said finally. Then: "They tell you he's gonna be all right?"

"That's what the doctor said." She looked back at Jesse. He was swathed in gauze, blindfolded with bandages. He had taken a severe crack on the head, causing the temporary loss of sight as well as a profound weakness and lots of pain. She knew little about medical matters, but she understood the dangers of such an outrage to his system. She also wondered about psychological damage. He had been performing in an air show competition here in Casper, Wyoming. Pitting his skill against that of younger pilots. Doing just the sort of thing he had told her he was planning on giving up. "What do you think, Charlie?" she asked.

"Depends, I'd say." Charlie pushed away from the wall and walked over to the window. "He's already blaming himself, you know. Awhile ago, coming out of all that dope they been pumping into him, he told me he wasn't likely to ever fly again. Said he screwed up. Said it was his fault for flying when his mind wasn't all on business. Said he coulda killed people. If the plane had gone down while he was maneuvering over the crowd, he's right."

"Never fly again!" Nan felt her heart clutch. "It's his life!"

"Yeah." Charlie continued to stare out the window. "I know that better than you do."

Nan could think of nothing at all to say in reply.

Jimmy and Jesse's parents called in almost hourly to check on his condition. Knowing both Charlie and Nan were there and having been assured that Jesse was in no mortal danger, the other members of his family agreed it wasn't necessary for them to make the long drive across the state to Wyoming. Jimmy was running the video store for Nan, and the Rivers's farm needed the full-time attention of the others.

Walker, however, did come for a quick visit to make sure both his friends were all right.

"I want to marry him," Nan told the minister a few hours after he arrived. They were having coffee downstairs at the hospital coffee shop. Jesse had been awake when Walker first saw him, but had fallen asleep after exchanging a few lame jokes with his friend. "I decided that the afternoon of the Fourth of July. Then, after I went to California, I was sure. But I can't tell him that now, can I?"

Walker shook his head. "That's a tough one. You know what he'll think."

"He'll think it's out of pity, won't he?"

"Likely." Walker put down his coffee cup. "Nan, Jesse's got about as much pride as anyone I know. He'd probably rather never see you again than think you were only staying because you felt sorry for him. You're going to have to be very careful and very sure you know what you're doing. More important, you're going to have to make sure *he* knows what you're doing and why. Really knows."

Nan agreed.

So, although for the next week she was rarely away from Jesse, she said nothing at all to him about their future or her feelings. Instead, she told him stories.

She surrounded him with dreams and images, fiction and fantasy, anything to get his mind off his condition and the circumstances that had caused it. She gave him her love without limits or ties to bind him. She gave him the best she had to offer. Not in the physical sense this time, but in the emotional. And she discovered that putting Jesse Rivers at the center of her life was good. She felt like a complete person for the first time that she could remember. She was being healed in spirit, she realized, while he was recovering in body.

Jesse slowly reentered the real world. His body healed quickly, obeying his orders not to malinger. His eyesight, the doctors said, would return soon as well. It was just a matter of time and getting enough rest. No one was talking permanent blindness, but he had a lot to think about, lying there in the dark. Just about everything he thought he had wanted in life was dependent on his vision. Now that was gone, however briefly. No guarantees it wouldn't happen to him again, next time forever. All he was sure of was Nan was at his side almost every moment he was awake. At his side, giving him love and comfort. Kicking his butt when he whined, and generally giving him everything he needed.

Except the assurance she would be with him permanently. That she was really with him out of love, and not just out of pity or guilt. Jesse tried not to think about it, but he harbored a growing suspicion that if he had just walked away from the crash or if it hadn't happened, she would still be in California. One night, when he couldn't stand the doubts any longer, he challenged her.

"I've got you figured out," he said. He was sitting up, the hospital bed adjusted for the position. Still blind, though the bandages had been removed a day ago, he knew she was seated cross-legged at the foot of the bed while she told him another story.

"Really?" She was drinking something. He heard the slurp of liquid in a straw. "How so?"

"Like the heroine in *Arabian Nights,*" he said. "Remember? The lady has to tell a new story every night to keep from being executed?"

"Good grief, Jesse!" He felt the bed shift as she moved. "What a gruesome comparison."

"Well, in your case, your Scheherazade charade is only to keep you from being bored to death. Not executed."

"You think I'm bored?" She had stopped moving. He sensed she was sitting very still.

"You've got to be." He spread out his hands. "Hanging out here day after day, night after night. You've been in California with all your old friends. Where the action is and all. This place has got to be driving you right up the wall."

"I didn't know that." She moved just a little. "I thought I was enjoying myself, now that I know you're in no danger."

"Well, you can't be!" He sat up straighter, his heart beating faster out of anxiety. "I'm doing all right. Why don't you just go on back and—"

He didn't get to say anything else. She shut him up with her lips on his. She held his head in her arms and straddled his body with her legs, hugging his hips tightly with her knees. If they hadn't been in a hospital where anyone could walk in at anytime, Jesse knew he'd have taken her right then. He also knew, right then, that he was going to recover completely. No problem!

"I'm not leaving, because I love you, you idiot," Nan said when she let him come up for air, finally. "I don't want to be anywhere else." She curled against him. "Except, of course, somewhere a little more private."

Jesse groaned from sexual frustration, but he felt just fine. He put his arms around her and held her tight. "Tell me," he said. "I need to hear you talk about this."

She began to talk about her trip, a subject she had avoided until now. "California was exactly what I expected," Nan told him. "Fantasies is on its corporate fanny. I made a deal to buy out my video stock at just a few cents to the dollar of actual value. I have enough squirreled away to just barely swing it. It'll leave me high and dry financially, but I have ideas. Good ideas."

"Such as?" In his darkness, he still saw her leaving him. Moving to a place where she could count on surviving in her own business. Without the backing her old company had given her, he knew she'd never be able to make it staying in Hennington. He held her tighter.

"Ouch!" Nan wriggled free. "What are you doing? Playing like you're an anaconda! Bust my ribs, and I'll just end up in the hospital myself. I don't have time for that!"

"What do you have time for, Nan?" He eased back away from her and folded his hands on his chest. "Empire building or me?"

"Must I make a choice?"

"I don't know." He felt weary beyond words. "I love you, but I don't think I know you. I still haven't figured out what it is that you really want...."

A discreet knock on the door quieted him. "Visiting hours are about over," a nurse announced, "but there are some gentlemen here to see you, Mr. Rivers. They say it's official business."

Nan scrambled off the bed and straightened her clothing. Jesse swore quietly. Two men entered the room. "Suits?" Jesse asked Nan. She squeezed his shoulder affirmatively. He swore again, just as quietly as before, but with a lot more fervor.

The men were Federal Aviation Administration inspectors. Nan listened as they grilled her lover on the details he could remember about the crash and the events leading up to it. As she listened, cold perspiration ran down her sides. Jesse's accident could cost him his license, if it turned out to be his fault. Could cost him his livelihood! She started praying silently. Then, as she picked apart what she was hearing, she grew terrified. She tried reining in her imagination, but it was no use. She knew she was right!

Jesse felt her support, felt her strength beside him. Felt her love, too. For the first time, he felt it as a solid, lasting emotion he could count on. Her hand stayed on his shoulder as he talked to the officers, and after a while, he reached up and took it in his own, holding her as if she were a talisman of good fortune for him.

It must have worked. By the time the FAA men left, he knew he hadn't been responsible for the accident. Although they weren't able to let him off the hook yet, he sensed by their questions they were already looking elsewhere for the cause of the engine failure. He explained this to Nan.

She started crying. She was doing it in such a way as to keep him from knowing, but his senses were unusually alert, and he could tell. "Don't be upset, darlin'," he said, reaching for her. "It's all going to be okay."

Nan went to his arms. "You don't know that," she said, whispering her fears against his chest. "Jesse, those guys think someone tried to kill you."

Jesse tried to reassure her, help her put aside her fears, but he had made little progress by the time she left, literally chased out by an indignant head nurse. All the rest of the night, he lay in darkness, trying to absorb the implications of what she had said, trying to convince himself that she was only letting her overreacting imagination run riot again. Trying, but not succeeding too well. He finally fell into a troubled sleep.

The next morning, he could see. Images were blurred, and his doctor warned him not to strain his eyes. Tinted glasses for protection were to be worn at all times. After swearing to check in with his own physician in Rapid City, he wangled a reluctant release from the Casper hospital.

Nan was waiting for him when he was through with the paperwork. "I've packed up your stuff," she said. "Charlie's gone home. He and Mike are going to operate your business for a while, until you get back in the air. Jimmy is doing a wonderful job at my place, and—"

"You look beautiful!" He took off the glasses. She stood in front of the window, the bright Wyoming sunlight dimmed by the drawn shade, but the pale gold of her hair was as vibrant as he remembered it. No tight, fancy hairdo now. Her blond mane flowed freely to her shoulders. No power dressing, either. She had on a light silk tank top and a flowery summer skirt. Sandals, no stockings. She was more tanned than when she had left Hennington, but the high color on her cheeks wasn't caused by sun or cosmetics, he knew. She was excited or upset about something. Well, he was excited, too! "Let's get out of here and go someplace private," he said, moving closer to her, savoring the tension he felt building in him.

Nan blushed. "Jesse, I checked out of my room earlier this morning. I'm all packed and ready to go." She could see by the expression on his face and the tautness of his body that her carefully laid plans for the day were not likely to take place on schedule. She put her hand on his chest. "We don't have time for..." Her protest faded, and a new light came into her eyes. She stroked his chest lightly. "You look beautiful, too."

"Where're we supposed to be going in such a hurry?" he asked, surrounding her hand with his. "If both our businesses are being taken care of by folks we trust, don't we owe it to ourselves to recreate a little, instead of rushing on back to the salt mines?" He expected her to protest further, perhaps to give in for a little while to his sexual invitation, but then to press for a return to Hennington as soon as possible. He didn't want that, at all. He wanted her to himself, for as long as possible. Raising her hand to his lips, he kissed it and let his tongue taste her skin.

It tasted just as sweet as he remembered. And she didn't protest. Better yet, she said nothing about returning to Hennington or to work. In fact, she didn't talk much at all for the next few hours.

The late-afternoon sun was painting gold bars of light across the sheet when Nan woke up. Their earlier passion had been white-hot by the time they checked back in to her room at the motel, and there had simply been no point in trying to discuss anything, then. Now they were both spent and sated.

She looked at Jesse. He lay on his back, his forearm over his eyes, dozing. Perspiration was still beaded on his skin. After the way he had made love, she thought, he ought to be comatose! "You asleep?" she asked softly.

"Just considering it," he answered. "You have an alternative activity in mind?" He raised his arm and regarded her through half-closed eyes.

Nan sat up, tucking her legs under her and noting the feel of a strained muscle here and there. No wonder! She was in great shape, but this had been unusually demanding lovemaking. They had been extraordinarily athletic about it! "You couldn't possibly do any more today," she said. "No way. If you were a normal man, which, of course, you aren't, you'd be half-dead.''

"Ah, a challenge." He moved his arm and started stroking her knee. "I do love a challenge."

"Jesse, relax. I want to talk. What's with you, anyway? You're a wild man this afternoon!" His hand had moved down her thigh an interesting distance.

"I've been deprived."

"Depraved is more like it." She scooted away from his questing fingers before she could get too distracted. "Cut it out. I really need to talk to you."

"Oh, all right." He sighed and rolled onto his side. The sheet, which had been pulled up over his waist, slid down to midhip. Nan was sure that if she got close enough to pull it back up, she was not likely to get much conversation out of him. She would just have to control her own desires as well as his. "What do you want to talk about?" he asked. His eyes were smoldering slits of green, watching her.

"Us," she said. "This..." She patted the bed. "This is extraordinary for both of us, but it isn't what's going to keep us going for the next fifty years. At least, that's not all that will keep us going," she said, amending her statement. If he made love like this when he was thirty, he was likely to still be pretty formidable between the sheets when he was looking at the wrong side of eighty.

Jesse sat up, the sleepy, sexy look gone from his eyes. "What are you saying?"

"That we...um..." Nan paused. She was right on the verge of asking him to marry her. With some other guy, she would have gone ahead, she realized. But not Jesse. He'd want to do it the old-fashioned way. By the traditional rules. He wasn't just some other guy. She had to respect his ways, if she wanted his respect for hers. "We need to talk about my business," she said instead. "And yours."

"Oh." He lay back down, his eyes slitting again. His expression was neutral. "Talk on."

"Well." She shifted around, crossing her legs and arranging the sheet for modesty, silly though that was, considering all they had just done together. "I've done a lot of thinking. Not just on this trip, but before I found out I was on my own. I even kept a little journal of my ideas. For instance, I want to change the name of my enterprise to Videos for Fun. It gets across the clean image better than using the word *fantasies*, don't you think?"

She didn't wait for him to answer, but plunged ahead. "I can show it all to you when we get home. The problem with trying to operate as an independent in Hennington is the scant population. Even if everyone in town rented a movie every night, which they won't, I doubt I'd turn a profit, much less have enough operating funds to buy new products."

Here it came, Jesse thought. The big announcement. He shut his eyes. They were beginning to hurt. "So, where do you plan to move?"

"I don't."

"What?" He opened his eyes. "What?"

"Why move?" She grinned at him. "When I have the best delivery service in the state right at my fingertips." She wiggled her fingers in his direction. "So to speak."

"You mean...?" He was beginning to catch her drift. "If my plane could carry a weekly package for you, you could do business with almost anyone near a landing strip."

"Exactly." She smiled, then sobered. "Of course, I'd have to ask for credit for a while. Maybe up to a year, because of operating costs. I haven't figured what the freight cost would be, but—"

"Nothing." He slid down on the bed and reached for her, his big hands encircling her waist. "Your cost would be nothing." She started to speak, but he pulled at her, drawing her close and covering her mouth with his. After a while, he asked, "You really want to stay in Hennington?"

"I said so, didn't I?" She reached up and ruffled his already much ruffled hair. "All my good friends are there. I have a life there. I'm an accepted member of the community with a business that was operating well. Now, why should I move? You can't buy that kind of goodwill overnight, if ever. Am I the kind of idiot who'd move away from a business plus like that?"

"Beats me." Jesse slid his hand underneath her hips. "Now, let's see for a while how long you can stay still right here."

It wasn't for long.

They remained in Casper that night. Over dinner at an elegant Chinese restaurant downtown, Nan told him of her plans for the next few days. "I'd like to drive up north to my old hometown," she said, "and have you meet my family. I've met yours, but—"

"Great!" He covered her hand with his. Soon, he was going to find the right moment to ask her to marry him. The only thing holding him back was the desire to make sure she was sure. Her plans sounded fine and firm, but he had to be certain this was what she wanted, and not something she'd cooked up to accommodate her feelings for him. "I'd really like to meet your people," he said. "Thank them for you."

"I love you, Jesse," she said. Jesse felt he'd never really known happiness until this moment. He'd ask her later tonight, he told himself. Just savor the time a little longer.

When they returned to the room, the message light was blinking on the telephone. Suddenly overcome with a sense of dread, Nan almost didn't reach for the receiver. But she had to. She had responsibilities.

The message was that Walker had called. Another emergency. Since he hadn't indicated whether he wanted her or Jesse, she let Jesse make the call. She sat on the edge of the bed, watching his face. His expression darkened as Walker talked.

When he hung up the phone, Jesse said nothing for a long, impossible time. Then: "Nan, your store has been closed down. And Jimmy's been arrested for renting pornographic movies." He looked directly at her for the first time. "Do you want to drive the first shift, or shall I?"

CHAPTER SEVENTEEN

"I DON'T KNOW how it happened!" Jimmy hid his face in his hands. He wasn't crying, but was very near to tears. "I just don't know. There's no way it could have happened!"

"But it did!" Jesse was storming around the room, his tension level too high to let him sit down and discuss the crisis calmly. "And we've got to figure out how. Those movies didn't just appear by magic." He almost choked on the last word after he said it. Among the various evils Nan was being accused of by some public gossip was witchcraft and the practice of black magic. Given her surname, it was a cheap shot, as well as an insane one, and he knew just where it was coming from!

"No, they didn't," Nan agreed calmly. "But it doesn't have to be Jim's fault. Now, if you're finished yelling, please settle yourself, so we can get on with this."

Jesse glared at her, then looked embarrassed, then sheepish. Then he sat.

Nan looked around the room. Jimmy hadn't actually been arrested, but because he had been in charge of the store when the pornographic films were found, he was considered to be involved, even though he was a juvenile. She was the one in danger of prosecution. *Persecution* had already started. The films were of the most horrible type and had been found inside the most innocuous of the kiddie video boxes. Several children who had been watching rented movies unsupervised had seen things that had upset them dreadfully. Nan felt responsible and sick at heart.

"Forget the criminal charges of renting pornography to minors that might be filed," Lars told her. "Some of the parents are considering civil suits against you and your company." Nan nodded, feeling numb.

What was saving her for the moment was her long absence. It was almost impossible for anyone to believe the items had been in the video boxes almost three weeks ago without someone finding them before now. The kiddie movies were just too popular and went out nearly every day. The switch had to have been made within the past forty-eight hours at the earliest.

Which meant to Jesse that, aware of it or not, Jimmy had the clue to the mystery. His little brother was the key, but he couldn't find the lock to save his life.

They were all seated in a small meeting room at the town hall. Jimmy, Jesse and Nan, Walker, Lars and an old friend of Jesse's, Edna Wilson, a lawyer. Nan had asked him for a recommendation when she realized the legal implications of her situation. She was on her own now, without her parent company to bail her out, and she needed someone she could afford as well as trust.

"Lars is right," Edna said, making a note on a sheet of yellow paper. "The laws regarding obscenity are vague. In all probability criminal charges won't be brought. Civil suits for emotional damage are your most likely nightmare."

Nan felt all the starch go out of her. "I'm beaten, then," she said. "I can't argue with any parent whose kid saw that stuff. I'd feel like suing someone, too."

"But it wasn't your fault!" Jimmy stood up, his fists clenched at his sides. "You weren't even in town!"

"I'm responsible, Jim. It was my store."

"We all know who's really responsible," Jesse said darkly. "But nobody wants to say it. Neilson was quiet enough for a while, but he's practically doing a jig down Main Street today." He picked up a pencil on the table in front of him and started tapping it. "Nan could easily sue him for slander with the garbage he's spreading about her." The pencil snapped in several pieces.

"Jesse, Doug Neilson was out of town, too," Lars said. "I checked first thing. He was gone the whole week before the smut was found. Besides, there's no way for him to have gone into the store or sent any of his people to make the switches. Somebody would have noticed." He went on to tell how he had been interviewing customers and opponents of the store alike, trying to get the full picture.

Jimmy shifted in his seat, feeling as if his skin were crawling off him. He knew who'd had the chance to do it, and he didn't believe for a minute it had happened that way. Mr. Conners was his friend. He even liked Nan. He had made a point of telling Jimmy that he appreciated her letting Angel work. Mr. Conners was happy Angel was seeing just him and not dating around. No, it couldn't be.

Unless Mr. Conners had fallen asleep the other night, and someone had come in to make the switch. That might be the answer. But he hadn't said he slept. Said he was reading and working the whole time. Angel's father couldn't be a bad guy. No way!

Jimmy slouched in his chair and put his hand over his mouth to prevent himself from blurting out anything. David Conners was a stranger, and he knew Nan and Jesse weren't all that crazy about him. Jimmy would be in deep trouble if they found out Conners had minded the store even for a few hours late on Saturday. No one else knew, since no one had come in, according to Mr. Conners, and Charlie wasn't standing night guard now that he was having to take care of ALS business. So there had to be another explanation.

There just *had* to be! And it was up to him to find it.

The meeting finally broke up around midnight. Edna cautioned Nan not to talk to anyone about the situation, not to respond to any insults or threats, not to do anything, in fact. "Just be calm and patient," the lawyer told her. "Most of us are on your side, and the truth will come out eventually."

But the lawyer's words, sensible as they were, did not comfort Nan. The store was closed. The company had gone broke. That part of her dream was just as broken. Blown into dusty fragments by one malicious act. But there was something far worse.

She was no longer trusted in Hennington. She sensed it even in friends like Lars, who was treating her distantly and with studied politeness. She had gone to California and pornography had been found in her place. Her neighbors had been cool, barely acknowledging her return. At the grocery store that morning, she had been snubbed by several women, and the clerk had been brusque to the point of rudeness. And Nan wasn't sure she blamed any of them. Children had been exposed to shocking material due to her carelessness. Jimmy was still a child himself, and she shouldn't have left him in charge for so long.

Of course, Sue and Walker hadn't deserted her. Neither had Inge, who was highly incensed over the situation and had already gotten her small self in trouble by staunchly defending Nan. But they were just a tiny band of supporters. Not enough to change the attitude of the rest of the town. Besides, it wasn't their fight.

No matter what, it was all her fault, and she was prepared to pay. After they left the town hall, Jesse tried to stay with her that night, but she told him no. "I have to do some thinking," she said. "I hope you understand. I'd like to be alone for a while."

"I want to be with you and help." His eyes showed her how much her rejection hurt. "But if you don't think you need me, I guess I have to accept that."

She left it at that, without discussing it further. She needed him, all right. The big question in her mind was, did he need her? She was right back where she'd started: planning on leaving Hennington just as soon as she could. No matter what she did here now, she'd never be accepted as she was before. "I'll talk to you tomorrow," she said and turned away from Jesse. Turned away so he wouldn't see the tears. Just when she had been so sure they had a future together, this had to happen to destroy her dreams.

Jesse went home, his heart on fire with pain and his brain running in circles like a confused jackrabbit. Was this going to be the end of his hopes for their life together? He knew people were upset, but he also knew they were overreacting. No one could say that morally Nan was to blame. That was what counted here, not the finer points of the law. Even if she lost in court, no one would really hold her responsible. She just flat out hadn't been around. So she wasn't to blame. Jimmy, on the other hand . . .

Jesse slammed the front door and bellowed his brother's name. No answer. Damn! It was way after midnight, and he knew the boy didn't have a car. So where was he? Out with that girl? He reached for the phone and dialed Conners's motel room number. No answer there, either.

Jesse set the receiver back on the cradle. He sat quietly for a while, thinking and listening to his heart, hearing his feelings clearly for perhaps the first time in his life. After a bit, he focused back on the telephone. Then he picked it up again.

Nan answered the phone only after it had rung nearly thirty times. She was sure it was someone calling to scream at her, or worse, to cry about the harm done by her movies. She heard the tremble of fear and fury in her voice as she answered.

"Nan. It's Jesse. You've been crying?"

"Yes." She sobbed softly. "A little, I guess."

"Oh, honey." She could hear his breathing. "I wish to hell all this hadn't happened."

"But it did. That's reality. Aren't you all the time fussing at me to face up to it? Well, now I—"

"Nan, I want you to marry me."

"What?" She nearly dropped the phone. Her heart leaped with a surge of joy.

"Listen to me. I planned to do this with moonlight and roses, a bottle of fine wine and a great dinner, but I think this is a better time. I know your mind is telling you that the best thing you can do is pack up and leave. But that's wrong. Listen to your heart. I need you, Nan. I love you. I want to spend the rest of my life with you, and if we have to, we'll move to Tombouctou to make it work. Marry me, darling."

"Jesse, I... Don't you want to think about this? It seems..."

"I have thought, damn it! Now, yes or no!"

"Yes."

"Nan, damn it, I—Did you say yes?"

"Yes." She started to laugh and cry. "Yes! I love you, and I will marry you. How soon can you get here to see me say it in person?"

"I'll be right—Nan, I can't come over. Jimmy's gone. I even called Conners's room to see if he and Angel were out in her old man's car. There's no answer. They aren't there, either."

"That's odd." Nan sat down on her bed. "I would have expected Conners to tighten his loose leash on his daughter now. She was, after all, working the night the films were supposedly switched, even if Jimmy swears she was never out of his sight."

"You believe him?"

"Jesse, he's your brother. Would he lie? Even for Angel? Who, by the way, doesn't have the brains of a gnat, in my opinion. There's no way she's involved."

"You're sure about that?"

"Well . . ."

"Hold it, I think I hear him. The front door. Gotta go, Nan. I love you."

She stared for a moment at the now silent receiver. So, he had proposed! And hardly in a careful traditional way. Nan smiled. There was hope! They had the most important thing. Love! Nothing else mattered in the long run. Trouble would always be around in one form or another, but love could be stronger! Their love certainly would be! She hung up the phone and prepared for bed, her heart at peace for the first time in a long, long while.

"I'VE GOT TO TALK to you, Jesse!" Jimmy interrupted his brother's lecture on the idiocy of staying out late and not letting him know where he was when things were in this kind of mess. "Can you give up the big-brother bit for a second, please?"

Jesse quieted. His anger was only a reflection of his deep concern and fear. "Sure," he said, sinking back into a chair. "I'm sorry about blowing up. I just was worried about you."

"Me, too." Jimmy stared at his hands. "I think I know how the videos got switched."

"And you didn't say anything at the meeting?" Jesse blew up again. He stood and started pacing. "My God, Jim. You just let Nan swing there in the breeze. How could you do that to her?"

His brother didn't reply for a moment. "You realize that's the first time you've called me Jim?" he asked.

"What?"

"You called me Jim, not Jimmy. Nan has always called me Jim. Like I'm an adult. Now, I know I'm not yet, but she treats me fair. I didn't let her hurt on purpose, Jesse. She's my friend. I didn't say anything because I just didn't know until now. I'm still not sure I know everything."

"Didn't know what?" Jesse sat back down, his hands clasped tightly together. "Tell me, Jim. Please."

"David Conners. He had to be the one who made the switch. I didn't want to think about it, because of Angel. But after the meeting tonight, I took a walk. Kind of needed to think, you know. I went by the motel, but Angel and her dad weren't there. At least, no one answered when I knocked and the car was gone. That worried me, 'cause she's always been there before, no matter when I came by. Anyway, I hiked all the way out to the airfield. Charlie and Mike were still there. Jesse, why didn't you tell me someone tried to kill you?" He looked up, finally, and Jesse saw the tears in his eyes.

"I don't know that," he said. "Nan thought so, too, when she heard the FAA guys asking me questions, but—"

"They couldn't find you today, on account of you were still on the way here with Nan. But they called Charlie. Their investigation showed definite signs of sabotage. Deliberate, Jesse. Someone wanted you to die in that plane crash!"

Jesse blinked rapidly a few times, absorbing what Jim was saying. His eyesight was almost twenty-twenty now. It was his inner vision that was blind. "I asked Nan to marry me tonight," he said quietly. "She said she would."

"That's great!" Jimmy wiped at his eyes. "Look at me, bawling like a little kid."

"Tell me everything, Jim." Jesse settled back, his hand resting loosely on the arm of the chair. "And then we have to decide how to handle things."

"We do?"

"*We* do."

Jimmy looked at his older brother and saw the man for the first time. Saw him as a real hero. Jesse was big and powerful and dangerous. And he was taking Jimmy on as his partner. Not as his kid brother, but as his friend and equal. Jim started talking.

And things started to fall into place.

NAN TRIED to get comfortable on the cold, hard folding chair, but she couldn't. She wasn't the only one. Everywhere she looked in the big meeting room, people were shifting uneasily, squirming around on their seats. No wonder. Emotions were high. So was excitement. None of her videos offered a show as potentially dramatic as what might happen if tempers got out of hand here.

Lars had called the town meeting. Called it after being closeted with Jesse and Jim for what seemed like hours earlier in the day. It was a Tuesday afternoon, but the place was packed. Almost every family had a representative, she thought, estimating the numbers. Some had more than a single delegate. Far more.

Douglas Neilson and his group filled a good quarter of the space. They carried signs and banners declaring her to be evil and describing the evil of her videos. Nan felt sick to her stomach every time she glanced in their direction. They were quiet, warned as everyone had been by Lars and his officers that any commotion would result in immediate expulsion. But she could still feel the hatred they exuded. Most of them weren't bad people, she thought. Just small-minded and easily led. Neilson was another matter. He might be narrow in his views, but she didn't see him being led around by anyone else.

She didn't want to think about him, however. She wanted to think only about Jesse and his marriage proposal. The road before them was going to be terribly hard, but she believed in him. And, for the first time, she really believed in herself. They would do it together! Whatever it took, whatever it meant.

"You look remarkably happy for someone about to get burned at the stake," Sue said, smiling to show she was joking. Sue and Inge flanked her, one on each side.

"I'm just looking beyond my troubles," Nan said. "No matter what happens, I still have a lot to be thankful for."

"And where is he?" Inge asked. "I haven't seen Jesse or Jimmy this afternoon. Walker, either. I thought they'd be right here by you, too."

"They said they had something to do." Nan felt a little uneasy at their absence, as well. But she trusted Jesse. He had told her to have faith. That everything was going to be all right. She wanted with all her heart to believe, but it was difficult in the face of so much hostility.

The mayor got up and called the meeting to order. She banged the gavel, but there was the same kind of silence before her announcement as after. No one, it seemed, had anything to murmur or whisper about. She thanked everyone for coming, outlined the situation and invited Lars to the podium.

"As you know," the big policeman said, "we haven't yet issued any arrest warrants in this case." The silence of the crowd was suddenly broken by a loud hissing sound from

Neilson's group. Lars glared, and they quieted. "We intend to make arrests before the meeting is over, however," he added. Nan felt a cold chill run up her back. *Arrests?*

"Don't bother arresting her," a male voice cried. "Just tar and feathers!"

"Shut up, Les." The order came from a woman sitting near Nan. "Let the chief talk."

"I got a lot to say," Lars Handley said, "but it'll wait a little while. There's some folks coming in just now who have more important information for all of you." The big double doors of the meeting room opened, hitting the wall with a crash.

Nan turned to look. So did everyone else. Jesse, Jimmy and Walker came in. Between the two Rivers men was David Conners. The writer looked a little more rumpled than usual. Walker had hold of Angel's arm. She had her blond head bent.

A murmur of surprise and question ran through the crowd. The sound crescendoed as the five walked up onto the stage. A man called out, demanding to know what was going on. Another voice echoed him, then dozens were asking.

Nan had eyes only for Jesse. Ears only for what he was about to say. He looked in her direction for a moment, then out at the audience in general.

"Afternoon, folks," he said. "I thought you would like to meet the man who put the dirty movies in your kids' videos." He pointed to David Conners.

Conners cringed. Jimmy, who was grim faced and looked ten years older, had him in a firm grip. A low, menacing vocalization rose from the audience.

"You're lying, Rivers!" a man in Neilson's crowd hollered. "You been sleeping with the witch, and you're lying for her!"

Jesse smiled. It was a terrifyingly cold expression. "I am marrying Nan Black, but I'm not lying for her. Conners made the switch. He's confessed to it. He did it while his little girl was making sure my brother's attention was elsewhere." He looked over at Angel, his expression softening. She was crying softly, her head still bowed. Nan saw Jesse hesitate. Some people around her expressed whispers of disbelief in Angel's guilt.

Then Jimmy spoke, loudly and indignantly. "Don't you let her off the hook! She knew well and good what her father was up to! They were being paid to do it. She was taking money for being nice to me! She's just as guilty as her father. And somebody tried to kill my brother, too! I think it's connected. All of it!"

That outburst brought a corresponding hubbub from the audience. Then Angel blasted the situation into outer space. She raised her head and pointed her finger straight at Douglas Neilson. "He did it!" she cried, tears streaming down her face. "He came to my daddy and said he'd pay him lots of money to wreck her business, get her chased out of town. But Daddy never did hurt anybody. When she caught him that one night, he just shot out the window. He never hurt Mr. Rivers, either!"

"No!" Neilson was on his feet. "She's lying! She's just a little whore like the Black woman. Don't believe her!"

"Are we all whores?" Nan yelled, standing and facing the man. "Is that what you really think of women?" Behind her, she heard Inge agreeing in very colorful terms.

"Everybody, shut up!" Lars was on his feet, trying to regain control. "Settle down, people!"

"You're all the devil's spawn!" Neilson shrieked, waving his hands wildly. "The town is going straight to hell, if you believe the witches!" He started to lurch around and people stumbled over chairs and one another to get out of his way. Nan saw Jesse start to jump from the stage. Walker came over and put a restraining hand on his shoulder, stopping him.

Neilson seemed to run out of steam. He stood still, breathing heavily, his eyes still wild.

Then David Conners spoke. "I'm not a writer," he said, softly at first but with growing volume. "I'm an actor. I was out of work, looking for a job in Minneapolis, when Neilson came to me. He got my name from a mutual acquaintance. Asked me to play a part, do a little innocent sabotage, create a little harmless havoc." He looked at Nan, who was still standing. "Ms. Black, I was so scared when you caught me holding that gun, I didn't even think. Just had to get out as fast as I could. I'm sorry."

Nan just nodded.

"But you admit you put the wrong movies in the cases?" Inge asked, standing up, too. "You were the one? Not Nan?"

"It was me." Conners hung his head. "I'm so, so sorry. I had no idea the films were as bad as they turned out to be. He told me they were just too sexy for the kids, not that they showed the things they did! He said it was the one sure way to make certain she'd have to close her business. I swear, I didn't know. I wouldn't have done it for any amount of money, if I had!" His dejection vanished, and his tone rang with outraged sincerity.

"What about Jesse's plane, then?" Nan asked, reminding herself the man was an actor, capable of deceit by training. "Who...?"

"Douglas Neilson did it," Conners said. "He followed Rivers around until he got a chance to monkey with the engine of his plane. Said if he was out of the way, you'd give in and leave quicker. I think he hates Rivers more than he does you, but—"

He was interrupted by a yowl of rage and madness from Neilson. He was on the move again, heading for the exit. Lars signaled and the two police officers jumped after the fleeing man, but the pileup of chairs and the milling people prevented them from reaching him in time. He was out the side door in a moment. Nan looked up at Jesse. He was moving, too. He was not just standing and watching this turn of events!

"No! Jesse!" Walker and Jimmy shouted in chorus, but Jesse kept going, even though he understood the warning in their voices. He was cold as ice inside; the heat of his rage against Neilson had dissipated. The man was obviously insane and dangerous. He had to be stopped. Jesse headed for the back of the stage and the nearest exit.

People were pouring out of the building when he got around to the front. But there was no sign of Neilson. He felt a hand on his arm and turned, ready to fight.

"It's me!" Nan stared at him in alarm. "What are you doing?"

"*We* are going to catch Neilson," Jesse told her, sure now what he ought to do. "Where's your car?"

A short while later, they were at his hangar, and she was helping him push the old Piper Cub onto the runway. The big plane was gone. Mike and Charlie were out making deliveries. "Get in," he told her. "I need you to be lookout."

"What? Jesse, what are you planning?"

"We're going to find Neilson and tell Lars where to send the troops! He's crazy-dangerous, and the sooner he's trapped the less likely he is to injure anyone else. Now, get in the plane!"

Nan obeyed.

They flew low, barely skimming the trees at first. She felt her insides draw up inside her into a small, cold huddle. Suddenly, she remembered why she was so afraid. He had told Charlie he might not be able to fly again! She knew his eyesight still wasn't normal. The plane shifted in the air and roared skyward. Well, he sure as hell was flying now! No turning back!

Jesse banked, turning in a wide circle around Hennington until he had scanned all the roads, including the unpaved ones. He couldn't see Neilson's truck on any of them. Leaning forward, he tapped Nan on the shoulder. She lifted the side of her earphones. "Look for a plume of dust," he said. "My eyesight's still blurry."

"Oh, that's great!" Nan clutched the strut on her right side. "And you're flying?"

"Just look for a single truck, moving like the devil's after him. That'll be Neilson. Don't worry. I can do this blind."

Nan looked. It beat thinking. From behind her, she heard the clicks and crackling voices of his radio. He was talking with Lars. She scanned the ground below. Nothing.

Then she saw it. "There he is," she screamed, pointing. "He's driving north!" She screamed again as the small plane banked at an impossible angle. She held on to the struts for dear life, but rose slightly in her seat so she could look back at Jesse. He was flying with one hand and using the other to hold the radio microphone. She settled back and closed her eyes, fearing they would end up as a joint grease spot on the ground.

But he flew as though he had radar built into his head. She heard him yell for her to hold on, which she was already doing for dear life. Then the bottom dropped out of her stomach.

Jesse buzzed the truck, saw Neilson's crazed eyes look up in fear and rage, buzzed it again. The little Cub wasn't built to stand too much fancy flying, but he was stretching it to the limit. The important thing was to slow Neilson down.

Stop him if possible. Jesse turned the plane, banked and headed down the highway toward the truck.

Nan saw the truck coming at them at an impossible speed. Jesse seemed determined to ram it, head-on. She started to scream again, but from behind her she heard him yell.

"Remember this? Just like when we first met!" he hollered.

She did, suddenly recalling that awful moment months ago when she had thought he was going to run his plane right into her. And just as suddenly, she knew it would be all right. Laughing, she leaned into the gravitational pull as Jesse slipped the plane out of the truck's path just in time. Neilson's truck slid off the road and slowed, plowing into a clump of sagebrush. Close behind, she saw the flashing lights of the Highway Patrol. Jesse circled the scene.

Neilson, clearly dazed, got out of his truck and was immediately surrounded by cops. One of the officers waved up at the plane. Nan felt Jesse make the wing waggle signal during one more pass over the scene. She sighed in relief, feeling her taut nerves finally relax. It was over.

Off to her right, she saw the red-gold rays of the setting sun as it slid down the horizon toward the west. She looked back at Jesse, knowing she was going to marry an authentic hero, not a fantasy figure who would fade away under the harsh light of reality. He grinned and gave her the thumbs-up sign.

Then they flew home.

CHAPTER EIGHTEEN

NAN WATCHED herself in the full-length mirror as she adjusted the fit of her wedding gown. It wasn't white. She'd been married in white the first time and didn't want any reminders of that disaster. The dress she wore now was pale blue. She liked it a lot.

It hadn't been her choice. She had been so busy with restructuring her business and setting up delivery service around the region that the plans and details of the wedding were left to others—others who were more than willing to pick up the reins and run! She smiled at the reflections in the mirror and smoothed the gown over her hips.

"It's perfect!" her mother said. Milda Wilkes had been staying with her for two weeks now, helping with the dress Inge had made and assisting Judith Rivers and Jane in arranging for the ceremony and festivities. "More than perfect," Milda added. "Inge, you are a genius with a needle!"

"I had a good model," Inge said, blushing with pleasure at the praise. "Nan is no problem to sew for. A perfect figure, as you know."

"Hopefully, that will change soon," Judith stated. "I want grandchildren. The quicker, the better."

Nan gave her future mother-in-law a wry smile. By now, she was used to Judith's forthrightness. "I make no promises," she said. "Not to anyone but Jesse. So don't be holding your breath."

"Never make a promise to a husband about kids," Sue warned cheerfully. "Look what happened to me!"

"You ought to be grateful," Milda stated. She started to help Nan unbutton the long row of fasteners down the back of the gown. "You have wonderful children."

"I am," Sue replied. "Indeed, I am!"

Nan listened as the women chatted about children and married life. She was, after all, buying in to the whole domestic package and needed all the inside information she could get. But that wasn't really bothering her anymore. She knew her love for Jesse was what she had been blindly seeking all her adult life.

He made her complete, and he also made it clear she did the same for him. They weren't alike, didn't agree on many issues, but their love was growing more solid every passing day. The differences only added spice!

"I hear little Miss Angel Conners is going to be living with a foster family in Pierre while her father does his community service time," Jane said, changing the subject. "They certainly got off easy."

"It's hard to blame her for anything," Nan said. "She really is innocent to a great extent. Just misled by her father's schemes to make some quick money. And he never thought of it as a criminal thing. Just as kind of a game, a role he was playing."

"Still," Judith added, "if you'd pressed charges, it wouldn't be so much of a game for either of them."

"That's why I didn't. The real villain was Douglas Neilson, and where he's going, he can't harm a soul."

"Criminally insane," Inge murmured. "Who would have thought it?"

"Anyone whose child was terrorized by him has thought it," Sue answered, her expression grim. A silence settled over the group for a moment.

"Conners's child was a victim, too," Nan said. "I hope the foster home she's in will help her see right and wrong more clearly than her father did."

"Walker knows her caseworker," Sue said. "He's confident things will go well for Angel. She was really shaken to the core by the whole terrible experience."

"So was my son," Judith added. "But he seems to have come out of it okay. He's seeing that Andersen girl again."

Nan smiled. Both of Judith Rivers's sons seemed to have come out okay. Jesse had recovered completely and was flying like a bird every day. Almost every day, anyway. The aerobatic competition days were over, he told her. From now on, stunt flying was only for fun, not for the danger and thrill. That suited her, but she was glad he had made the decision on his own and not because of pressure from her. One of the best things about their relationship was an agreement not to interfere in each other's dreams, but to help whenever possible.

And Jesse had certainly helped her. A few days after Neilson's arrest, while they were planning delivery schedules, he made an announcement. "I know now what it is you really want, Nan," he said. "And I'm happy I'm going to be able to help you achieve it." He had a mischievous twinkle in his green eyes.

"Well, don't keep me in suspense," she had replied. "I can hardly wait to know what it is myself!"

"Building. You want, no, you *need* to build. You're a growth junkie, so to speak. I called you an empire builder once when I was angry, but I was right. You don't really care where you do it, just so you can expand on and develop a project indefinitely."

"Is this good or bad?"

"It's you. So it's good. Let's just relax and see where it takes us, okay?"

She couldn't argue with that. Nor could she argue with the fact that her lover was getting to know her as well as or better than she knew herself. She thought about Jesse as she continued to talk with her mother and her friends. While she still found him exciting to the extreme when they were alone, playing their lovers' games, she now felt serene and secure. Her life from now on was based on the solid foundation of his love. He had no greater gift to give her than that!

"Anybody home?" Jesse appeared at the door, a big grin on his face. All the women except Nan flew at him, warning him away while they were finishing fitting the wedding gown. Nan, who was wearing only undergarments now, just stood there and smiled back at him. As he retreated, he called over his shoulder, "I'll be by at seven, okay?" She waved acknowledgment. Seeing him made her feel so wonderful inside, Nan thought.

But as the day progressed, a sense of unease began to grow in her mind. It grew, and she could never get alone for long enough to think it out. To study it and figure why she was being bothered. Family seemed to swarm all over her, almost suffocating her.

The traditional bachelor party was planned for later that night, but first both families and all the special guests gathered for a dinner. It was pleasant enough, fun, really. But as the event wore on, Nan began to feel even more uneasy.

She loved Jesse with every fiber of her being. No doubt in her mind or heart about that. But all this *tradition* was beginning to get her down. Her father and mother acted as if this was the greatest thing she'd ever done. Her sister and brother and their spouses and kids crowded around, wishing her well. Judith Rivers told anyone who would listen and many who didn't that Nan was going to be quitting work soon to start a family. Jane gave her a conspiratorial wink every time they heard that phrase together, but it didn't help the sense of being dragged into other people's dreams. Dreams that were not her own!

Even Jesse seemed caught up entirely in this marriage stage play. He treated her with courtly charm, but he wasn't being himself at all. By the time he left with a group of other men who were clearly intent on continuing the party in a far more rowdy manner, she felt very alone and a little desperate.

"Prenuptial jitters?" Sue asked quickly, drawing her aside a few minutes after the departure of the "boys." "You look like you just decided this is all a gigantic conspiracy against you."

"Is it that obvious?" Nan couldn't even smile. "Actually, I feel like running away as fast as I can."

"I did." Sue regarded her calmly. "I was halfway to Denver when Walker caught up with me the night before our wedding."

"You are kidding me!"

"No." Walker appeared at his wife's side. "She isn't. If you think Judith is sizing you up as a Rivers brood mare, you ought to have heard what my mother said to Sue. She made it clear the only good Sue could ever do me was to give me children. She does not approve of Sue's writing, and when she left me to go back to college, my mother nearly had apoplexy!"

"Mother Walker and I do not get along," Sue added cheerfully. "But we tolerate each other. I think you and Judith will reach a level of understanding eventually, also."

Nan frowned. "But you did what she wanted, didn't you?"

"No, I did what *I* wanted. Of course, I always wanted our children, even when we feared we couldn't have any." Sue linked arms with her husband. "Of course, Walker did take some part in making the dream come true."

"The fun part," he added. "Listen, Nan. I know you've been this route before and it didn't work out. But marriage is more than just the union of two people who love each other. You and Jesse are making a commitment to society, both large and small."

"I guess you're right. But I still feel sort of trapped."

"Normal enough," Sue said. "It'll pass. Nobody ever said this was an easy life, did they?"

Nan smiled. "No, they did not."

Although her conversation with the Petersens helped her achieve some perspective and composure, Nan was still upset when she went to bed. Her mother had fussed and bullied her into an early night, declaring that all brides must be rested and fresh for the day of their marriage. Great, Nan thought, tapping her fingers on the sheet. She was being treated like a tender young virgin. Hardly a reflection of reality. Her mother was operating out of a fantasy, that was for certain! Just as Judith was. No way was Nan ever giving up work for family! She could have both, and Jesse knew it, too.

She relaxed a bit, thinking of him. He wasn't perfect, but he was near enough. She thought of the way it had been when they hunted down Neilson together. Partners! That was what they were. He had taken her along on a dangerous flight, expecting her to do a job. And she had.

Her eyes closed. So, their relatives were being pains. It didn't matter in the long run. They were going to be fine! She turned over. Only, it would have been nice if she had been able to talk about this with him instead of getting counseling from Sue and Walker and dealing with it by herself. Face it, she was jealous of his time with his buddies. And wasn't that as bad as being upset with the pushy attitude of his mother and hers? She needed to be respected for who she was; so did he. If he needed to blow off his last blast of bachelor steam, who was she to resent it? He had a right. Didn't he?

She rolled back to her other side. Would they have a naked dancer jump out of a cake at the bachelor party? Was that why Walker hadn't gone? Was it that sort of affair? She pictured Jesse carousing with other women and found the idea hurt deeply. She *was* jealous! How could she complain about traditional values and expectations, when she was practically wallowing in them! She turned onto her back, listening in the darkness to the ticking of the old alarm clock by her bed and to the tapping of a tree branch against the window.

Tree branch? Nan threw back the sheet and sat up. There was no breeze blowing tonight. What was a tree branch doing at her window? A tingle of alarm filled her. What if it was one of Neilson's followers, intent on doing her harm just before her wedding day? What if his insanity hadn't been limited to himself, but had spread among those who agreed with his aims, including destroying her and Jesse?

No! She settled back, cursing her overactive imagination. She had seen for herself how deeply dismayed Neilson's group was when they learned the vicious extent of his actions. Even Lester Gray, the second in command, had shamefacedly apologized in person. No, she no longer had anything to fear from those people. She just wanted Jesse and was constructing a scenario that required him to appear and rescue her! How silly! Another useless hero fantasy!

"Nan!" The voice whispered her name with urgency. "Nan, over here. At the window."

She almost shrieked aloud in surprise. Jesse was outside her bedroom window, tapping softly on it with his finger and motioning her to come over. Nan got up. "What in the world are you—"

"Shh!" He waved his hands. "Don't wake up your mother, for goodness' sake! She'll have my hide if she catches us. Then she'll turn what's left of me over to my mother for the coup de grace."

"What?" She went over to the window and raised it all the way. "What are you doing? And what are you talking about? Jesse, are you drunk?"

"Sober as a judge." He grinned up at her. "Really. I left the party before things got too wild. I think I was kind of a damper on the festivities, anyway. I wanted to be with you."

"You did?" She knelt, her face now almost level with his. "I wanted you, too. But Mom made me go to bed. She would have sulked if I didn't, and I figured you'd be deep in debauchery, anyway."

"Listen to us." He reached in and took her hand, kissing her palm. "Full-grown adults, who are being treated like kids. You're expected to go to your chaste bed for the last time, and I'm supposed to...well, celebrate my last free hours."

Nan giggled. "It is silly, isn't it?" His kiss tingled on her skin. "It's as if we belong to everyone else, not to each other."

"Oh, we belong to each other, all right." His tongue licked at her hand. "Come on. Let's go." He gave her a tug.

"Where? What are you doing?" She pulled back. "It's after midnight."

"I know what time it is." Jesse reached up and grabbed her under her arms, lifting her out the window. The September night air was chilly against her skin, and she wore only a thin cotton nightgown. "It's time we made love and then got some sleep. Tomorrow's going to be a busy day."

"You're crazy," she said, wrapping her arms around his neck. He still had on his suit from the dinner party, but his tie had gone and his shirt was partly unbuttoned. "Let me down."

"No." He turned and started walking to the street and his truck.

"Jesse!"

"Be quiet. You'll wake your parents." He paused and kissed her. Nan was suddenly very warm.

He carried her around the truck and set her on the passenger seat. "Where're we going?" she asked. "We can't go to your home. You have relatives packed in there to the ceiling, just like I do."

"I know." He got in and started the engine.

"So?"

He smiled. "I thought we'd return to the scene of our first meaningful encounter. Sort of relive it for old times' sake, if you get my drift." He regarded her for a long moment, his eyes telling her everything she needed to hear from him. He promised her the past, present and future with his eyes. Nan felt even warmer. The doubts and anxieties left her. This time, she knew, they were gone for good.

He drove out to the airfield, neither of them saying anything else. Nothing else needed saying. He turned on the stereo, and soft classical music played. Nan reached over and put her hand on his thigh. She heard him give a sigh of pleasure.

He parked the truck by the hangar and carried her inside. "Too much junk on the ground to make bare feet safe," he said, when she protested she could walk by herself. "Besides, I kind of like this. Makes me feel like one of those heroes in your old movies."

"I just feel a little silly," she said, not feeling silly at all, but rather so sexy she could hardly stand it. "I'm out here with you in only my nightie. What if someone comes looking for you?"

"They won't. I made it pretty clear that I wasn't having fun." He carried her over to the big Cessna. "Anyway, I'd already made these plans for tonight." He set her down on the wing and walked over to the hatch. He took off his jacket and tossed it aside. Then he opened the door. "See?"

Nan looked. Inside the cargo hold was a scene reminiscent of a sultan's seraglio in miniature. Jesse had strewn thick pillows of every size and description around on the floor and hung the bare walls with silk material. A low table with two glasses and a bottle of wine waited for them. He kicked off his shoes and jumped up into the doorway. Holding out his hand, he said, "Come on in. I guarantee your every fantasy will be delivered to you in this magic place."

Nan slid down the wing and took his hand. Her heart was beating ninety miles an hour, and her body felt as if a furnace was building inside. While she had been moping and worrying, he had been preparing this special delight for both of them. "Every fantasy?" she asked, slipping through the door next to him. He nodded. It didn't take her long to find out he was telling the truth.

MORNING BROKE into the hangar space in narrow, silvery streamers. Jesse had shut the door, but sunlight shone through the windows. A strip of it fell across Nan's face where she lay, sprawled on the bed of pillows with Jesse's arms wrapped around her from the side and behind. She blinked, remembering the ecstasy. Then she remembered the rest.

"Jesse!" She reached over and shook him. "It's morning. We're in deep trouble!"

He rolled onto his back, one arm thrown over his eyes. "What time is it?"

"I don't know. I didn't have much on when you kidnapped me last night, you know. My watch is still on my bedside table."

"Um." He sat up, rubbing his face. Glancing down at his own watch, he put his arm around her shoulders. "Don't fret, love," he said. "It's early yet. We've got plenty of time." His fingers started stroking her skin, suggestively and seductively.

She regarded him, trying not to smile. "Let me explain something to you, my dear, future husband. You will be related legally to my family in a few hours. It would be in your best interest, therefore, to keep on good terms with my mother."

"And if she finds out we've been acting like crazed alley cats on the eve of our wedding..."

"She'll have your liver for lunch."

"We're on our way." He let her go and got up, grabbing his pile of clothes.

Fortunately, no one seemed awake yet when Jesse helped Nan sneak back into her bedroom through the open window. She kissed him and watched until he disappeared, heading for his own place. Heading for the home she would move to once they returned from their honeymoon. She gave herself a glance in the mirror over her bureau and decided a long shower was the best way to erase the signs of the night's activities. As the water flowed over her skin, she relaxed and relished the memory of the long night hours.

Jesse wasn't as lucky. Although Jimmy was still snoring vigorously on the sofa and his father was apparently still asleep in the bedroom, Judith was up and about in the kitchen. When he tried sneaking in through the back entrance, she caught him red-handed.

"You look like something the cat dragged in," she scolded, keeping her voice low and handing him a cup of steaming coffee. "Are you going to be hung over for your wedding?"

"No, Mom." He sat down and sipped coffee. "I didn't drink much last night."

"Well, you look like you did." She regarded him with a baleful expression. "What's Nan going to think when you lift her veil and she sees the road map on your eyeballs?"

"I do believe she will understand."

Judith stirred pancake batter. "She's a good woman, Jesse. Strong. You can't be wilding around anymore like you have all your life. She won't stand for it."

"I hung up my 'wilding' the day I met her, Mom."

She looked at him. "Can you really do that, son? I mean, you've done what you wanted without worrying about anyone else for so long—"

"That's not true." Jesse set down his mug. "I've always loved you. Loved my family. I just didn't walk the road the way you thought I should. Nan and I are about to walk our own road together. Side by side. We've got enough love to make it all the way to the end, believe me!"

His mother stood still for another moment, then she said, "I guess I do, son. I guess I do."

Jesse stood up and gave her a big hug. They both turned away to hide tears of deep emotion. "How many pancakes do you want?" Judith asked when she was able to speak without her voice giving her feelings away.

"Just keep 'em coming, Mom," he answered, grinning at her.

Jimmy wandered in after a little while, drawn by the smell of bacon, pancakes and coffee. "Hi, big brother," he said, dropping into a kitchen chair, slouching there and regarding Jesse with a grin. "Where'd you get yourself to last night?"

"He was out drinking and carousing with his buddies," Judith said, her disapproval softened by their earlier conversation. "Just look at him. Don't you let yourself ever get that way, Jimmy."

"He wasn't with the guys, Ma." Jimmy reached over and picked up a pancake, which he ate. "I heard he stayed around for the bachelor stuff just a little while, then left." He gave Jesse a quizzical look. "So, where were you all night, then?"

"I was flying," Jesse said. He dipped a forkful of pancake in syrup and put it into his mouth. He closed his eyes and chewed. After he had swallowed, he repeated the words in a whisper with a slight change. "We were flying," he said.

NAN WALKED down the church aisle on her father's arm. Thad Wilkes wasn't given to expressing his inner feelings often, but he had almost reduced her to happy tears a few moments before, when he had told her how proud he was of the way she had chosen to live her life after the disaster of her first marriage.

"Didn't want to bother you about it, girl," he said. "You being stubborn and all. Never did want nobody else's opinion but your own. But that man you got hitched to the first time was just no damn good. Your judgment's improved. Jesse's a good 'un."

"I think so, too, Dad."

"He'll take care of you, you know."

Nan smiled at her father. He was tall and lean as a rail with sun-weathered skin, even though he spent much of his time indoors working at his grocery store. He was a lot like she was, she reflected. He saw things his way, and no one else's. Well, she had learned to give a little on that score. Now, she could love him as he was and not feel she had to fight to change him or her mother. "I know, Dad," she agreed, not saying that she was going to take care of Jesse as well. They were going to be more than wife and husband; they were partners. And partners took care of each other!

Her partner waited for her at the altar. Every line of his face shone with love for her, every inch of him made her tremble with desire.

Jesse watched as she walked slowly toward him. She was a dream, rooted firmly in reality. So beautiful, she made him ache inside. So wonderful, he knew he could never be happier. So challenging, he knew they would never lack for excitement in their lives. He knew he ought to remain solemn and dignified as she approached, but he couldn't. Jesse grinned, lit from within by the joy he felt.

Nan felt that joy, too. As she reached to take his arm, she knew that all her dreams and fantasies had finally found a place to land. That place was wherever she and Jesse were together.

Harlequin Superromance®

This August, don't miss Superromance #462—STARLIT PROMISE

STARLIT PROMISE is a deeply moving story of a woman coming to terms with her grief and gradually opening her heart to life and love.

Author Petra Holland sets the scene beautifully, never allowing her heroine to become mired in self-pity. It is a story that will touch your heart and leave you celebrating the strength of the human spirit.

Available wherever Harlequin books are sold.

STARLIT

Harlequin Superromance®

CHILDREN OF THE HEART
by Sally Garrett

Available this August

Romance readers the world over have wept and
rejoiced over Sally Garrett's heartwarming stories of
love, caring and commitment. In her new novel,
Children of the Heart, Sally once again weaves a story
that will touch your most tender emotions.

You'll be moved to tears of joy

Nearly two hundred children have passed through
Trenance McKay's foster home. But after her husband
leaves her, Trenance knows she'll always have to
struggle alone. No man could have enough room in his
heart both for Trenance and for so many needy
children. Max Tulley, news anchor for KSPO TV is
willing to try, but how long can his love last?

"Sally Garrett does some of the best character studies
in the genre and will not disappoint her fans."
Romantic Times

**Look for *Children of the Heart* wherever
Harlequin Romance novels are sold.** SCH-1

This August, don't miss an exclusive
two-in-one collection of earlier love stories

MAN
WITH A PAST

TRUE COLORS

by one of today's hottest
romance authors,

Jayne Ann Krentz

Now, two of Jayne Ann Krentz's most loved books are
available together in this special edition that new and
longtime fans will want to add to their bookshelves.

Let Jayne Ann Krentz capture your hearts with the love
stories, MAN WITH A PAST and TRUE COLORS.

And in October, watch for the second two-in-one
collection by Barbara Delinsky!

Available wherever Harlequin books are sold.

Back by Popular Demand

Janet Dailey

Americana

A romantic tour of America through fifty favorite Harlequin Presents, each set in a different state researched by Janet and her husband, Bill. A journey of a lifetime in one cherished collection.

In August, don't miss the exciting states featured in:

Title #13 — ILLINOIS
        The Lyon's Share

    #14 — INDIANA
        The Indy Man

Available wherever
Harlequin books are sold.